SWORN TO A DEMIGOD

ROMANCING THE SEAS
BOOK THREE

ATHENA ROSE

COPYRIGHT

Edited by Vanda O'Neil
Cover Design by Lara Wynter
Published by Burton & Burchell LLC

This book is written in U.S. English

AVA

*A*va looked out at the horizon as they sailed toward their destination.

A mountain on a strip of land grew with every stroke, bathed in the golden rays of the setting sun.

This would be where she found her husband.

Ava had spent many years yearning for the comfort of a man in her life. She wanted to be married more than anything in the world, and now that she had come so close to her heart's desire, she felt she could reach out and hold it in her palm.

Soon, they arrived on the old Greek island, and a small fishing village welcomed them. The locals spoke little English but acted friendly enough. Several of them pointed to the abandoned pier across the beach surrounded by jagged rocks. The locals warned them to avoid sailing too close; apparently, there had been sightings of a beastly man lurking near the shoreline.

Ava held her breath with anticipation. The fear in their eyes looked as clear as day, but it did not stop her from having hope. Soon, she would meet her husband.

A part of her wondered if he might take one glance at her and become dismissive.

What if he did not find her pleasing?

She cast the worry aside. Throughout her whole life, she had observed people and found herself most interested in lovers.

Her crewmates walked hand in hand, oblivious of her presence most days. At night, they made oohs and ahhs that she listened to. And she envied the way the men looked at their wives.

She longed to have that too.

When they were about to reach the shoreline, they saw him—a hulking figure with muscles like tree trunks and eyes that glinted in anger.

When their vessel approached the beach, the monstrosity of a man swaggered forward. His thick arms swayed, and he scowled deeply at them all.

Ava's eyes landed on Hercules for the very first time, and her stomach knotted.

He looked like a beast of a man with strong,

rippling muscles from head to toe. He wore nothing but a tiny pair of cotton shorts, and his thighs bulged out of them.

His dark eyes landed on her, and she wondered if he might smile. He did not.

The dinghy slid onto the sand, drawing to a halt. Ava climbed out of the tender and turned to face the man who towered over her, and his breaths came out hot and heavy.

"Who are you to disrupt my peace?" he growled as his hands balled into fists.

Captain Stone and Prince Edward brandished their weapons and made to move forward, but Georgette raised a hand and stepped up to Hercules instead. She eased the tension by bowing low and gestured for the others to follow her.

Ava curtsied, smiling shyly at the man, but he did not look in her direction again. Her chest grew tight.

"We have been sent by the goddess Isis to beseech the help of the great Hercules," Georgette said, straightening slowly. "Are you he?"

The man crossed his arms across his broad chest and smiled for the first time.

His skin shone like he was covered from head to toe in olive oil, and his complexion was a beautiful caramel shade as it reflected the sunlight.

He threw his head back and laughed. His thick, dark hair shook with the effort. "Isis sent you? Then I hope you brought me the gift she promised all those years ago."

"Indeed." Serena gestured to Ava.

Ava stepped forward. "It is my honor and privilege to be your wife." She spoke the sentence just as she had rehearsed with Isis so many times before.

Hercules hummed so low that the ground vibrated beneath Ava's feet. His penetrating stare moved up and down her body. Then he grumbled something inaudible and walked away.

"Do not follow me if you want to keep your heads," he shouted over his shoulder.

The group watched the demigod walk into a cave.

When he left, Captain Stone sighed. "Well, that did not go as planned."

Ava hugged herself. The sting of rejection burned her insides.

Serena nudged her. "Do not worry. Men are fickle beings. Demigods are even more so. I am certain he is just tired. We shall try again when he returns."

"I do not think I please him. Am I not pleasing to look at?" Ava asked, worried.

Captain Stone and Prince Edward started to

argue, but both of them promptly went quiet under the furious stares of their wives.

"Let us make camp. Serena, I have a favor to ask of you," Georgette said.

Prince Edward and Captain Stone busied themselves collecting wood from the boat to make a fire.

Screna and Georgette huddled further down the beach.

Ava pretended not to listen, but she tucked her hair behind her ear so that she might hear their conversation more clearly.

"I know you hate me," Georgette began.

Serena scoffed. "I do not hate you. I simply do not like you."

Georgette sighed. "All right. But we are about to embark on a hazardous journey. We will face unworldly creatures, and I was hoping you could teach me how to use my siren powers."

Ava snorted, and the two women looked at her. She turned away, blushing.

After a pause, Serena spoke up. "No. You do not need to know them. Besides, it took me years to conjure a simple handkerchief. From what I have heard, you already mastered the art of healing."

Georgette sucked in a breath. "Please, Serena. I need a way to protect Mannington that does not involve me watching him die every time. My soul cannot bear it."

Serena hummed as she frowned at Georgette. "How much do you love him?"

"Is that a sincere question? Is it not obvious how earnest my affections are for him? I would give my life for him."

"Would you give your immortality?" Serena asked.

Ava's heart jolted. Before a second thought could change her mind, she ran to the two women. "Serena, you cannot be thinking—"

Serena shrugged. "Why not?"

Ava dragged her hands through her hair. "It is forbidden magic, Serena. With unknown consequences."

Georgette frowned, looking from Serena to Ava like she was following a tennis match. "What is this forbidden magic you speak of? Is it the same Isis spoke of?"

Ava nodded. "Serena and Prince Edward practiced a binding ritual."

Georgette looked over her shoulder at the two men moving around on the boat and turned back to meet Ava's pointed look. "What does a binding ritual do?"

Serena held up her palm to show the light scar. "You combine blood. He is now part siren, and I am part human."

Georgette made a sound of amazement. "Will you do it for us?"

Before Serena could reply, Ava grabbed Georgette by the shoulders. "Please, do not do this. I shall teach you how to enhance your powers. I am sure you will pick it up quickly."

But Georgette kept looking at Serena with widened eyes full of hope. "Will you do it, Serena?"

"Please! Think about this!" Ava shook Georgette. "You are sacrificing your immortality. One day, you shall die!"

Georgette shrugged. "Last year, I thought I was human and expected to die one day. In any case, I would rather live one full life with my husband than exist for an eternity alone."

Ava let Georgette go. Her words had cut deeper than she could ever know. "Do what you will."

Ava kept her distance as Serena performed the ritual.

Captain Stone and Georgette knelt before her like a bride and a groom.

Ava winced and turned away when they made the

cuts. She tried to block out the sounds of their chants as they performed the forbidden ritual.

She focused instead on the mouth of the cave. Her heart fluttered faster than the wings of a hummingbird.

When she could no longer bear it, she stood and headed for the cave, knowing that the two pairs of lovers would be too caught up in their sacred activity to notice her absence.

At the entrance, she peered inside the dark space and listened for Hercules. She could only pick up on the steady inhale and exhale of a person sleeping.

Ava curled her hands into fists at the humiliation of coming all this way, only to be rejected at first glance. Her body trembled with terrible fury, and she boldly strode forward.

When she rounded a corner, the cave opened up. A gust of ice-cold air blasted her, and a candle flickered to her left.

Hercules lay face down, fast asleep on a bed far too small for him.

Angry and disappointed, Ava marched forward and poked his back. He continued to sleep, blissfully unaware of her presence.

Ava pranced around, pretending to be in distress.

She shrieked at an imaginary spider and pretended to trip and twist her ankle.

When Hercules did not stir from his sleep, she let out a scream as though a savage beast had entered the cave.

Still, Hercules slept on.

Ava's mouth fell open as she looked upon the great Hercules, her supposed husband. She had spent years in solitude, always watching people from afar and never enjoying the touch of a hand. Or even a kiss on the cheek.

Many of her siren sisters were too caught up in spiteful attacks on men to notice Ava, and Isis only spoke to her when she needed something.

It was why Ava had often agreed to spy for Isis, doing her bidding gave her a sense of purpose and a hope that one day her cold mother would show appreciation to her oldest daughter.

Isis had promised Ava love and acceptance in the world's most glorious hero if she saved herself and did as she was told. She dutifully suppressed her yearnings for connection and obeyed her mother's every command.

But it was for…what?

Nothing.

All she faced from Hercules was more isolation.

Though it was not her nature to be anything other than cool and collected, the built-up frustration and the humiliation of Hercules's rejection brought out a side of her that she worked hard to repress.

Ava turned into her most terrifying form and let out a bloodcurdling scream. She clawed at Hercules's back, shrieked at him, and unleashed decades of disappointment.

Finally, Hercules jolted awake, his face flushed with color. He sat up, panting.

When his focus rested on her, Ava calmed enough to return to her human form. She placed her hands on her hips, and her blood still boiled.

"I have waited over one hundred years to be married. I have never been with a man. Not a kiss or a handhold, not even a hug. Isis promised me a husband who would give me great satisfaction. And after waiting so long, you reject me? No, sir. You do not reject me, I reject you!" She summoned her deepest scowl, shook a fist at him, and then swiveled to walk out.

But quick as a flash, the candle blew out, thrusting her into darkness. She stopped. A heavy hand clutched her waist, and hot breath touched her neck.

"Ava. It has been close to a millennium since the

last time I felt this alive." Hercules's voice sounded like honey and drenched her senses in sickly-sweet warmth. "I am sorry to have disappointed you, my lady." This time, his breath tickled her other ear as he moved around her.

A flood of tingles set off a chain reaction in Ava's body as his fingertips grazed her arms.

"You will have to forgive me, for I have been alone for more than a thousand years. I did not know my error."

"Then you accept me?" Ava asked.

Hercules growled, dragging Ava's hair away from her neck.

She nearly fainted at the touch. Her senses ran wild, and her imagination concocted all kinds of scandalous things she expected Hercules to do next. They were alone in a dark cave, after all. She had admitted to being his virgin bride. What would he do about it?

As though he had heard her thoughts, Hercules's hand left her body.

Ava shivered at the absence of his warmth.

Candlelight filled the cave once more, illuminating Hercules's intense eyes. He did not look at her face. Instead, his gaze traveled over her body. This time, he looked at her with more care and attention.

"I accept Isis's gift. What ludicrous mission has she got in mind?" he asked.

Ava led Hercules back to the beach, where the others sat beside a roaring campfire.

Everyone jumped to their feet as he approached, and Hercules raised his palms.

"Forgive my rudeness earlier. I am not accustomed to having company." He wrapped an arm around Ava and squeezed her waist. "Tell me about this quest."

Ava sucked in a deep breath. "We need to retrieve all of the bones of Osiris and return them to Isis. The problem is, each burial site is guarded by a monster."

"Ah." He rubbed his chin in thought.

"Will you lead us?" Serena asked.

Hercules looked at the faces watching him and gave them all a grim look. "Are you prepared to die for this mission?"

"Yes," everyone replied in unison.

Hercules shrugged. "Then I will lead you."

Excitement and anticipation grew as everyone talked in whispers.

Hercules walked toward the sea and waved his broad arms in a circular motion. A portal opened up in thin air.

Georgette's wide eyes flew from the portal to

Hercules to the group around her. "We're going *now?*"

Hercules looked back at her with a smirk.

"Oh, no. Not yet. We need supplies. Weapons. And I will not go anywhere without my golden mace."

Captain Stone frowned. "Where is it?"

Hercules jabbed his thumb toward the blue portal and grabbed Ava by the hand. "My wife and I need to pay my uncle a visit."

A measured silence passed by before Prince Edward asked the question on all of their minds. "Who is your uncle?"

Hercules saluted them and tugged Ava to the edge of the portal. "Hades."

Ava's heart lunged as they fell through.

AVA

*A*va's heart drummed in her chest. Each beat echoed the anticipation she felt as she ventured into the Underworld with Hercules. The air felt dense, laden with a cold mist that wrapped around her like a shroud. The very essence of the Underworld tried to seep into her pores and made her skin tingle with an icy touch.

Eerie silence met every step they took, broken only by the distant wails of lost souls and the soft crunch of their footsteps on the ashen ground. The vastness of the realm stretched out before them in an endless expanse of shadow and obscurity. Light seemed to be swallowed whole, only to be regurgitated as ghostly blue flames. These flames danced sporadically in the distance, and their ethereal glow cast eerie illuminations on the jagged rocks and barren plains.

As they delved deeper, peculiar formations dotted the landscape. Towering obsidian pillars rose from the ground. Ancient runes etched their surfaces and pulsed with a faint luminescence. These structures hummed with energy—a power both alluring and foreboding.

The scent of the Underworld was heavy with of a mix of damp earth and something metallic, like the aftermath of a thunderstorm. Every now and then, a gust of wind would carry whispers, fragmented memories of those who once lived now trapped in this liminal space between life and death.

Beside her, Hercules moved with a purpose, and his familiarity with the terrain became evident. Yet, even he seemed to tread with caution. His eyes constantly scanning their surroundings, alert to the mysteries and dangers that the Underworld held.

Ava clung to his presence, drawing comfort from his strength. For in this realm of shadows and echoes, where time seemed to warp and reality moved like fluid, she realized that the tales she had heard of barely scratched the surface of the Underworld's true nature.

Every few steps, Ava found her gaze irresistibly drawn to Hercules.

In the muted, otherworldly glow of the Underworld, the contours of his muscular physique stood out with stark clarity, each sinew and tendon defined, as if sculpted by the gods themselves. The dim light played tricks on her eyes, casting shadows that accentuated the dips and curves of his well-chiseled form, making him appear even more formidable.

The scars that crisscrossed his chest did not just look like blemishes on his skin; he wore them like badges of honor. Each one told a story of bravery and of battles fought against insurmountable odds. They spoke of a warrior who had faced the fiercest of foes and emerged victorious time and time again.

To Ava, they formed a testament of his resilience and indomitable spirit.

But it wasn't just his physical appearance that captivated her. His eyes, deep-set and intense, were like windows to a soul that had seen centuries unfold. They shimmered with a wisdom that came from lifetimes of experiences, of triumphs and heartbreaks, of love and loss.

And then his scent wafted around her in a tantalizing blend of musk, reminiscent of a wild forest after a rainstorm. Raw and primal, it evoked images of untamed landscapes and fierce battles.

The fragrance was so heady, so potent, that Ava felt herself being pulled toward him, like a moth to a flame. It was a sensation she had never felt before, a dizzying mix of desire and admiration.

As they journeyed deeper into the Underworld, Hercules moved with a grace that belied his size. He took measured steps, exuding a quiet confidence with a relaxed posture and a steady gaze. But in moments of heightened alertness, his muscles would tense, his eyes would narrow, and he would move with a predator's precision, ready to spring into action at a moment's notice.

Ava couldn't help but wonder what it would be like to truly know the man behind the legend.

They approached a chasm.

The bridge before them looked like a marvel, constructed from what appeared to be bones, each piece intricately interwoven to form a pathway. It shimmered and shifted as if not entirely solid, yet it held firm under their weight. As they began to cross, the River of the Dead stretched out below them. Its waters remained dark and still, reflecting nothing but the sorrow of the souls trapped within.

The souls, mere wisps of what they once had

been, moved with a languid grace. Their ethereal forms glided silently from side to side. They seemed to be searching for something just out of reach, perhaps a memory of a life once lived or a love once cherished.

Ava's heart ached as she watched them.

Isis always said that compassion was her weakness.

She leaned closer to Hercules and spoke in a voice barely above a whisper. "What becomes of these souls, Hercules? Is there no end to their torment?"

Hercules paused and fixed his gaze on the river below. After what felt like an eternity, he finally answered her, his voice low and filled with a sorrow Ava had never heard before. "They are trapped in a cycle, forever drifting between hope and despair. Some find their way out, while others... remain." His words sounded cryptic, leaving Ava with more questions than answers.

Ava considered it, thinking about the war that waged between sirens and men. How many of those wisps had once been powerful sirens, soaring through the seas, now fated to be trapped within such depressing waters for all eternity?

The thought of her fallen sisters possibly being

amongst those lost souls sent a shiver down Ava's spine. She remembered their laughter, their songs, the bond they shared that stretched beyond time and distance.

The idea of them being trapped in this endless purgatory felt unbearable.

"Do you think...?" Her voice faltered. "Do you think any of my sisters are down there? Or did they manage to escape this fate?"

Hercules looked at her, and his eyes searched hers for a moment. But he remained silent, offering no reassurance or confirmation. His reaction spoke volumes, and Ava felt a chill settle in her heart. Nothing sounded louder than the noise of silence.

The path they treaded gradually widened, leading them to an enormous cavern. The ceiling soared high above, lost in shadows, while intricate carvings adorned the walls. Each depicted tales of old, of gods and mortals, of love and betrayal.

The air grew colder, and an oppressive stillness enveloped them, broken only by the distant murmurs of the creatures within the belly of the Underworld.

As they stepped into the grand throne room, Ava's breath caught in her throat.

The sheer scale of the chamber felt awe-inspiring. Torches lined the walls, and their blue flames cast an eerie glow that reflected off the polished obsidian floor. But the throne at the center truly captured her attention. Crafted entirely from obsidian blocks chiseled into the shapes of bones, it looked both magnificent and macabre.

Hades sat upon the throne.

Ava had heard tales of the god of the Underworld, stories that painted him as a fearsome, monstrous being. But the figure before her defied those tales.

Hades looked strikingly handsome. His hair, slick and black as the night, cascaded down to his shoulders, framing a face both stern and regal. His torso, bare and rippling with muscles, gleamed under the torchlight, while his sharp eyes, piercing and calculating, scanned the room and missed nothing.

A host of hooded figures surrounded him, and each stood with an unnatural stiffness. Yet, all of them bowed in reverence, and their voices raised in chants and hymns, worshipping their lord.

Despite the adulation he received, Hades appeared disinterested, even detached. His fingers tapped rhythmically on the armrest of his throne, and his gaze, though sharp, seemed to be focused on something far away, as if the proceedings of his court were of little consequence to him.

Ava felt a knot of tension in her stomach. They walked a fine line between diplomacy and danger. She cast a sidelong glance at Hercules, hoping to draw strength from his presence, but even he seemed to tread carefully in the presence of the god of the Underworld.

The path leading away from the throne room was a labyrinth of winding corridors, each more foreboding than the last. The cold, unyielding stone that formed the walls seemed to absorb the dim light and cast long, stretching shadows that played tricks on Ava's eyes.

Every step they took echoed eerily, and the sound bounced off the walls and melded with the distant, mournful cries that permeated the air.

As they progressed deeper, they passed countless doors, each one unique in its design. Some ornate, adorned with gold and precious stones, while others were simple, made of rotting wood and rusted iron. But what they all had in common were the sounds emanating from within. Wails of despair, angry shouts, soft sobbing, and other, more indescribable noises that sent shivers down Ava's spine.

She couldn't help but wonder what torments awaited behind each door, what souls the doors trapped in eternal suffering. But she would be glad never to find out.

The weight of the Underworld pressed upon her shoulders, dragging her down. It made every step a monumental effort. The air grew thicker, harder to breathe, and a sense of unease settled in her chest. She sensed the eyes of unseen entities watching them, their gazes heavy and malevolent.

Hercules, noticing her discomfort, reached out, took her hand, and gave it a reassuring squeeze. His touch felt warm, a stark contrast to the coldness around them. Though a simple gesture, she felt monumental gratitude for it.

As they approached a particularly large door, Ava felt a pull, an inexplicable urge to see what lay beyond.

She reached out, her fingers wrapped around the brass handle, and pulled with all her might.

But the door remained steadfast, refusing to yield to her siren strength.

Frustration bubbled up within her, but before she could react, Hercules stepped forward.

"Allow me, my lady."

With a smirk that hinted at both amusement and confidence, he took a few steps back and charged at the door.

The impact made a thunderous sound that reverberated throughout the corridor.

To Ava's astonishment, the seemingly impenetrable door shattered like fragile parchment under Hercules's strength, revealing the mysteries that lay beyond.

The sheer opulence of the room looked overwhelming.

Ava felt as if she had stepped into the heart of a dragon's hoard, surrounded by unimaginable wealth.

Gold coins lay in vast heaps, spilling over ancient chests inlaid with gemstones. Delicate tiaras, necklaces, and rings were arranged on velvet cushions. Their stones caught the dim light and reflected it in a myriad of colors. Ancient weapons, their blades encrusted with jewels, hung on the walls, alongside shields and armor that bore the insignias of long-forgotten kingdoms.

But as magnificent as the treasures looked, a sense of unease gnawed at Ava.

The room, for all its splendor, felt like a trap, its riches a lure for the unwary. Every creak of the floorboards, every rustle of their clothing, seemed amplified and echoed ominously in the vast chamber.

"Hades keeps his most prized possessions in this

room," Hercules muttered, looking around. "Now, let's find that mace."

Despite his words, Hercules tossed the fine pieces of silver and golden amulets like they were useless rags. They fell with a clatter, and the sound jarred Ava's senses.

She cast furtive glances at the room's entrance, half-expecting to see Hades or one of the cloaked figures. Her heart raced, and she found herself mentally retracing their steps, trying to figure out if they could make a quick escape if needed.

In stark contrast to her anxiety, Hercules seemed completely at ease. The tension that had marked his demeanor earlier had vanished, replaced by a cheeky grin that Ava hadn't seen in a while. He swaggered around the room, his movements confident and self-assured, as if he were in his own palace rather than the heart of the Underworld.

It seemed as if the sight of the treasures, reminders of battles won and adventures had, had rekindled a spark within him.

"Is this mace a sturdy staff?" Ava searched the treasures and had no idea what to look for.

"This mace," Hercules's fingers traced the air as if he could conjure it from memory, "is like no other.

Crafted from the purest gold, it gleams even in the darkest night. And the spikes…"

His eyes gleamed with mischief as they landed on her. "They're not just for show. Each one is honed to perfection, sharp enough to pierce the toughest armor."

He paused, and his expression turned somber. "Hades took it from me during a battle long ago. It wasn't just a weapon; it was a part of me. I am truly lost without it." The pain in his voice sounded palpable, and Ava had a surge of sympathy for him. She reached out, placing a comforting hand on his arm, hoping to offer some solace in this place of shadows and secrets.

The vast room closed in on them as they scoured every corner, looking for the elusive mace.

Frustration mounted in Hercules's eyes. His jaw clenched, and his fingers twitched.

"We've looked everywhere." Ava's voice tinged with desperation. "Maybe it's not here. We should regroup with the others and come up with a new plan."

Hercules turned to her, and his eyes burned with determination. "I've faced monsters, gods, and all manner of challenges," he growled. "I won't be bested by Hades's tricks. That mace is here, and I intend to find it."

Before Ava could respond, a cold, mocking laughter echoed through the chamber. "Oh, Hercules," a voice dripped with condescension. "Always so headstrong."

They both spun around to find Hades leaning casually against the doorway, and the golden mace gleamed in his hand.

His presence commanded the air around him, and his aura exuded power and control. Two cloaked figures flanked him with their faces obscured, but their eyes glowed with malevolence.

Hercules, without hesitation, charged at Hades, his eyes locked onto the mace.

But the two figures intercepted him with surprising agility and raised staffs.

As they clashed, Hades lifted a red jewel, and its inner light pulsated.

The moment Hades held it up, Hercules staggered. His strength visibly waned, and his movements became sluggish.

Ava watched in horror, and her mind raced.

Hercules had a weakness. She needed to intervene, to find a way to tip the balance in their favor.

But before she could act, Hades spoke, and his

voice dripped with malice. "You want this mace, nephew?" Hades twirled the weapon with ease. "Very well. But everything has a price."

Ava stepped forward. Her voice came out firm despite the fear gnawing at her. "What do you want, Hades?"

Hades turned to meet Ava's hard stare, and his eyes widened with recognition. "You're a daughter of Isis and Poseidon." His nostrils flared as though he had stepped on something sticky. "I thought I could smell a siren down here."

Ava prickled under his words. She had been unaware that sirens had a particular scent.

Hades's dark eyes took in her form, and she wanted to recoil, but instead she stood firm and clenched her jaw.

Finally, Hades chuckled. "I daresay the stars have moved in my favor." He tossed the red crystal in the air and caught it.

He motioned for his guards to step away, and they obeyed, allowing Hercules to stand tall and catch his breath. "All I need to do is borrow your little siren here." Hades grinned at Hercules.

Hercules scowled at him. "What do you need her for?"

Hades tutted. "Now, now, my nephew. That is no

way to speak to your uncle. After all, I'm only trying to help."

He slinked his arm around Ava's shoulders, and a strong woody aroma flooded her nostrils. "I just need her to sing a little song for me. Just one. Then you can have her and the mace."

Hercules and Ava exchanged looks as they considered the deal. It sounded simple enough.

If singing a song would win Hercules's freedom and get his beloved weapon, then it would be worth it. But Ava could not imagine what use Hades had for her voice other than to draw a man to the Underworld.

Yet, if that was the case, surely Hades was powerful enough to drag any human to his realm should he desire.

As though he could read her mind, Hades answered the question. "There's someone I've been expecting for a long time now, and yet he has evaded me for many years. But your enchanting voice will lure him into the depths and right to where he belongs."

Ava stiffened. She had no interest in killing. But then she looked at Hercules again and bit her lip. "Who is the poor soul I am to sing to?"

Hades waved a hand aside. "No one you know.

He is not special or of particular importance. The world will not miss him, I assure you."

Ava sucked in a breath and shut her eyes.

Just one soul. Someone of no importance. In exchange for her new husband and the key to starting Isis's quest.

She opened her eyes and gave Hades a resolute nod. "I agree to your terms," she said, determined. "Just one song."

Hades's face lit up as he grinned delighted at Ava. "Excellent. I'll draw you a map to the island. The man you shall seek is called Adonis."

HERCULES

The distance between Ava and Hercules grew with each step. Oppressive silence filled the space that seemed to magnify their separation.

Hercules strained against Hades's grip, and his voice echoed down the corridor as he called out to Ava. "Hades is not known for playing an honest game. Stay strong!"

Ava's voice, sharp and defiant, cut through the gloom. "Worry about yourself, Hercules! I've faced worse than Hades's trickery." Fire filled her words, and they became a sharp reminder of the fierce spirit she had displayed in the cave on the island.

A brief smile tugged at Hercules's lips. The

memory of that encounter warmed him despite the cold surroundings.

Ava had stood her ground with an unwavering voice and determination in her eyes that had taken him by surprise. If anyone could handle the challenges of the Underworld, she could.

But as the distance between them grew, so did Hercules's concern.

He might have faith in Ava's strength and resilience, but the thought of her facing the dangers of Hades's realm without him by her side gnawed at him. He had met many adversaries in his time, but Hades was unlike any other.

Cunning, manipulative, and with a penchant for mind games, the god of the Underworld was a formidable foe.

Hades tightened his grip, which jerked Hercules from his thoughts as Hades pulled him into a dimly lit cell.

The walls seemed to pulse with a malevolent energy, and the air thickened with a sense of foreboding. But Hercules refused to be cowed. He might be in Hades's domain, but he would not be broken. He would find a way to reunite with Ava and escape the clutches of the Underworld.

And Hades would rue the day he crossed paths with the son of Zeus.

The room into which Hades threw Hercules looked unlike any he had seen before. Here, the dark, obsidian stone walls seemed to absorb the scant light, giving it an oppressive feel. Strange, ancient symbols were etched into the stone, their meanings lost to time, but their presence added to the room's eerie ambiance.

The air thickened with a dampness that clung to Hercules's skin, and a faint, musty odor permeated the space, hinting at the age and neglect of the chamber. In the center of the room, a solitary torch flickered, and its flame cast dancing shadows that played tricks on the eyes.

Hades had ensured that Hercules's confinement remained not just physical but psychological.

The cold and heavy chains that bound him had been adorned with thorns that bit into his flesh as a constant reminder of his captivity. Every movement sent a sharp sting of pain up his arms, a cruel touch added by Hades to ensure his discomfort.

But what drew Hercules's attention the most was the ruby crystal.

Positioned deliberately on the door's ledge window, it formed the room's focal point. Its deep red hue glowed with an inner fire, casting a blood-red illumination that bathed the room.

Hercules could feel its energy and power even from a distance, a malevolent force that seemed to reach out to him, seeking to drain his strength and will. The crystal pulsed rhythmically, almost as if it were alive.

It became a stark reminder of his vulnerability in this place, and of Hades's cunning and resourcefulness.

The god of the Underworld had left nothing to chance, ensuring that Hercules was not just imprisoned but also weakened, making escape all the more challenging.

Hades leaned in, his voice dripping with mockery. "Do you remember the last time we faced each other, Hercules? You, with all your might, brought to your knees by this little gem." He chuckled, and the sound echoed eerily in the confined space. "I must admit, watching the great Hercules fall was quite the spectacle. It reminded me of Achilles during the battle of Troy."

Hercules gritted his teeth. The memory of that defeat still felt fresh in his mind.

Hades tried to get under his skin, to break his spirit, but he wouldn't give him the satisfaction.

A smug grin twisted Hades's face. "A haggard old witch gave me this ruby. She said it would be the key to your downfall. And she was right."

He frowned, looking at the crystal. "But she also said that when you become a true god, it will lose its power over you."

After a second or two, he shrugged and grinned back at Hercules. "I daresay, I'd like to see that. But for now, it looks like you're nothing but a pathetic demigod. A fraud."

Hercules smirked, refusing to let Hades see his discomfort. "You've been lurking in this dreary place for so long, Uncle, that you've resorted to schoolyard taunts. How the mighty have fallen."

Hades's smile faltered, and his eyes narrowed. "At least I've not been hiding alone on some remote island, wallowing in self-pity."

Hercules met his gaze defiantly. "I'm not alone."

Hades tilted his head, and his expression turned contemplative. "Ah, the siren. A curious choice. I'm surprised you're ready for another relationship. I believe you swore off women after what happened to Megara..."

Hercules's face darkened, and anger bubbled up within him. "Don't you dare speak her name."

A cruel smile spread across Hades's face. "Struck a nerve, have I? Even after all this time?"

Hercules took a deep breath, forcing himself to remain calm. He needed to change the subject, to keep Hades from delving too deep into his past. "What's your obsession with Adonis? I thought you two settled your differences."

Hades's eyes flashed in a clear warning. "Tread carefully, Hercules. I have the power to end you with a mere snap of my fingers."

Hercules nodded toward the ruby. "Without that ruby, you wouldn't stand a chance against me. And you know it."

Hades's smile vanished, replaced by a look of pure malice. He leaned in close, and his voice came out a low growl. "You'd do well to remember your place, nephew. Or you might find yourself joining the lost souls in the River of the Dead."

With that, Hades turned on his heel and left. The door slammed shut behind him, leaving Hercules alone with his thoughts and the ruby's glow casting eerie shadows on the walls.

Hercules panted as he cast his eyes at the damp stone floor. But his mind replayed events that once again sliced open old wounds in his heart.

He gritted his teeth until his jaw ached, and he fought against the hot tears prickling his eyes.

The all-too familiar screams played on repeat in his mind. Just as they had over and over for more than a millennium. It would drive anyone to insanity.

He shuffled, and his bare back pressed against the rocky wall of his cell. A sharp pain smarted through him as the abrasive rocks grazed the places where Ava had slashed him with her claws.

He welcomed the pain. Shutting his eyes, he let out a long breath.

The pain felt like both a punishment and a welcome distraction.

He dragged his back over the wall and grunted. Drops of blood rolled down his torso, leaving a burning trail in their wake.

Perhaps Hades was right, he pondered as he zoned in on the sharp throbbing ache in his body. Ava's outburst made him forget himself for a moment. Now he saw with perfect clarity just why he had isolated himself for so many centuries. And why he deserved to stay hidden in the shadows.

He slumped forward, heaving big breaths as his muscles ached from decades of grief and tension.

Even if Ava did succeed and Hades released him,

Hercules considered the idea that perhaps he sat right where he belonged after all.

Another memory flashed before his mind, and he groaned as if possessed.

If memories could cause physical pain, he would have perished from a million cuts to his very soul. By the time his memories stopped repeating, nothing would remain of him but a wisp. Like an eternal wail of lament and sorrow.

He had been foolish to agree to join people on a quest. If they knew what he was capable of, what he had done out of self-preservation, Ava and her friends would cower in fear at the very sight of him. Just as anyone who knew him did.

Anyone except Hades, of course.

But no one had more malice in their heart than the Nether King. He knew suffering and delighted in it. That had likely been why he had taken Hercules's mace, knowing how much it would destroy his nephew to be parted from it.

Hercules balled his big hands into fists like two rocks, and he pounded the ground until it trembled, and his knuckles bled.

Then another thought sparked a different feeling inside of him. One so ancient to him, so alien, that he had almost forgotten what it was.

Ava's pretty face came into view, and he thought about Hades putting his grubby hands on her.

Knowing that Hades loved nothing more than to play with his prey, toying with their hearts and causing sheer torture to them... He realized that if he did not get out of the cell and find Ava, then Ava's fate might end up worse than Megara's.

Hercules grunted and shook himself. The whisper of his lost love's name drenched him in lava-like emotion.

He wrenched his wrists until the manacles nearly tore the flesh from his bones. Thick congealed blood covered them as he roared like a lion, and the rock wall began to crack as he yanked forward.

Finally, with a defining crunch, his wrists and thumbs snapped, sending a fresh rush of throbbing, maddening pain through his senses. But his broken bones let his hands go limp enough to wriggle out of his cuffs.

He huffed deep breaths, relishing the agony, and slumped against the wall. With a final deep breath, he rested his mangled hands on his thighs.

He looked up at the tiny crack in the ceiling that let in a soft glowing light.

No one could tell the time in the Underworld, but Hercules knew that it moved differently from Earth.

He sucked in long breaths, willing his strength to heal his wounds. Then he rested his head against the wall and shut his eyes, dreaming of happier times.

"I will find you, Ava," he murmured like a prayer. "I promise."

CAPTAIN STONE

"*I* can't believe they just left us here!" Georgette stared at the place where the portal had once opened.

Captain Stone paused to look at his wife in awe.

The ocean breeze washed over her, pushing her wavy, blonde locks back, strands of hair flying away from her face, and even with a deep scowl, she had unparalleled beauty that held him in a trance.

Serena, the siren with fiery red hair, scoffed at her, which snapped him out of it.

"Count your blessings Hercules did not have us go with them, *sister*." She spat the last word like poison. "The Underworld is no place for the living."

It had only been a few minutes since Hercules

and Ava had gone and Georgette and Serena had already broken into an argument.

As the sisters exchanged heated words and dangerous glares, Prince Edward and Captain Stone exchanged wary looks. They busied themselves by packing up the camp. Neither of them felt the need to say it aloud: stay out of it.

The news that Georgette and Serena were twin sisters had him reeling, but the more he watched them scowl at each other, pacing with their long hair flowing behind them with grace despite the aggressive way they moved… he could see it. The two held resemblance with each other; not just in looks but their mannerisms too.

And the more time they spent together, the more they seemed to draw out each other's hot headedness.

And as his sight set on Georgette's flaming cheeks, moving to her slender fingers curled inward as she came to a stop until she shook a fist in the air, his nether regions tensed.

He smirked.

He delighted in seeing his wife in this mood, and it felt refreshing to see her bad temper not directed at him for once.

She was too deep in conversation with Serena to notice him staring at her, so he crouched by the campfire, stoking the flames with a stick as he read her body like a book.

Her narrow shoulders tensed far too high to be natural, and her legs would be knotted up with tension. She looked wound up with conflicting emotions: fear, confusion, and anger…

He would enjoy pacifying her tonight.

Flashes of inappropriate thoughts crossed his mind. His hands clenched, and he bit his lip as he pictured her sprawled out on the narrow bed in their cabin.

Her plump breasts on full display with soft nipples gleamed in the lamplight. By the time he finished teasing her, she'd thrash like a wild maven.

He'd clamp her legs apart and dive in to pleasure her until she shook and screamed, begging him to claim her.

But he would not stop until she tumbled over the edge, over and over until she felt listless, satiated, and panted.

He could almost taste her as he thought about it, and his mouth went dry.

Georgette turned, and her sharp eyes met his.

He swallowed and forced a straight face. If she knew what thoughts crossed his mind, she would direct her fury at him for not taking her seriously.

To his dismay, Serena directed her attention his way, too. "Keep your disgusting fantasies to yourself, pirate."

Captain Stone stiffened. "I didn't say anything," he said, as he silently wondered if he had somehow uttered his private thoughts by mistake.

He glanced at Prince Edward who shrugged back. He found Georgette again who looked at Serena with a furrowed brow.

It suddenly dawned on him that he was no longer an ordinary human.

He glanced at the bandage on his hand, where he'd cut his palm for the binding ceremony. Now that he had siren blood running in his veins, he would never be the same.

Could Serena read his thoughts?

Serena made an exaggerated sigh and folded her arms. "No, you didn't say anything, but your mind screamed about all the things you want to do to *her*." She shot Georgette a dark look. "Thank the gods you two haven't developed your telepathic abilities yet." She looked from Georgette to Prince Edward.

"We will be able to read minds?" Georgette asked. For the first time, she sounded hopeful.

Meanwhile, Captain Stone could only think about

how horrifying it was that his sister-in-law could listen to his private thoughts.

A moment of silence went by, and Prince Edward's face paled as he stared into the campfire like he had a vision. His thoughts must have been obvious to Serena because her mood shifted, and she cleared her throat.

"We should prepare for Hercules's return, so we are ready to leave."

Captain Stone jumped into action, happy for the change of subject. "Right, we shall need supplies. I will take the dinghy to the next island and—"

"I'll go with you." Georgette placed her hands on her hips.

Captain Stone pressed his index finger to his mouth as he thought about it. "I think I would prefer it if you stayed at the camp with..." He stopped when Georgette reached his flank and held him under her hard gaze.

"With whom?" She gestured to Serena before pointing at Prince Edward. "My vengeful sister who hates me or my ex-fiancé?"

"I said, I don't hate you." Serena rolled her eyes, but Georgette ignored her and walked around Captain Stone until her bosoms touched his chest.

She knew what she was doing. Her touch sent a

zing through Captain Stone's senses, and it took everything not to clutch her hips.

His hands twitched.

"Do not tell me you have forgotten everything we've been through?" Her voice a low murmur as her eyes flashed dangerously.

Captain Stone glanced at his brother who had suddenly busied himself by the campfire, sharpening a stick with his knife.

Serena watched them with her arms folded, listening to their every word. It did not matter how quiet Georgette tried to speak; the barest whisper would land on a siren's ears like a thunderclap. Especially when she eavesdropped. Not that it mattered now that she could hear their thoughts.

By the way Serena looked so intently in their direction, she obviously hung onto every word of their exchange, and Captain Stone changed his mind.

Though he did not like the idea of taking his wife into unknown territory, it had to be better than leaving her with his brother.

After all, no matter how much he professed to love Serena, Prince Edward did utter Georgette's name while he bedded her. An atrocity that Captain Stone felt certain Serena would never forgive. But he did not know if she harbored animosity toward Georgette on the matter.

In any case, he didn't entirely trust either of them.

He found Georgette's dewy eyes and swallowed. "Of course, my love. You are right."

The air calmed, and Georgette's shoulders dropped as she lifted her chin. "Well, then, Serena, stay here with Edward and look out for Ava and Hercules… if they return, call out to us. Now that we're all…" She turned to give Captain Stone and Prince Edward a confused look. "Am I to assume that our husbands are part-siren? Is that what we call them?"

Serena scoffed and tossed her hair back in a way that reminded Captain Stone of Georgette.

"They are part-Triton." Serena shrugged. "It seems there is so much you do not know."

Georgette hissed and marched to her sister. "That is precisely why I asked you to teach me."

Serena pointed an accusatory finger at her. "Do not talk to me like that. I performed the binding ceremony, did I not? I am under no obligation…"

Georgette made a noise of frustration and dragged her hands through her hair. "I was hoping you would do it out of decency, not obligation."

Serena's face screwed up. "How dare you!"

The air sizzled with tension as the two sisters struck up another argument.

Captain Stone and Prince Edward exchanged looks once more.

Captain Stone felt unsure whether he indeed possessed the ability to read minds or if it was just so blazing obvious. But he knew that Prince Edward shared his thought: their women needed to be tamed, and it would be beneficial to all of them if they spent some time apart.

"Come, my lady." Captain Stone roughly grabbed his wife by the shoulders and marched her away. "We must go to the other island before the markets close."

Serena and Georgette simmered down, but Captain Stone could still hear their grumbles as he took Georgette back to the boat.

When they reached half-way to the neighboring island, Captain Stone lowered the sail and let the boat slowly bob in the crystal-clear waters. He sighed deeply and gave Georgette a hard look. "Tell me what's really going on in that pretty head of yours."

He reached for Georgette's cheek.

Her mouth fell open as she looked at him. "Nothing. Why do you ask me in that tone?"

Captain Stone cocked his head to the side as they

bobbed on the glassy surface of the water under the blistering sunshine.

Sweat gathered in the swell of Georgette's cleavage and her upper lip.

Captain Stone moved over, lowered his mouth to her bosoms and sucked on the glistening sweat. Then he brushed his thumb over the sweat above her upper lip. He hovered close so they could sit and breathe each other's air for a few moments.

The tender moment melted Georgette's harshness, and soon tears welled in her eyes and tumbled down her cheeks.

It felt like witnessing a wall crashing before his eyes; Georgette's harsh exterior vanished, and she looked so vulnerable.

"All that has happened… all that is to come… I have hardly had a moment to sit and contemplate it all." She pressed her fingers to her temples with a sigh and edged away, but Captain Stone swooped her up into his arms and settled her in his lap.

"My dearest Georgette, it pains me to see you so tortured." He kissed her cheeks, and her salty tears lingered on his lips. "Perhaps we should stay here, and I can work on easing the tension in your body while you…contemplate it all." He winked, and a shadow of a smile crossed Georgette's face.

"It's about my father," she said just as Captain Stone began kissing her neck.

He promptly withdrew, and his arousal disappeared at her words. They felt like a kick to his gut. "Ah…"

He stared at a small rip in her cotton trousers. He played with the frays with his fingers, while Georgette leaned in and rested against his chest. Her body trembled, despite the strong sunlight beaming down on them.

Captain Stone cradled her and stroked her hair as she succumbed to grief.

"Lord Harrington was a…"

Well. Lord Harrington had not been a good man, Captain Stone thought. The man had gambled away Georgette's dowry, lost his estate, and always smelled of hard liquor.

But he had been someone close to Georgette and someone she loved. Even though he could not understand why she cared for him now that she knew the truth, he understood that finding him hanging from the rafters in their home must have been a terrible shock.

No daughter should have to find her father in that state. No matter how poor of a father he had been.

Georgette lifted her head to give him a deep,

sorrowful look. "Lord Harrington was not my father," she whispered, but the words landed on Captain Stone like a smack to the face.

The revelation numbed him.

He had supposed that Isis shared such information when they learned that Serena and Georgette were, in fact, twins. But at the time, he was far too concerned with the events at hand to listen to anything Isis had to say.

Especially as he still mulled over what his experience with Hathor meant.

Why did she want him to destroy Isis's tower? Did she know what lay under it? Was Hathor on Isis's side, or did she have other malicious intentions?

He cleared his throat. Now was not the time to ponder such things.

He brushed a cluster of strands of hair away from Georgette's tearstained cheek and tucked it behind her ear. "Do you need to talk about it?"

Georgette turned away and leaned against him again. "No. I suppose I don't," she said in a strangled voice.

"Then what do you want?" Captain Stone asked, rubbing her back.

Her muscles felt lumpy and knotted, longing to be worked on. If there had not been other sailboats in the distance and daylight exposing them, he would have taken care of her right there.

He craned his neck to the door of the tiny cabin. "Come on, love." He tightened his grip on her body and stood up, holding her close to him.

Georgette wrapped her arms around his neck and looked around them as the boat swayed under his heavy steps. "I thought you said we needed to get to the markets before they close," she protested as Captain Stone carried her to the cabin door.

He kicked it open and descended the narrow steps to the small bed nestled within.

"The market can wait. Your body is more twisted than a bundle of sailor's rope. You're not of use to anyone in this state. I'm going to unwind you."

To his relief, Georgette did not argue when he flipped her on her front. In fact, she wriggled down the bed on her stomach, resting her cheek on her forearms, and waited.

"Very well. Do your worst." She relaxed into the bed.

"Good girl," Captain Stone growled. He took no time in loosening her shirt and lifting it up, revealing her tight cotton stays beneath.

He carefully tugged on the ties and discarded the garment on the floor. As soon as it landed, he turned his attention to Georgette's bare back. Her shoulder blades poked out and almost touched from the tension. She always stayed on high alert.

He would enjoy watching her loosen up under his touch.

The air flooded with the sound of Georgette's sighs as Captain Stone dragged his calloused hands over the plains of her back.

She exhaled and softened under his touch, and when he placed tender kisses down her spine, she melted like butter left out on a warm day.

The boat rocked lazily in the calm water.

Captain Stone tugged on the waistband of Georgette's trousers and undergarments. When he got them over the globes of her shapely bottom, Georgette lifted herself on her elbows and huffed.

"All of my adolescent life, I believed my mother to be a saint... a loving, loyal wife to my father—who *isn't* my father, by the way—and then I discover that not only is she alive, but she discarded me like a used handkerchief."

Captain Stone listened as he rubbed her buttocks, grazing his thumbs along her hip bones. "Hmm," he said low and deep before leaning in to kiss her tension away.

He took two of his fingers and slid between her legs to brush against her core.

When he dipped his fingers inside, it felt like tucking into a pot of warm honey. His arousal strained against his trousers.

But Georgette had not finished talking. She rolled on to her back, exposing herself but seemed too distracted with her thoughts to take the moment seriously.

To Captain Stone's dismay, she yanked her shirt over herself and pulled up her trousers again.

He nearly howled when she crossed her legs and sat up.

He could smell her, yet he had to sit and listen. He knew it. But every fiber of his body wanted to claim her instead.

"Now, I'm to believe that my real father is the god of the sea and that that grumpy siren out there is my twin sister? And for some ungodly reason, Poseidon, our father, kept her but didn't want me? Mannington, do you have any idea how it feels to be rejected by both of your parents?"

Hearing his name on her lips felt like a jolt to the heart.

Struck by the seriousness of the conversation, Captain Stone swallowed.

He opened his mouth to speak; after all, he knew exactly what that felt like.

His parents acted like he had died when he left his royal life to become a pirate. When they saw him again, many years later, they barely glanced in his direction. Even when his own mother did look him in the eye, her nose wrinkled, and she looked like she had stumbled in horse manure.

But then he shut his mouth, sensing this was not the time to talk about himself.

This was about her.

Instead, he cupped her face, wanting to kiss all of the hurt away. "It is a lot to take in, my love," he murmured, before pressing his lips to hers.

She molded to him, clutching his back like he was the only thing stopping her from drowning in grief.

Their kisses grew wet and salty. When Captain Stone drew back for breath, Georgette was crying again.

"What kind of mother curses her own children? Can you think of anything more twisted?" she whispered.

Captain Stone held his breath and glanced at Georgette's hand resting over her stomach.

Not many weeks had passed since they lost the

baby. The emotions, the pain, the raw suffering…it all felt so intense.

It killed Captain Stone that he couldn't erase all of it. He would sell his soul for a tonic that wiped memories.

"Georgette," he whispered, like a man dying of hunger. Slowly, he lowered to his knees and grazed his thumbs along the waistband of her trousers. "Please."

Georgette sniffed and took a deep breath.

She loved it when he begged, and usually he possessed more pride than to bow to anyone. But he would walk across the surface of the Earth on his knees until they bled if that would soothe his wife.

She had endured more pain and suffering than any human he had ever known, and he could do nothing about it.

The knowledge brought sheer agony to his heart. His chest twisted and ached.

Her eyes darkened, and she nipped her bottom lip as she surveyed him.

He tore his shirt from over his head and grabbed her hand, placing it over his beating heart. "Tell me what you will have me do? You want to talk, I shall listen. You want to unleash a thousand beasts on your parents in an act of revenge, I shall make the arrangements. You want me to—" He stopped when Georgette's mouth landed on his lips.

She threw her arms around his neck and kissed him with more passion. "I want you to make me stop thinking about it."

Captain Stone almost growled with delight. Now, *that* he could do.

She slid her hand into his trousers, gripping him in a way that sent a rush of pleasure through his whole body.

"Give me a reason to believe there is still something to enjoy in this world," she whispered against his mouth.

Captain Stone roughly pulled her trousers down and gripped her bottom while he stroked her tongue with his. He acted rough, messy, and unapologetic as he claimed her.

When he entered her, she bit his shoulder and dug her nails into his biceps.

The pinch made him tense in a delightful way, and he roamed his hands all over her clammy body.

The only time that anything made sense in the world was when they were connected. There could have been nothing but fire and brimstone outside that cabin, and it would never compare to the blazing heat between him and his wife.

They rocked the boat and shattered the quiet sea air with Georgette's screams.

Captain Stone grinned to himself as he fisted her hair and pulled her head back. "That's it, my love. Let go, you're safe." He planted kisses down her neck.

Georgette melted against him and grew rigid as another wave of pleasure rippled through her.

She had him in a death grip, and Captain Stone bit her earlobe, certain that just one more stroke would cause him to tumble over the edge of reason and cease to exist.

When they felt spent, they lay together, naked, with not even a hair's width between them.

Georgette sighed and nestled into the bed as Captain Stone lazily stroked her arm. He nuzzled her neck and held her so tightly that she grumbled about it. But her protests did nothing to stop him from holding onto her like she might disappear if he let her go.

"I do not know why your parents did not keep you," he whispered. "I cannot fathom why Poseidon would let you go and keep Serena. But there is one thing I am certain…"

He flipped Georgette around to look at him and cupped her teary face. "You are the most precious treasure on land or sea. They will bitterly regret their choices… I know you are the most beautiful, wonderful, powerful force in all of the world, and I shall not rest until you know it too."

Georgette opened her mouth to reply but lurched back with a frown, and her gaze shifted to the side.

"What is it?" Captain Stone asked. But then he followed her line of sight at the dark figure standing in the doorway.

"My apologies for breaking up such a tender moment…" the hooded stranger began.

Captain Stone reached for his knife but paused when the stranger slammed a large steel axe on the floorboard with a thud. The blade glinted dangerously.

"I suggest you get dressed. In the name of the All-Father, you are now prisoners of Hakon."

SERENA

*S*erena sat and hugged her knees as she looked out at the rolling sea, imagining the portal opening up again and Hercules walking through with Ava.

She had heard stories about the great Hercules and his golden mace. He would never go anywhere without it.

What in the world happened for Hades to have it in his possession?

From the tales she heard of Hades, the trickster, it would be unlikely that he would simply hand it over.

And if that was the case, then Hercules and Ava could very well be gone for a long time.

But even with that knowledge, she could not bring

herself to take her eyes off the sea. She clung to the tiny hope that she was wrong. Any second now, the portal would reappear.

Hours went by, and though her limbs grew stiff, desperate for relief, she did not move.

"That's everything packed away. And we are alone for once." Prince Edward wrapped her up in his arms. His warmth felt like a welcome contrast to the crisp sea breeze that floated over her body.

He dragged her hair away from her face and buried his face in her neck. His stubble grazed her skin in a way that sent tingles through her.

He whispered in her ear, blowing hot breath over her cheek. "And the sun is beginning to dip below the horizon…"

Serena sighed while her husband left a trail of kisses down her neck.

Prince Edward's kisses soothed her, but they left a bitter sting.

Nightmares plagued her sleep, of him calling out Georgette's name again. And this time in her mind, he would be caressing her, touching her. Confessing his undying love… to Georgette.

The fact that Georgette was her twin sister made everything worse.

It had become hard enough to be told that the two shared blood, but a twin?

She wondered how different it would have been to grow up with a sister in Atlantis, to have a play mate and someone to confess secrets or get up to mischief.

Perhaps in another life, one where they had not been separated, where they hadn't been loved by the same man, they would have even been friends.

Prince Edward's broad hands dragged over her shoulders, and he dragged his calloused thumbs over her arms in small circular motions, thrusting any thought out of her mind. "Come, my love." He tugged on the wide neckline of her gown over her shoulder and pressed his lips to her skin. "There is a cave waiting for us."

She purred as a wave of warmth washed over her, and her eyes fluttered closed.

But then she snapped them open and shook her head. "We must stay and wait for their return."

Prince Edward picked Serena up and swiveled her to face him. He clutched her breasts and tweaked her nipples through the cotton of her dress.

He kissed her again—harsh, needy, and demanding.

It was the way she had always wanted him to kiss her, and once again her mind emptied of all thoughts as raging heat pooled at her core.

She licked his upper lip, and he sucked on her tongue.

The sun's last ray illuminated the darkened sky in hues of orange and red. The Earth seemed to move more slowly while they kissed on the beach.

But while the world slowed down, they moved at an accelerated pace.

They removed each other's clothes like a pair of wolves.

Prince Edward probed her, teasing, gentle.

He hovered and pulled back from her mouth to look deeply into her eyes.

His blue eyes looked like the ocean on a summer's day, and they twinkled at her in the setting sun.

The sand irritated Serena's back as he lay her down, and the blasted grains got everywhere. She squirmed and scowled as they invaded every crevice of her body.

Prince Edward retreated, and a deep crease formed between his brows. "What is wrong, my lady?"

Serena tried to push off the sand from her, but it clung to her sweaty form.

Prince Edward must have sensed the problem because he craned his neck to look at the dark sea and back at his beloved. A wicked smile played on his lips.

Serena's heart melted.

His jawline could cut rope, and a dimple creased on his left cheek when he grinned.

As much as she hated what he did to her in the past, he was the most handsome man and knew exactly how to please her.

Before she could ask what put him in such a playful mood, he picked her up and carried her to the shoreline.

"I told you we should keep watch…" she began.

"We shall not stray far," Prince Edward interrupted her. "There's something I've been wanting to try… ever since I…" He trailed off as he lowered her into the water.

He winked before he swam out to the open sea, and his head disappeared from view.

Serena began to swim forward, looking for him, when a pair of rough hands grabbed her thighs.

She cried out in shock, but then she let out a shuddering breath as a flood of delicious pleasure rippled through her senses.

Prince Edward stayed in the water and worshipped Serena with his fingers and his lips.

His hot tongue snaked over the contours of her body and swirled around her most sensitive parts.

The water carried her, and the shocks of pleasure had her flying to another dimension. The only thing keeping her from disappearing entirely was Prince Edward's hands on her thighs.

He became her anchor.

When she trembled with euphoria, she slipped below the water to meet Prince Edward's gleeful face.

They hovered in the sea; a pair of naked lovers wrapped up in each other's arms. Meanwhile, all manner of fish and sea life roamed around them.

Prince Edward kissed Serena in the water, and ice-cold air shot through her body.

"Remember when you did this to me? You were so innocent then." Prince Edward spoke to her thoughts.

Serena could hear his thoughts so clearly when they were under the sea. The ocean magnified their powers tenfold.

Serena succumbed to the kiss and wrapped her legs around his waist.

"I remember, my prince." She swayed to meet the tip of his erection. It touched her core, and she nearly squealed with excitement.

Prince Edward grasped her hands and entered her with more force than Serena expected.

She gasped against his lips as a temporary sting took hold. But then the pain gave way to a gush of love.

He kissed her face, her neck, her cleavage… All the while he connected with her. Each thrust became harder than the last.

When she released, she ripped her mouth from his to take a deep gulp of water.

For sirens, their emotions, thoughts, and sensations felt so much stronger when they were in the water.

Serena turned primal, thrashing and clawing Prince Edward's back until the water around them turned crimson with his blood.

Prince Edward did not stop, and Serena did not want him to.

She wished they could be like that forever.

But just as Prince Edward prepared to thrust again, something shot through the water and forced them apart. The object sailed toward the darkness below.

It whistled past Serena's ear, and she only caught the silver glint before it disappeared.

"What on earth...?" She thought, looking wildly at Prince Edward for an answer.

He looked up as his dark brows knitted together. Then he grabbed her hand and dragged her through the reddened waters.

Serena finally noticed that her claw marks on his back had not turned the sea red. A lifeless body slowly sank to the depths of the sea.

A strong vibration emitted through the waters, and Serena's heartbeat picked up. *"Edward, I..."*

Soon, they reached the shore, and Serena followed Edward to their campfire and the piles of clothes waiting for them.

The air felt heavy with smoke and explosions.

Bewildered, Serena pulled on her dress and undergarments while she looked out at the darkened horizon.

"In the name of the gods, what is going on?" Prince Edward finished buttoning his shirt.

Serena waved her hand over them, causing their bodies to become dry within the blink of an eye. Then she tried to make sense of the scene before them.

Ships flooded the waters between the two islands in the midst of a battle.

"Look, it's our ship!" Prince Edward pointed to

the center of the commotion. It was surrounded by strange vessels.

He met Serena's concerned gaze.

"Captain Stone is the king of the pirates. There's no need for alarm…" she began.

But Prince Edward shook his head.

"No. Something is terribly wrong…" he muttered, pointing at the strange ornate ships.

He recognized the elaborate designs carved into the wood and the strings of human bones that waved in the air in place of a flag. "They are not pirates." A look of grim horror took over his face.

Serena frowned. "I don't understand. They're not naval officers, nor are they sailors. So, if they are not pirates, who are they?"

Prince Edward began to pace, cursing all of the gods.

Serena grabbed his arm. "What is it? Who are they, Edward?"

He halted, dragged a hand through his hair, and huffed. "I have no idea how this is possible, but I swear on my life that those ships belong to Vikings."

"Vikings?" Serena parroted, but she shook her head in disbelief. "There haven't been sightings of Vikings for almost a thousand years."

Prince Edward grabbed her by the arms. "I know.

But now we are seeing them. Listen for the others, can you hear anything?" He searched Serena's face as her gaze found the floor.

She frowned deeply, but her breath hitched with a yelp, and she blinked at him.

"Something terrible has happened. They need us."

AVA

*T*hick clouds shrouded the night sky and blotted out the stars and moon.

In the absence of warmth and light, an uneasy chill rushed over Ava, sending the hairs on the back of her neck on end.

The sensation felt unusual; she was not accustomed to feelings of fear and uncertainty. But she had never been in a situation like this. After all, she finally got what she wanted: a husband.

Cruelly, Hades snatched him and locked him in the darkest depths of the Underworld.

Now, she had been tasked with a most ugly mission to get him back.

Ava had, regretfully, killed men in the past.

When she was young and impressionable, her

mother, Isis, told her grim stories about the wicked-ness of men and how they treated their dogs better than women. She had convinced Ava and all of her sisters that men needed to be purged from this world. Without them, there would be peace and harmony. With them, only suffering and pain existed in the world.

Now, Ava understood her mother's true motiva-tions. A goddess, bound to an island in immortality, doomed to live forever isolated from the world?

She felt bitter after losing the love of her life, and the daily torture she suffered could drive anyone to madness.

But as Ava watched the humans more closely, she saw something else in men.

She had been there when Captain Stone thought Georgette had perished in a shipwreck. He collapsed to his knees on the beach and sobbed.

It had been the first time Ava had seen a grown man cry, and it touched her soul.

Then Ava heard the shrieks from pirates who dared to touch Serena as Prince Edward tore them limb from limb with his bare hands.

Men acted like rogues, yes. Sometimes, they behaved in brutal and cunning ways. But when love motivated them, they could do the most dastardly and wickedly romantic acts.

Since Ava witnessed this, she made a vow never to kill another man.

But this time she needed to. Just one more.

Then she and Hercules would be reunited, and she wondered if, perhaps they could go somewhere private for him to perform some wicked acts on her before they returned to the island.

The thought stirred a new sensation in her core, and she suppressed a grin.

She stared at the freshly drawn map in her lap as she rowed in the boat Hades gifted her.

Usually, she would traverse the waters in siren form, allowing the heat of the ocean to fuel her. But something felt unnerving about the stillness of the water that had her remain in the small boat.

She turned back to give Hades one last look, as though her soul hoped to find that this was just another one of her nightmares.

Perhaps the movement would jolt her awake.

Instead, her gaze met with Hades. His sharp eyes glinted in the darkness, and a soft blue swirl of light encircled him. "Good luck, Ava. I will be watching."

His words sent another chill crawling up her

spine, and the blue circle of light suddenly fizzled into nothingness, casting Ava into total darkness.

She sucked in a breath and shut her eyes, relying on her hearing to navigate forward.

Leaves rustled on the island ahead. Somewhere in the dead of night, a badger ventured out in search of grubs to eat. An owl hooted lazily, and a family of bobcats snored.

Listening to nature soothed Ava's soul enough to let her clear her mind and focus on what she needed to do.

This special task meant a lot to Hades. Of that, Ava felt certain.

His last conversation with her replayed in her mind.

"Many years ago, a boar killed Adonis—a most humiliating death for a hunter. But his lover, Aphrodite, struck a deal with Zeus to resurrect him and grant him immortality. The price? He must spend four months a year as my servant in the Underworld. But alas, he has evaded me for centuries. The spineless fool has given his soul to dark magic, surrounding his pathetic dwelling in a curse that forbids me from entering. That is where you come in."

Hades bent over his stone desk. A flicker of blue

candlelight illuminated the contours of his chest as he drew long strokes of ink on a piece of parchment.

When he finished, he bent down until his lips were level with the fresh ink, and he blew.

A chilling air floated over the parchment and settled on Ava. She hugged herself and swallowed.

The dangerous glint in his eyes when he looked up froze her in place. He smirked, and she found something both charismatic and cold about his smile.

For the first time in her existence, she stared death in the eye, and she could not wait to be out of his sight.

Somewhere far away, Hercules groaned, drawing Ava back to the present.

She grounded herself in the sounds of wildlife on the nearing island, and the boat slid across the water as if it had a life of its own.

A dark and ominous island loomed over her as the boat reached the shore.

Ava clutched the map in her hands like a lifeline as she navigated her way through this dark and treacherous place.

She stumbled over rocks and roots but kept going despite the fear that threatened to overwhelm her.

Finally, after what felt like hours of walking, Ava arrived at the center of the island.

An eerie silence surrounded her, and she felt as though the island itself watched her every move.

Fatigue overwhelmed her limbs, and Ava thought it better to wait for the sunshine to help her navigate her way. After all, it was impossible to know which way to turn in the darkness.

She found an ancient sycamore tree, and its trunk looked hollowed out, as if nature had created a place of refuge and safety.

There, she nestled in, and let her mind stop spinning long enough to succumb to sleep.

*M*any hours passed, and Ava woke to a stern voice above her head. "What are you doing on my land?"

Ava jumped and blinked into the setting sun to look at a tall, handsome man with deep green eyes.

He towered over her like a giant.

She took a moment to look at his broad shoulders and chiseled jaw.

His piercing eyes seemed to look right through her. He held a bow and a sword in his hands, and from the way he carried his weapons, he looked to be a skilled hunter.

She opened her mouth to speak but no words came out. Fear had taken hold of her, and now she could only scramble to her feet and stare at him in awe.

The man narrowed her gaze on her. "Well?"

Eventually, Ava found the courage to speak up. "If I may, are you Adonis, the great hunter and ruler of this island?"

It slightly sickened her to speak with such adoration, but she knew the only way to coax a man to his demise required a little ego-stroking first.

However, dishonesty was not one of her strengths, and in truth, she held no respect for the man.

After all, she was tasked to drag him to his doom, the less emotion that came into it, the better. If she allowed herself to like the man, even a little, it would make her mission so much more difficult.

The man relaxed the tension in his stance and lowered his shoulders. "Yes, I am Adonis. What do you want from me?"

Relief flooded Ava at her luck.

She did not have to brave whatever curse surrounded the castle after all. Instead, Adonis had come to her. Now, she just needed to lure him to the water.

Ava flicked her hair back and gave him a serene smile. She worried that she acted too obvious and that Adonis would surely sense the fear behind her eyes.

"My name is Ava. I'm honored to be in your presence. I was told that you could help me find my friend. She was last seen on the beach, and as you are the greatest hunter in the world... I thought your tracking skills could help me."

"The greatest hunter in the world..." Adonis narrowed his eyes. "Where are you hearing such nonsense?"

"Is it really nonsense?" She had to think on her feet.

Her ears pricked up at the pitter patter of tiny feet somewhere nearby.

Adonis read her like a book, and as quick as a flash, he had an arrow nocked in his bow aimed directly at her.

Ava held her breath. A feeble arrow would be no match for siren skin. But if Adonis shot her, the act would be over.

She just thought about a backup plan when an arrow shot through the air and sailed past her cheek.

Ava's heart thrummed as she spun around to see where it went.

A quail lay lifeless on the forest floor. Adonis's arrow stuck out of it and pinned the bird to the earth.

Ava turned around to catch Adonis's smug smile, and he strode forward to retrieve his prize.

"This friend of yours…" He snapped the quail's neck with a flick of his wrist.

His burning gaze landed on Ava as he casually plucked the arrow from his catch and wiped it on his jacket. "How long have they been missing?"

Ava swallowed as she tried to think of a story on the spot. "A few days," she said. "I'm so worried about her, and I fear that the longer I do not find her, the more likely it is she is in danger."

Adonis hummed as though he weighed her up.

She fixed her smile.

Then he chuckled softly and waved his hand dismissively in front of him before speaking again. "Very well! Come with me."

Ava released her breath.

Isis had been right about one thing: when it came to women, men would believe anything so long as women dressed it in a little flattery.

She followed Adonis through the overgrowth.

He cut a path through it, swinging his sword with

so much power it acted like a part of his body. The vines split so easily that it showed Ava his brute strength.

The man was not to be messed with.

Of course, a mere mortal would be no match for a siren. Her strength overpowered any human. She could simply reach out and snap his neck. But he wasn't a mere mortal, was he. Besides, the glint of a silver blade at his hip made her refrain from making a move.

It would be foolish to attack a hunter, even more foolish to attack an immortal one. She might have the strength, but he'd have better reflexes, and all it would take was one swipe and her neck would split open, spilling her life force in seconds.

Finally, they stepped out onto a road that led out onto the beach, and her heart sank.

A castle stood taller than any building she had ever seen with spires that seemed to reach the clouds.

She frowned. "Forgive me, sir. But why are we not looking for my friend's tracks on the beach?"

Adonis laughed. "You are lucky I found you when I did. Walking in the forest at night is dangerous at the best of times, but tonight is a full moon. You don't want to be wolf meat, do you?"

Ava stiffened. She had heard of werewolves but never seen them.

Her experience on distant lands was limited, as she much preferred to be in the ocean or on the Isle of Imerta. No wolves lived there. Isis made sure of that.

She rested her hands on her hips. "Bedtime stories do not scare me anymore," she said. "I'm sure we'll be fine. Besides, if we do encounter a wolf, with your skills, I am certain it would have an arrow in its eye before it reaches us."

A glimmer of a smug smile crossed Adonis's lips. But he then settled into a resolute frown.

"In any case, we shall begin our search in the morning. You are welcome to spend the night in my palace. I shall have the cook prepare a broth. If we are to traverse the jungle and search for your friend, we will both need to be rested with our bellies full."

Ava wanted to argue, but she could not come up with another word to challenge Adonis's logic.

However, she eyed the castle warily and swallowed. She did not want to cross the boundary and find out what—if anything—happened to sirens who dared to enter his cursed land.

Hades had explained that dark magic laced the boundary designed against men only—a sign of arrogance with a hint of misogyny, Ava thought, for any man to assume that women were not to be considered a danger.

But a sneaky thought played in the back of her mind that Hades merely relayed heresy, and that the curse might simply referred to man as all humanity.

She had no time to dwell on such thoughts.

Adonis marched forward with long strides, and Ava had to run to keep up with him.

As they reached the wall, she peered through the iron gates to see the gardens filled with statues.

The statues depicted men wearing all manner of clothes. Some wore simple clothing, like a shepherd. A few had suits of armor. One raised a sword.

If Hades had been wrong about the technicality, she would soon meet the same fate.

And a horrible thought struck her: perhaps Adonis had not been fooled by her story. Perhaps he had suspicions and lured her right into a trap.

Then she thought back to Hercules shackled in the cell. Without his godly strength, he would be helpless, shackled, and in pain.

She shut her eyes for a moment.

"Are you all right?" Adonis asked, his words laced with concern.

Ava kept her eyes shut and took a deep inhale. "Just catching my breath." She lifted a hand.

As she considered the risks, her heart won.

She could not in good conscience shrink away from an opportunity to save Hercules. After all, he was her husband. A good wife would not think twice about risking her life to save the man she loved.

Of course, Ava did not love Hercules; she barely knew the man. But she wanted him to be around long enough for her to grow to love him.

She had no other option and sensed that Adonis was a stubborn man. She would have to cross the threshold and stay in the castle for the night.

If she did not turn into another garden feature.

She settled on the plan that she would kill him tomorrow. After all, all immortal beings had a weakness. She just had to find his.

Besides, a warm meal and a soft bed were a luxury she had not experienced for a long time.

Adonis opened the gate, and it swung forward with an ear-splitting squeal. Then he gestured for Ava to walk through.

She took a deep breath and stepped forward, bracing herself for what might happen. She caught Adonis eyeing her closely; the twitch of his mouth had her concerned.

But to her relief, nothing happened. She walked through the gate and into the castle without a problem.

She glanced over her shoulder at the tiny strip of beach in the distance, and her heart sank as the gates closed behind her.

Ava breathed a sigh of relief, grateful that her charms had worked. But she could not shake a sense of unease as she followed him.

Adonis led her through the castle, and their footsteps echoed loudly in the empty halls. He moved like a lion with long, confident strides, and his deep breaths came out in puffs like a grizzly bear.

They climbed a spiral staircase, and Ava's heart pounded in her chest.

What if she had made a mistake coming here? She had no way of telling whether Hades had led her into a trap.

Perhaps Adonis was a mad man who took Ava to her destruction?

She swallowed and shook the thought away.

Unless he led her to a room filled with steel spears, she still possessed enough strength to overpower him should things take an ugly turn, or at least strength enough to give her a fighting chance.

"Wait here." He opened a door to a small room.

A fine, four-poster bed stood in the center with white drapes falling like waterfalls around it.

Ava glanced around the room and smiled at Adonis.

"I'll send some handmaidens to your room, where they will help you bathe." He wrinkled his nose.

Ava froze, clamping her arms at her sides as she felt self-conscious.

Before she could even reply, Adonis marched away. She stayed rooted on the spot, listening to his fading footsteps.

Later, a pair of timid girls no older than fourteen came in. Each carried two pitchers full of steaming water. They entered and left the room several times, filling the small tin bath that sat in front of the roaring fireplace.

Ava took no time to undress and pick up a small towel. She scrubbed her body until her skin felt raw and lathered up her hands with the bar of soap that smelled of lavender.

When she finished, the handmaidens helped her into a sheer nightdress and tucked her into bed. They brought in a small bowl of piping hot broth. It had chunks of meat bobbing in it, and Ava wondered if it was the quail that Adonis killed that night.

But her stomach grumbled, and she wasted no

time in picking up the silver spoon and eating every morsel.

Once she settled, she shut her eyes, wriggled under the fine silk sheets, and sighed. The taste of warm spices from her meal lingered in her mouth, and her stomach felt delightfully content.

She had not expected this luxury.

Soon, guilt crept in, weighing her deeper into the bedding.

Somewhere far away, Hercules lay on a cold stone floor, probably starving.

And when she allowed her hearing to tune into the faraway sounds on the Earth, she could still hear the faint cries of her sisters.

It became an ugly reminder of the war that raged on. And Isis's mission was more important than ever.

She yanked the covers up to her chin, squeezed her eyes shut, and tried to block out the sounds of devastation that haunted her.

When sleep refused to come, she blinked up at darkness and listened to the strange creaks and footsteps from outside her door.

Minutes rolled by, and soon the golden strip of light beneath the door grew black, and the sounds died down. She could only hear faint snores now.

Her heart raced as she thought about where

Adonis might be. She thought about finding his room, sneaking up to him while he slept, and slitting his throat.

Then she could merely carry him to the ocean for Hades.

But her stomach churned at the thought.

She was not a monster. Something about murdering a man in cold blood while he slept felt wrong.

Though she could almost hear Isis's voice in her mind. *Stop wasting time on frivolous quests and find my dear Osiris.*

But even as the words crossed her mind, a vision played out in her minds' eye.

A mountain the shape of a camel loomed over a sleeping giant of some sort that was coiled up like a snake. But the details looked too vague to make out exactly what it was.

At last, the warm bath and meal did their job in relaxing Ava just enough for her to finally release her tension, and sleep took her away to a world of strange, twisted dreams.

AVA

$\mathcal{M}$orning came, and the handmaidens opened the shutters to let in a flood of golden light.

Birds chirped outside, and for a flicker of a moment, Ava felt content. She could not remember the last time she felt so at ease.

But as soon as her mind began to spin, the familiar entrails of guilt and worry wrapped around her throat once more.

As her handmaidens helped her into her clothes, Ava forced a smile and made small talk. They dressed her in a pair of sturdy boots with cloth trousers and a fur vest over her cotton shirt.

She frowned at herself in the floor-length mirror.

Ava did not feel accustomed to wearing such

bland, neutral tones. But she looked like a hunter, and today, Adonis would become her prey.

The attire could help her focus on the horrid task.

Adonis found Ava in the main hall, and his gaze trailed over her body in a sweeping motion before the corner of his mouth lifted.

Ava took this as a sign of approval, but she did not like the way he leered at her. "Are we ready to go?" She motioned to the doors.

"Not quite. I need something." He nodded to the grand staircase. "Will you join me?"

The question sounded simple enough, but something about his demeanor kept Ava on edge.

His nostrils flared, and his eyes snapped on her breasts for a moment. The tip of his tongue slid across his upper lip.

When he reached the stairs, he took two at a time, and a nervous energy pulsed from him that made Ava's heart palpitate.

She followed but kept a distance, wondering what the man thought about to put him in such a good mood.

But when they reached a small wooden door, he halted to glance at it.

Curiosity filled Ava as she watched his fingers graze the brass handle for a moment, and his face darkened, as though he thought about going inside. But then shook himself and pressed on.

When Ava passed the door, she strained to listen for any noises or for any clue of what might be behind the mystery door. But she could only pick up on the slow steady breaths of someone sleeping.

Finally, they reached a tower at the top of the castle.

Adonis pushed open the door, revealing a small room with a table in the center and a strange device standing by the window. It looked like a giant spy glass with all manner of strange cogs and workings.

"What is this place?" She looked around.

Adonis set down his bow and dragged his hand over the scruff of his beard as he approached the scattered papers on the table. "I have drawn maps of every corner of this island, and many islands across the seven seas," he began.

Ava traced the intricate drawings and thumbed through the stacks of parchment. "This must have taken many years to do," she whispered, amazed.

Adonis's stern look cracked into a flicker of a smile. But then he crossed his arms over his broad chest. "Centuries."

Ava stepped back, frowning, as a horrifying thought struck her. "You are a god?" Hades had not mentioned that, only that he'd been granted immortality. Because if it was true, then her mission would be futile. Everyone knew that a god could not be killed.

Neither could a siren song charm a god. Her powers would be utterly useless.

Did Hades just send her on a mission expecting her to fail?

Adonis averted his gaze and shrugged. "I can see why you come to that conclusion." He surveyed the papers again. "Some call me a god, others prefer the word 'demon,' but…"

"But what do you call yourself?" Ava reached for his arm.

When her fingertips brushed his skin, a vision illuminated her mind's eye.

Lush rolling hills of green, snowdrop flowers on a hill, and willow trees with long swooping branches billowed in the breeze. Then in the distance, a child with tight brown curls slashed the air with a stick.

Innocent laughter flooded her mind, and the happy scene grew dark.

The flowers vanished. And nothing but bones sat at the feet of a man. The man held a bow in his right hand and a glinting silver sword in the other. The sky looked black, and his head hung low.

Ava lurched back with a hiss as she took a sharp breath.

When she saw Adonis's eyes again, her heart filled with terrible sorrow.

"You're in terrible pain." Ava hugged herself as though to soothe the ache that did not belong to her.

Adonis's thick brows knit together. "Who are you?" he asked. "How can you speak to me as if you know everything about me?"

Ava tried to steady her nerves as she buried the sadness and grounded herself in the moment.

She inhaled and picked up on the scent of the slightly damp wood in the corner of the room, the salty breeze that floated in through the open window, and the steady thump-thump of Adonis's heart.

She dragged her thumbs over the cotton material of her shirt. "I feel and see things," she said, finally.

Adonis studied her for a moment as though he tried to decide whether to trust this woman or not.

She wondered what he saw. Did he see a harmless woman wearing plain clothes, with wild hair that hung in waves to her waist? Or did he see an imposter, someone in disguise who knew far more about him than she should who had malicious intent?

He must have settled on the first option because

his face broke into a polite smile. "I'm sorry," he said. "I have already forgotten... May I know your name?"

Ava swallowed.

None of this made it easier for her to carry out the mission. But she pressed her fingernails into her palms and pictured Hercules locked up in the Underworld. It was the only image that gave her strength to stay on course.

"Ava," she whispered.

"Ava...?" Adonis coaxed her for more.

But Ava did not have a last name, or a title. "Just Ava."

Adonis smiled properly now, and it reminded her of the child in her vision. "Well, Ava, I don't know how you do it, but I feel compelled to trust you."

Ava did not respond. She knew how. It was one of her gifts. Something that her mother took great delight in using for her own selfish gain.

But the fact that it worked on him gave her hope. Perhaps Adonis was a demigod. Perhaps her mission would not be ill-fated after all.

Adonis tapped the maps with his index finger. "Where was your friend last seen?" he asked.

"Friend?" Ava asked, snapping out of a daze.

"Oh." She played with her hair. "I'm sorry. I can't

help but notice that you're all alone here. No friends or family, just servants and cooks."

Adonis's eyes flashed as he looked down for a moment, and the side of his jaw bulged. But then he met her stare with a confident smile. "I'm not alone."

Ava knew that.

She wondered if the question might prompt Adonis to tell her who lived behind the door they passed and what made him react the way he did to the sight of it.

But instead of giving her any answers, Adonis's face turned neutral, and he rolled up several pieces of parchment.

"I have a confession to make, Ava. I have no intention of going to the beach. I cannot help you find your friend."

He spoke gruffly and avoided eye contact. But even without looking into his eyes, Ava picked up on his twinge of guilt. "But perhaps these maps will serve you on your quest. They are useless here."

Ava cursed Hades for putting her in this situation.

The man clearly felt tortured by something in his past, and if he had walked the earth for centuries, then he was no mere human.

How could she possibly carry out what she came to do? She could see how Adonis had evaded Hades for all these years. He would know better than to go near the sea.

She hesitantly took the scrolls from him and placed them in her satchel.

An awkward silence flooded the air, and she took a moment to wonder how to lure this mystery man out of his home.

"Very well. May I borrow a boat? I shall pay you a handsome price." She reached into her satchel for her leather pouch. She pulled out a handful of gold coins, but Adonis's dull eyes looked at them like they were old buttons.

"I'm afraid not. I never go to the shoreline, and I suggest you stay far from there too." He crossed his arms across his broad chest.

Ava frowned. "Why?"

Adonis dipped his head to give her a piercing stare, and for the first time, Ava thought the man could see her soul.

She swallowed as clouds of guilt rose up and choked her throat. But she stood her ground and held his gaze, refusing to break her resolve.

"Have you not heard?" He nodded to the window. "There's a bloody war out there. If the pirates do not get to you, the sirens will."

A chill took hold of Ava as she wondered if Adonis knew he spoke to one.

His words weighed heavy in the space between them.

But the tense moment evaporated at the sound of a loud thud from beneath their feet. Adonis's eyes widened, and his nostrils flared. "I do not mean to rush you, but it is quite important that you leave... now."

His gaze darted to the dusty floorboards. It seemed that he strained to hear even the slightest sound.

Ava did not need to strain; she could hear another thump followed by a crash, like a suit of armor tumbling to a stone floor.

Adonis gestured to the door. "I am sorry I cannot help you anymore. Please, use the maps. They will serve you well. And take any provisions you need on the way out. The kitchens are on the left when you reach the bottom of the staircase."

Ava opened and closed her mouth soundlessly as Adonis ushered her out.

"Thank you for your hospitality," she forced out, burying the disappointment rising within her.

As Ava exited the castle, a wave of sorrow washed

over her. She had failed to convince Adonis to come out of hiding.

She walked down the castle steps with her head lowered, her satchel heavy on her shoulder.

Walking through the forest, she longed for the warmth of the sun on her skin, but the thick over-growth blotted out its rays.

The journey back to the beach took all day, and when she finally stepped onto sand, the sky had been blotted in ink, and clouds shielded the stars from view.

It seemed to reflect her hopelessness.

Without Adonis, she could not free Hercules. And without Hercules, she could not return to her sisters, Serena and Georgette.

The burden of her mission pressed down on her as she trudged across the vast beach toward the shoreline.

When she arrived, Hades already stood there with his back turned to her as he stared out into the ocean. He stood barefoot, and the foamy tide washed over his ankles.

Ava approached him slowly.

He spun around, splashing water around him.

She could feel his dark gaze on her as she neared

him. "I couldn't get Adonis to come out of the castle."
She tried to keep the defeated tone out of her voice.

Hades was enigmatic and cool in his reaction. He
stood still and menacing, and shadows cloaked his
face as the moon reached the highest point in the sky.
"Did you see anyone else in there? The palace." He
kept his voice a whisper.

Ava studied Hades for a moment and nodded.
"There were maidens. He mentioned having a
cook…"

Hades shook his head. "Anyone else?"

Ava thought about it. "Yes, there was someone
sleeping in a room that Adonis seemed to be secretive
about. Do you know who it is?"

Hades's face lit up in a sinister smile, and the
moon illuminated his pearlescent teeth. "Now, listen
carefully," he said in a low voice. "There's someone
inside that castle who I need to get to. And you're
going to help me."

GEORGETTE

eorgette's heart thundered as she quickly dressed under the cold stare of the intruder with the battle axe.

As she waited for Captain Stone to finish buckling his belt, she took a good look at their captor.

His cloak fell open enough to see he only wore a pair of tan-colored trousers and thick sheepskin boots. Black tattoos lined his skin from his bald head to his firm pectorals. The tattoos painted strange pictures, like caveman drawings that depicted battles of old. At the base of his skull, he had a long braid of hair that draped over his chest like rope.

"Come," he barked.

Georgette glanced at her husband, and Captain Stone lurched forward to attack, but the intruder brandished his steel axe and held the blade a hairs' width from Captain Stone's nose.

"I've got orders to bring you to the Jarl. But he will not care if I just bring your head instead." The man's grin revealed his blackened teeth. "Try it. I dare you."

Captain Stone backed down, and the strange man gestured for them to step out of the cabin.

A rush of cold sea air slapped Georgette's cheeks. It smarted, telling her this bizarre situation was not a dream. But even though she knew it, her mind could not comprehend what she looked at.

A fleet of archaic-looking ships invaded the waters. Smoke darkened the sky as a full-scale battle broke out.

Canons blasted as ships fired at each other.

What was going on?

As Georgette's eyes scanned the flotilla of ships, her mouth fell open.

These vessels did not look ordinary; they bore the ancient, almost mythical design of Viking longships. Dragon heads adorned the bows. Their wooden scales seeming to writhe in the misty sea air.

Fierce men, adorned in fur and steel, brandished weapons and barked orders in a guttural tongue that echoed across the waves.

The wind of an era that should have been long passed filled the tattered and battle-worn sails.

"Vikings? I thought they were dead." Georgette's voice barely sounded audible over the din of clashing metal and war cries. "This cannot be real."

Captain Stone, equally perplexed but ever so stoic, sighed. "These are mysterious times."

Before either could further contemplate the surreal tableau, and how it was possible, the strange man walked them to the deck and shoved them onto the Viking's ship.

A sea of eyes from rogues followed them as two mountain-like men wrapped a length of rope around them.

The air stank of gunpowder and tobacco.

And when the men roughly tied them up, a wave of putrid body odor wafted to Georgette's nostrils. She wrinkled her nose and resisted the urge to cough. But the smell clung to the back of her throat.

She thought that if the Vikings did not kill her with their barbaric weapons, the stench would certainly finish her off.

She struggled against her bonds in an attempt to find Captain Stone's hand. She could just graze his rough knuckle with her baby finger. But his touch soothed her, nonetheless.

The rough hemp chafed at Georgette's wrists, grounding her to a reality she still struggled to comprehend.

Then, who could only be Hakon, the Jarl of this seafaring brigade, approached. The monstrous man had an untamed bramble of a red and gray beard, and his eyes looked as unforgiving as the northern winters.

"Be still as stone, or you will meet the wrath of Thor himself," Hakon warned in a gruff voice.

"What do you want?" Captain Stone barked.

As if on cue, a sudden commotion from the boarding plank interrupted the tense atmosphere.

"I vow to the gods that if you touch a hair on her head…"

"Shut up," someone snapped.

Georgette's ears pricked up at the familiar voice.

"You'll stay your hand, níðingr. For we are as many as the stars, and my reflexes rival those of the swiftest wolf. If you move, I'll slit your throat and soak her pretty dress in your blood."

Georgette's chest tightened as the seriousness of the situation settled on her like a weight. She craned her neck to catch a glimpse of what was happening.

Vikings shoved Serena and Prince Edward unceremoniously onto the deck, and each of their hands had been bound.

"What are you doing here?" Georgette couldn't hide her surprise to see them.

"Rescuing you," Serena replied through gritted teeth. She staggered forward, struggling to maintain her balance as the Vikings tied her beside Georgette.

"You're doing a marvelous job, indeed." Captain Stone's voice dripped with sarcasm.

Serena mumbled, "Well, it's a work in progress," under her breath.

Georgette couldn't see her, but she could picture her cheeks stained in humiliation. Nothing more mortifying existed for a proud siren like Serena than to lose a fight. Especially during a rescue mission.

Georgette only wondered why they bothered; she thought Serena would have been delighted to see her demise.

Prince Edward's ears grew red, and he would not so much as look up from the ship's deck as the Vikings tied him next to his brother.

Hakon slammed the butt of his axe onto the deck with a thud.

Everyone's head snapped up to look at him.

"Do not struggle or even think of escaping. Your

fates are sealed! You are chosen for the blood offering to the All-Father."

"An offering? To your god?" Georgette's voice trembled, yet her mind whirred with plans and possibilities. This was not her first time almost being a blood sacrifice.

But her thoughts diminished under the steely glare of the brutish man who glared at her.

"Ja, and your flesh and bone will please the All-Father and bring us favor." Hakon sneered at them.

Captain Stone's fingers wrapped around Georgette's baby finger and squeezed.

She held her breath as a wash of calm took over.

They would get out of this. After all, the Vikings looked great in number, but they had no idea just who they dealt with.

The four of them had strength and magic that no mere mortal could comprehend.

And yet, the Vikings outnumbered them and had steel weapons on hand. Escape now would have been unwise. After all, they needed to wait for Ava and Hercules to return.

They only needed to bide their time and wait for the perfect moment.

"Yes, sister." Georgette almost jumped at the sound

of Serena's voice in her mind. *"Have courage. These pathetic humans have nothing on us."*

Georgette tried to look back to catch a glimpse of her sister, but she could only see a wisp of red hair in the corner of her eye. *"I can hear you!"* she thought with surprise.

Serena's laugh entered her mind. *"Well done. You're not completely useless after all."*

The deck creaked under Hakon's sturdy boots while he droned on about their impending doom, but Georgette focused too much on Serena's voice in her head to listen to him.

"So, what is the plan?" she asked.

"They won't sacrifice us on this ship. They're taking us somewhere. And when they do, we'll find our opportunity."

"What do you have in mind?"

"I'll distract them, while you aim for the ginger's throat. You know how to grow claws, right?"

Georgette sucked in a breath. *"You say it like you think I'm capable of killing."*

Serena sighed audibly this time, which prompted Hakon to stop talking and squint at her as though he found her to be the most repulsive thing he'd ever seen.

"Do my tales weary you?" His voice sounded like thunder rolling over a tsunami. "Would you prefer I end your torment? Shall I split you open and let your insides kiss the daylight?"

"Don't you dare threaten my wife!" Prince Edward roared.

Georgette couldn't help but smile at the aggression in his voice. Behind the passion, she could just make out a hint of desperation.

"Edward. There's no need for that." Serena's tone sounded surprisingly soft.

Hakon's eyes narrowed as he looked at the four of them. "You best bind your tongues if you want to keep your heads." With a final glare, he nodded to his men and walked away.

Hours rolled by, and the captives watched the Viking crew at work. They moved with surprising grace, considering their appearance.

When night fell, they disappeared below deck for what sounded like a party. One scrawny kid with a mop of orange hair slumped moodily by the rail. It seemed he drew the short straw and had to keep watch while the rest of the men enjoyed their drink.

"Georgette, can you hear me?"

Georgette jumped at the sound of Serena's voice in her mind once again. *"Yes."*

"Good. I have a plan, and I need you to tell Stone when these barbarians are not looking."

The thought of having a plan to escape made Georgette giddy and took away the terror that had made her arms numb and lips tingle. She took a long, steady breath.

"All right, Serena. I'm listening."

*A*va's eyes narrowed at Hades. The moonlight casted an eerie glow on his face.

"Who am I to rescue? And why is it so crucial for you to get to them?"

Hades sighed, and his face softened for just a moment. "Persephone. I confess, I had ulterior motives when I asked you to lure Adonis out. The truth is, it's only Persephone who I care about. She's my reason for everything, and she's trapped in that castle against her will."

The name echoed in Ava's mind like a haunting melody. "Persephone... but why would Adonis—"

Hades cut her off. "We don't have time for the why. Will you help me or not?"

Ava clenched her fists, her internal battle clear on

her face. Finally, she nodded. "Alright, I'll go. But only if you vow to release Hercules. I can hear him. I know you've locked him up somewhere awful."

Ava's footsteps echoed through the stone corridors of the castle as she retraced her steps up the spiral staircase. She remembered the door Adonis had hesitated before, the one he'd refused to open earlier.

Taking a deep breath, she approached it.

Her fingers tightened around the hilt of a small dagger she had concealed in her satchel—a tool she had hoped she wouldn't need to use. She delicately inserted the thin blade into the lock and maneuvered it with the skill of a rogue, albeit an amateur one.

A subtle click sounded, and the lock gave way under her touch.

Ava pushed the door open. It creaked with the weight of its own secrecy.

Her heart pounded in her chest as her eyes fell upon a figure lying on a bed draped with silks of emerald and gold.

The woman looked ethereal in the dim light that filtered through a veiled window. Her strawberry-blonde hair framed her face like a halo, and tendrils of it lay gracefully over her pillow. She looked innocent, a stark contrast to the disquiet Ava felt within these walls.

With tentative steps, Ava approached her, and her gaze swept over the woman's tranquil face.

This had to be Persephone. The recognition didn't come from a place of memory, but from a place of inherent knowing, as if the air around her whispered her name.

Gently, Ava shook her shoulder. "Persephone, wake up. We have to go."

Just then, a cacophonous sound echoed through the halls, snapping Ava's attention back to the imminent danger.

"Who dares to infiltrate my home?" Adonis's voice thundered with a fury she had not heard before.

Persephone's emerald-green eyes blinked, and she looked around as Ava tried to coax her to leave with her. "Who are you? What are you doing?" she asked.

"There's no time. You must come with me. I'm rescuing you." Ava grabbed her by the wrist.

Persephone begrudgingly followed and ran to keep up with Ava as she hurried down the staircase.

Adonis's thunderous roar echoed in the halls.

Persephone's eyes widened as the sound of Adonis's voice reverberated through the stone walls.

For a moment, she looked torn, and her gaze flickered back toward the door. "Adonis?" she mumbled, as though the name alone could provide sanctuary.

She halted and looked puzzled at Ava like she weighed her up. "Rescuing me? From what?"

Ava's heart pounded in her chest; they didn't have the luxury of time.

And Persephone appeared too groggy to think properly. It was the only logical reason for her response.

With a wave of her hand, Ava cast a hypnotic spell, and her voice tinged with urgency. "Follow me, Persephone. Your life depends on it."

Caught in the spell, Persephone nodded, and her eyes filled with vacant trust.

They both bolted out of the room. Their footsteps sounded muffled by the lush castle carpets, but not enough to escape the keen hearing of Adonis, the world's greatest hunter.

They navigated the labyrinthine corridors, every turn a gamble, every step echoing with risk.

Ava sensed Adonis's presence like a wolf on their trail, and his rage painted the walls a shade darker.

He came close—too close.

The women emerged into the garden, a sprawling maze of hedges and flowers bathed in the ethereal light of the moon.

They wove through the greenery, and the scent of jasmine felt heavy in the air. The garden's beauty seemed surreal; a paradise paradoxically tinged with danger.

Ava's eyes widened as she sensed a shift in the air —the hair-raising sensation of being watched and hunted.

They had reached the boundary of the castle grounds, the mythical line that separated Adonis's domain from the world beyond.

Suddenly, the twang of a bowstring cut through the air, a sound so perfectly tuned it could have been a note in a death symphony.

Time seemed to slow as Ava turned.

Her eyes met Adonis's just as he released the arrow. Its steel tip glinted menacingly in the moonlight.

Just as the arrow nearly found its mark, Hades appeared as if materializing from the shadows. He stepped in front of Ava, and the arrow shattered against his chest, splintering into a cloud of dust.

The air hung thick with the aftermath, charged with palpable tension.

Hades's eyes met Ava's for a fleeting moment— grateful yet tinged with an infinite sadness—before turning to Adonis again.

"Hello again, Adonis," Hades said.

Adonis's face paled, and he opened and closed his mouth soundlessly. He nocked another arrow and sent it flying, but it too turned to dust on Hades's sculpted chest.

Adonis stepped forward, yelling like a dying animal, and his panicked eyes flitted between Persephone and Hades.

"Persephone! Persephone!" He laced his voice with desperation. "Come back to me! Don't leave me here."

Ava's heart ached at the glistening tears that rolled down Adonis's cheeks as he reached the boundary.

Hades stood there, holding the golden mace in one hand, waiting. His composure so calm, so sure, in complete contrast to Adonis's panic.

Nostrils flaring, the hunter puffed air with anger as he seemed to think about his options.

"Stay in your cage and live your life, Adonis." Hades waved his hand in the air as if to cast aside any doubt.

But Adonis did not look at Hades. He could not take his eyes off Persephone, who looked back at him with a confused frown.

"Adonis, I…" Her voice trailed off.

But her voice made Hades spin around and look at her with an expression Ava could not read. Was it repulsion? Devastation? Or just plain fury? Ava could not be sure.

"Do not talk to him," he snapped at Persephone.

She clutched her dainty necklace with a gasp and stepped back.

Ava frowned.

Was Persephone not the love of Hades's life? Her reaction did not match his story.

"Persephone! Please…" Adonis begged; his voice sounded hoarse now. "Come back…"

"Let her go, Adonis. Or come out and fight me. If you win, you can have her."

Adonis puffed out his chest and finally looked at Hades again with a firm nod. "Very well." His voice held a note of finality that had Ava's stomach in knots.

She stood beside Persephone, and her breath caught in her chest as she watched what would be the most epic challenge of all time.

In the realm of shadows and moonlight, the two titans, Hades and Adonis, clashed in a dance of fury and sorrow.

Each movement formed a stanza, and each blow

became a line in a poem written in real-time, inked in the language of power and pain.

Steel met steel.

Their weapons sang a dirge, mourning losses that could never be reclaimed.

Sparks flew like errant stars, displaced from the heavens, as they parried and lunged.

Adonis struck with the grace of a winter wind— swift, biting, indiscriminate.

But Hades moved like the stillness of the abyss, the unfathomable depths where not even wind could reach. His counterattacks came patient and inevitable, like the passage of eons in his dark realm.

Around them, the air pulsed with an energy both ancient and immediate.

Neither of them needed words. Their conflict spoke a language older than time and told a story that transcended mere mortals.

Ava watched, entranced.

Their movements looked so beautifully dark and dangerous, that she wished she was a skilled writer so she could write poems like Homer of this epic fight.

A cold chill rushed over her, knowing that she watched history unfold; a long-suffering feud finally reaching its conclusion.

As she watched them fight, she could not be sure which side she hoped would win.

If Adonis destroyed Hades, then she could simply take the golden mace and return to Hercules.

But then again, if Hades won, he would hand it over.

With a final, echoing clash that resonated through the fabric of the universe itself, the duel found its last verse, the line that would bring it to a close.

An ear-splitting screeching noise of steel splintering flooded the air as Hades smashed Adonis's sword with the golden mace.

Ava's mouth fell open as Adonis's eyes widened and grew hollow as he watched the shattered pieces of his sword fall to the ground.

Now Ava knew why Hercules wanted—no, demanded—to have his mace back. She saw with her own eyes the devastation it could bring.

A pause fell, as heavy as the culmination of ages, and the battle ended—not with a declaration, but with a look, a fleeting moment of recognition from Adonis that spoke of finality, of things broken and never to be mended.

His eyes searched for Persephone one last time, who stared at him with her mouth hanging open.

Then, with one lazy swing, Hades smashed the side of his face with the mace.

Death came in an instant, and Adonis dropped like a statue on the ground. Thick droplets of blood oozed from the jagged gash along the side of his skull.

Silence stretched on as if the whole world stopped turning on its axis and every living thing paused.

Hades stood proud and victorious over Adonis's dead body before he turned to smile at Persephone. But his face darkened when he looked upon her.

The silence shattered with an earth-shattering scream—the cry of a woman whose heart had splintered and broken into a million pieces.

She clutched her face in terror, and her eyes flooded with tears.

"What have you done? What did you do?" she shrieked.

AVA

"*P*ersephone…" Hades dropped the mace with a thud and charged toward her, reaching out.

The hush in his voice surprised Ava.

For a moment, she thought about picking up the mace and making a run for it. But for some reason, her body froze, and she watched an intimate reunion she felt she had no right to witness.

Hades wrapped a shaken Persephone in his arms. "Persephone." He said her name like a prayer.

Persephone looked up at Hades with her face screwed up and cheeks soaked in fresh tears. "I know you. You are Hades!" she shrieked and pulled away from him. "You're the one he warned me about!"

Hades's face contorted in anguish. "Persephone, it's me—"

"Stay away from me!" she screamed, and her body trembled. She pushed feebly against his chest, but he would not let her go.

"Who warned you?" Hades's voice stayed barely above a whisper.

"Adonis, my husband," Persephone spat the words, each one a dagger to Hades's heart.

Ava could sense his pain.

"He told me you'd come for me, that you'd trick me and that you were not to be trusted! And you killed him. You killed my husband!" She started to sob uncontrollably now, retching, and shrieking like a woman who had just lost the true love of her life.

The sounds twisted Ava's stomach into tight knots as she thought perhaps, she had made a terrible mistake.

The look of heartbreak that crossed Hades's face was unmistakable. Then he shut his eyes with a resigned breath.

He waved his hand, and Persephone's eyes fluttered closed, and she collapsed into a deep, magical sleep.

Hades gently picked her up and cradled her in his

arms like she was the most precious jewel in the world.

Turning his eyes back to Ava, he looked at her as if seeing her for the first time. But then his face darkened. "Take the mace. We're going back."

Ava hesitated. Her mind raced, wondering why in place of elation, she felt hollow.

She got what she wanted, but the experience changed her. She wasn't sure if she wanted to take the mace and return to Hercules or run into the woods and spend the next thousand years crying over the hand she played in the situation.

Hades sighed, and the weight of millennia seemed to settle on his shoulders in that moment. "Ava." Hades's words snapped her out of her guilt-ridden thoughts, and she took the mace, trying not to look at Adonis's body.

For a moment, she stood beside him.

The drops of blood on the spikes of the mace gleamed in the moonlight.

With that, Hades gestured his hand in a sweeping motion, creating a swirling vortex of dark blue energy —a portal.

"Come." His sadness broke Ava's heart.

He stepped into the portal, still holding the

sleeping Persephone in his arms, and Ava followed close behind him.

Ava stood in the dimly lit chamber of the Underworld, and her eyes locked onto Hades.

After settling Persephone in a bed and locking the door, he turned to Ava and gave her a look that reflected his prior self.

The god of the dead held a smirk on his face that sent shivers down her spine once more.

She wondered how he could be so cool and collected considering the terrible act he had just carried out.

"You've done well, Ava. Persephone is back where she belongs." Hades gestured to where the woman lay, still in a dreamless sleep.

Ava clenched her fists.

Had she known what twisted plans Hades had for her, she would never have agreed to the deal.

But she could do nothing to change it now, not without help.

She pressed her index finger hard against his bare chest. "You promised to release Hercules and hand over the golden mace. I've upheld my end of the bargain. Now it's your turn."

Hades chuckled; a sound as cold as the realm he

ruled. "Ah, but you see, I've changed my mind. I like you. You have gumption and a backbone. I think I'll keep you in our realm for a while. Besides, I may need your assistance in helping Persephone to settle in."

Ava shook her head. "Find someone else to do your dirty work. I've done what you asked. Free Hercules at once or—"

"Or what?" Hades's eyes flashed dangerously. He towered over her, strong and oppressive. Even the fury of a siren would be no match for his strength.

Dark chains materialized from the shadows. They wrapped around Ava's wrists and pulled her away from him.

Ava struggled, while Hades flicked his wrist, and an invisible force enfolded her and flew her through the endless tunnels of the Underworld.

The air crackled with his electric laugh as he followed.

Finally, she halted, suspended in the air with her wrists bound, staring at an iron door.

It fell open with a maddening crunch, and her eyes met Hercules, who was similarly bound and slumped in the corner.

Her heart fluttered. She welcomed the sight of him, like candlelight in a storm.

But his spirit was low, broken. It made her heart bleed.

When Hades tossed her into the cell, she fell and scraped her knees on the rough stone floor.

But Ava refused to cry out or show any evidence of pain. She turned around.

Hades looked triumphant and bold in the doorway.

"You treacherous snake!" Ava spat.

Hades shrugged. "I am the god of the Underworld, my dear. Deception is in my nature. Now, one more thing…"

He snapped his fingers.

Adonis's body materialized in the cell. He lay on the stone floor, and the stench of death filled every crevice of the tiny space.

Ava held her breath, looking at the man.

His eyes looked vacant, and his face dripped with congealed blood and brain matter.

Ava found it unfathomable that just moments ago, the man looked strong and burst with determination, and that now, he had become nothing more than a shell.

Just as the thought crossed her mind, a blue wisp floated from Adonis's pale lips, and a faint howl of agony landed on her ears like a thunderclap as the wisp floated away.

Hades reveled in his victory as he wielded Hercules's golden mace. His eyes glinted with joy, and he stared at the maroon droplets and brain matter that adorned the mace.

"You didn't have to kill him." Ava's hoarse voice was tinged with disbelief and shock.

Hades looked at her, and his eyes became colder than ever. "He defied the laws of the Underworld. He had to be punished."

Hades lied. The love between Adonis and Persephone had been undeniable. Perhaps Hades loved Persephone in a twisted way. But it wasn't pure and true. His love was more like an obsession.

It sickened her to the core that she had any part in his ugly games.

"But to kill Adonis? To take him away from Persephone forever?" Ava's voice broke.

She believed nothing would be more torturous than the idea of two lovers ripped apart for all eternity.

Now Persephone belonged to the hands of the cruelest god in all the lands. And it was Ava's fault.

Hades shrugged. "Collateral damage."

His harsh words struck deep in Ava's heart. She

felt a rage building within her, a fire stoked by betrayal and loss.

Before she could say anything, a grunt came from beside her. She looked to see Hercules stand to his feet. "Come on, Uncle. Ava has given you what you want. Give me the mace and let us go."

Hades tapped his lips and waved the bloodied mace in the air. "Actually, I've grown rather fond of this thing. It's brutal." He cocked his head to the side and gave a wicked grin. "And I've decided I need Ava. So, what will it be, Hercules? Let Ava take your place, or stay here together?"

Ava opened her mouth to protest. Those could not be the only options.

But Hercules scowled at Hades with a growl. "Let us go, you filthy—"

Hades tapped the red jewel glowing on the wall. "Don't strain yourself, Hercules. We know what this does to you."

Hercules paused, and his eyes turned into narrow slits, but he didn't say anything.

Hades shrugged. "Very well. I take it that you are both staying for the time being. Do make yourselves comfortable. If you behave, I may have one of my minions bring in a bed. Eventually." He winked at

Ava, who wanted to claw his devilish eyes out, but her body refused to obey her.

Instead, she watched, dumbfounded, as Hades kicked Adonis's lifeless body before he waved his hand and it disappeared. Yet, the smell lingered.

"Well, I'll let the two of you enjoy some time alone. A thousand years should be long enough for you both to calm down. Then we'll talk about the mace."

Hercules roared while Ava screeched obscenities at Hades.

But the god rested the mace on his right shoulder and hummed to himself as he vacated the cell, the heavy door swinging shut all on its own.

Ava panted, staring at the three iron bars at the square opening in the door, reeling.

She turned around and noticed Hercules's bloodied wrists hanging at a strange angle.

He grunted as he cracked them into place again.

"You're hurt," she whispered, edging closer.

Before she could get a better look, Hercules shrugged and moved them out of sight. "I'll heal. I always do."

"It looks bad... How do you know?" Ava could not bear the thought of an infection taking hold of

Hercules and having another man dying before her eyes.

She wondered if that would be Hades's wicked plan for her.

Hercules grunted again. "Because I am a demigod. Some call it a blessing. I call it a curse... but I cannot die."

"Why is that a curse?" Ava backed up under Hercules's piercing stare. The look he gave her made her blood cold.

She swallowed, sensing that this was a sensitive topic. So, she opted to move away from it.

"Well, our friends are waiting for us. And we're stuck in this filthy cell for the next thousand years. What do you expect to—" She fell silent, a wave of nausea rushed over her at the reality of their situation.

Hades had truly trapped them. Without Hercules's godly strength, they could not escape.

As Ava and Hercules sat in their dark cell, the weight of their failure dragged their shoulders down.

Ava thought of her friends and allies in the world above.

She wondered if they would look for them, and what they would do if they knew Hades had betrayed them both.

"We will get out of here." Hercules's voice filled with a conviction that Ava needed to hear.

A tear rolled down her cheek as she looked up at him and met his reassuring smile.

The demigod stood there as a beast of a man, and tattoos painted his broad, defined chest. His eyes sparkled, despite their hopeless situation.

He needed to say nothing else to fill her with renewed hope.

She nodded. "You're right. And when we do, Hades will wish he'd never crossed us."

GEORGETTE

hey sailed for weeks across the sea.

Georgette's stomach swirled despite the still waters as she played out all of the worst-case scenarios that faced them.

The Vikings offered them meat and beer, as one of them said, "To fatten them up for the All-Father."

Finally, the Viking Island loomed closer as a dark silhouette against the darkened sky and Georgette cast a wary look at Captain Stone, knowing that their moment of escape was coming.

All stayed quiet on the ship. Several of the men had gone below deck. On this night, the kid with orange hair had stolen a bottle and drank it until he slumped to his knees and passed out.

Georgette listened to the rumbling voices beneath her feet.

They had been drinking. Perhaps an unwise decision considering the fact they had unwittingly kidnapped four people with supernatural gifts. All of whom were biding their time for the perfect opportunity to run.

Georgette and Captain Stone exchanged a knowing glance.

Serena had overheard the men discussing what they planned to do, as her sense of hearing was far superior to Georgette's.

The ship had almost reached the island when Serena told her it was time to act.

With a sleight of hand, Georgette managed to free herself and Captain Stone.

She sent a mental thanks to the Governess who had forced her to sit for hours day to day doing needlework and untangling complicated knots for so much of her younger years. It was the first time that skill came to good use, and it might just save their lives.

She hurried to release Serena, while Captain Stone made for Prince Edward, but before he could work on the knots, Prince Edward grunted and snapped the rope in a swift motion.

Georgette caught her husband cocking his brow at his younger brother.

"If you could have done that all along, why the blazes did you let them tie you up?" he hissed.

Prince Edward glanced at Serena and did not reply, but Captain Stone seemed to read his brother's thoughts.

Georgette wondered if they had been able to communicate mentally as well. Or if Captain Stone just knew his brother through and through.

"I see. You are not the one calling the shots, it seems," he said, unable to hide the amusement in his voice.

Serena scowled. "Quiet. We have one chance at this, and I'm not interested in staying here for a moment longer. The crew has been ordered to kill us if we try to escape. So, I suggest we make haste."

Prince Edward crept to the young sleeping Viking. He picked up the lantern at his side and hurled it into a stack of furs and dried meats. Fire caught instantly, and the flames danced like wild spirits in the night.

The ensuing chaos served as the perfect distraction.

"It's now or never," Captain Stone whispered.

With hearts pounding louder than war drums,

they made their leap of faith into the icy waters below, swimming furiously toward the shrouded sanctuary of Viking Island.

But just before they reached the shore, Georgette stopped.

"Wait. Why are we going to the very place they plan to slaughter us on?" she asked.

The others stopped swimming and bobbed in the waters, looking at her.

She pointed to the horizon. "We should shift and swim as far away from here as possible."

Captain Stone hummed as though he liked the idea, but Serena spoke first. "In case it slipped your mind, we were just captured by Vikings who have been talking about a prophecy and were hired to kill us. Are you not at least a bit curious about these people?"

"How did you…?" Georgette began to ask, but then she remembered that Serena had eavesdropped on the conversations for the whole journey. She must have learned enough to pique her curiosity, but not enough to satisfy it.

"We should learn everything we can about these people," Prince Edward said. "Like, how did they find us? And why are we so important to them?"

Angry shouts flooded the air as the roaring fire took hold of the Viking ship.

The sight warmed Georgette's heart. She hoped they would all burn.

Prince Edward had a good point, though.

But Serena had answers to Prince Edward's questions, too. "There was another clan who wanted to take us, too."

"They were fighting over us?" Georgette asked, aghast.

"It appears that you already know a lot about these people," Captain Stone said. "Perhaps Georgette is right. Now that I am in the water, I feel different. Maybe we can…"

"We have no time for you to go on a journey of self-discovery. You can explore your new abilities later," Serena snapped. "Besides, where do you suggest we go? The world is at war. We have no ship. Or money…"

"I am still King of the Pirates," Captain Stone interrupted. "We'll go to Tortuga and…"

"I admire your enthusiasm, Stone." Serena's tone did not have even a hint of admiration. "But you'll be dead long before we reach the Caribbean. You're practically a baby right now."

She turned to Prince Edward. "Neither of you

are strong enough yet to swim such long-distances. And anyway, you cannot seriously think I'm going to walk away when we are this close to answers."

"Answers to what?" Georgette asked. "We should get back to Hercules's Island, they must be back by now! Or have you forgotten what Isis said?"

Serena made a sound of frustration and slammed her fist in the water, sending a wave over the others. "I cannot explain it. But I feel that these people are tied to our mission. I am certain that they will hunt us down. I want to know who they are working for and who else might be tasked to destroy us and why."

Silence fell on the couples as Serena's logic hung in the air like a dark cloud.

"Fine. We'll go to the island and learn what we can. Then, we'll steal a ship and get as far from this place as possible," Captain Stone said.

Swimming through the frigid water with arms that felt like lead, Georgette finally reached the jagged shoreline of Viking Island.

Captain Stone, Serena, and Prince Edward followed close behind.

After they all scrambled onto the beach, they all took a moment to catch their breath.

Georgette could not stop shivering, and Prince Edward shook so much his teeth chattered.

"Here." Serena waved her hand over all of them. In an instant, her sopping wet hair went dry and fell in glossy curls below her bust. It dried the rest of them too.

Georgette patted her braid and her stomach. She felt shocked at the soft, dry cotton under her fingertips. It was as if none of them had been soaking wet only moments ago.

She made a mental note to ask Serena to teach her how to do that later.

Serena pointed to the black smoke that hovered above the tree line in the distance. "Come on. There's a bonfire over there, and I can hear people chanting."

A moonless sky hung heavily above them. A smoky haze veiled the stars that seemed to rise from the island itself.

Dark forests loomed like walls of shadow, and peculiar monoliths of unknown origin dotted the landscape.

As they navigated the woods, twigs snapped under their boots, and all manner of exotic birds watched them, perched on gnarly branches in the trees.

Serena's face lit up like a child on Christmas morning. "We're getting close."

A line of blazing sticks illuminated a pathway leading into the heart of the island. The flickering firelight seemed to beckon them like a spectral guide into the depths of a long-forgotten world.

With no other option but to follow the path, they ventured deeper into the island.

The flames of the torches flickered and danced in the wind, casting grotesque shadows that seemed to lurch from the undergrowth.

As they grew closer, a low hum and chanting grew louder. Georgette's heartbeat matched the drums, and the hairs on her arms stood on end.

Walking toward the danger felt like a foolish thing to do, and yet Serena strutted, swinging her arms with purpose and a look of triumph on her face.

Georgette wondered how this woman could be so different from her and yet be her twin. It seemed that Serena feared nothing.

Finally, they arrived at a clearing. They stayed near the edge and hid themselves behind the overgrowth as they peered in.

Fires blazed, and tattooed men wearing animal furs danced around them.

A towering idol of Odin marked the space. The one-eyed visage had been carved into weather-worn stone.

"It seems we have a welcome party," Captain Stone mused aloud.

Georgette looked over her shoulder, flinching at a strange sound from behind them. "I can't shake the feeling that we're being followed," she said.

"Do not be paranoid, sister. No one knows we are here." Serena flicked her fiery red hair back. The bonfires reflected on it, bringing her tresses to life like she had flames on her head. Her eyes lit up as she watched the Vikings dance and chant.

Suddenly, a loud horn blew, sending scores of birds soaring into the sky. Everyone around the fire stopped what they were doing and turned around as one as if to greet someone.

Georgette moved to the side to get a better look, but too many men blocked her view.

"Hakon, how dare you return to this place empty-handed," a gruff voice shouted. It sounded like a lion's roar and sent all manner of wildlife scurrying away.

Georgette tensed next to Captain Stone.

He, obviously sensing her nerves, slid his hand around her waist and drew circles over her hip. The touch soothed her just enough to slow down her breathing and listen.

"I promised you four lambs, I give you four lambs," Hakon shouted back. There was a series of thuds. "And be happy with that, Borik. The boat caught fire and is lost to the sea."

"You know I did not talk about actual lambs, Hakon. I was clear in my instructions…"

Georgette sucked in a breath and exchanged a look with Serena.

Her sister smiled at her triumphantly as her voice entered Georgette's mind again. *"Now we have a name. They are working for Borik."*

But her smile faded. Serena whipped around with a hiss, and her nails elongated into claws. "Get off me!"

A full-scale fight broke out as a group of Vikings struck them with long sticks of some sort.

Captain Stone tried to shield Georgette from a brutish man who towered over them all like a giant. But more Vikings kept coming, like a colony of the deadliest ants.

Finally, strong hands seized them from behind and dragged them to the idol where Hakon was now nowhere to be seen. Had he left after being scolded?

A wave of cheers and laughter crossed the endless sea of faces.

"Told you, you can't escape the gods' will." Hakon growled, materializing from the shadows like a wraith. "See, I told you, Borik. I have the lambs."

Georgette wondered how a literal sacrificial lamb might feel like now. But the thought shifted to the seriousness of the situation. *"Is this part of your marvelous plan, Serena? What do we do now?"*

"Quiet. I'm thinking."

Rough hemp ropes cut into her flesh. Each one became a grim reminder of their impending fate.

Georgette scanned the sea of men, wondering which one was Borik. If she was going to die, she at least wanted to look upon the man who ordered her death.

But no one stood out.

Instead Hakon stepped forward. "I intended to make your deaths quick and painless, but after sinking my boat to the bottom of the ocean, I shall make you suffer." His eyes flashed dangerously.

Georgette looked over to Captain Stone. He was nothing more than a dark silhouette now, but his eyes glowed like diamonds at her.

She wanted to do something. To break free and run to him. But the more she wrestled, the more her hands soaked in her blood.

Hakon laughed. "You can try to escape, but these ropes have splintered bones woven in, so every time you move, you only cut yourself even more."

A wave of dark laughter followed the announcement, sending a chill through Georgette's body.

She pictured Ava and Hercules, wondering where they were and if they could hear her thoughts. *"Ava, please. We need your help! Ava!"*

"You do not think I've already tried that?" Serena's voice interrupted her mental pleas. *"She is probably still in the Underworld. We cannot reach her until she's back in the land of the living."*

The Vikings lit fires in front of each sacrificial victim.

The heat made Georgette break into a sweat. But her heart swelled as she could now see her husband's face. The anchor-shaped tattoo on his neck appeared.

She thought back to the treehouse where they made love for the first time. She remembered dragging her finger over his warm skin as she traced his tattoo.

She shut her eyes and let sweeter memories flood her mind.

Her mind went back to when Captain Stone rescued her from pirates and took her to the cabin, stripped her bare, and tenderly washed her with a damp cloth.

He had insisted on seeing for himself that she had not been harmed.

She thought to the moment she about married Prince Edward, and how she believed that her beloved Captain Stone had perished at the hand of Isis on Imerta, only for him to barge into the church and roar, "I object."

Georgette had faced certain death before, and someone always rescued her: Captain Stone.

As Hakon raised a ceremonial dagger high above his head, Georgette looked at her husband.

His eyes met hers, and in that fleeting moment, a mix of regret and defiance flashed between them.

Bound and seemingly defeated, it looked like they had no escape this time. And no one would come to save them.

"By the All-Father, we offer these lives to thwart the prophecy and gain favor in the battles to come." Hakon's voice boomed across the clearing, echoing against the walls of tall trees and monoliths.

Just as the blade began its downward arc, aimed at Captain Stone's heart, a distant horn sounded—a haunting melody that hung in the air, causing even Hakon to pause.

But that slight hesitation was all they needed.

As Hakon hesitated, distracted by the haunting sound of the horn, three more Vikings, not from Hakon's crew, burst into the clearing.

They looked younger, their armor less battered, and their eyes filled with fire that Hakon's men seemed to have long forgotten.

"Einar! Hilde! Astrid! You're too late. The honor is with my clan!" Hakon roared, gesturing toward Serena and Prince Edward.

But the young Vikings hesitated. "Jarl Hakon, these are strange times. The gods' messages are unclear." One of them stepped forward and leveled his gaze at the towering chieftain. He had thin arms and a mop of unruly brown hair. "Hathor has come to us in a vision. We should not be so eager to spill their blood."

"Hathor?" Captain Stone repeated.

Georgette frowned, surprised by his reaction.

He looked at the Vikings with rapt attention.

"They cannot be talking about Hathor; the Vikings do not worship Egyptian gods." Serena's voice entered Georgette's mind again.

Hakon confirmed by saying as much. He grew dismissive of the young clan, but when he turned back to Captain Stone, Prince Edward lunged at him.

Edward had used the momentary distraction to reach into his coat, pulling out a small, ornate dagger. He cut through Serena's bonds, who immediately moved to free Georgette and Captain Stone.

Captain Stone grabbed Hakon's head in his broad hands.

"Nei!" Several of the Vikings shouted, and their voices laced with horror.

Hakon grunted and wrestled under Captain Stone's grip, but a second horn call echoed—this one closer, filled with urgency. The Vikings, even Captain Stone, looked at each other in bewildered silence.

Another clan entered the clearing, all of them female with black markings on their faces.

"Hathor came to us along with Odin himself. We have read the signs wrong about these people."

"We've sailed through time and tide to be here," said a tall woman, her voice low and growly. "What if these four are not offerings but omens? Signs of the very prophecy we try to avoid?"

"The prophecy does not speak of captives and prisoners, but of gods and men fighting alongside each other to avert doom," added one from the other clan, his eyes meeting each of theirs in turn. "Maybe we've read the signs wrong indeed. Maybe these four as destined for something greater than to be lambs for the slaughter…"

"We are no lambs," Serena hissed. She bared her pointed teeth and spread out her claws in a powerful stance before the Vikings.

Gasps filled the air as Serena stood before them, strong and defiant. Her hair raged like flames, while blue swirls of energy formed a circle behind her.

Georgette and Captain Stone exchange a look and nodded to Prince Edward.

Somehow, Serena had created a portal. The energy inside it drew Georgette like a moth to a flame.

"They're going to run. Get them!" Captain Stone's hands still clamped Hakon's face.

To everyone's surprise, an ugly crunch echoed in the clearing, and everyone watched aghast as Hakon's body fell to the ground with a thud.

Georgette's heart thundered as Captain Stone picked up the warrior's axe, his expression blank, as if he had just snapped a twig. But then all chaos ensued.

It seemed that her husband's actions had dissolved any argument as to whether or not they should be executed. All eyes narrowed on the four of them, and even Serena looked at Hakon's body, at his neck twisted in an awkward angle, and seemed lost for words.

The three Viking clans waded forward with their weapons raised and teeth bared.

But Georgette, Captain Stone, Prince Edward, and Serena lifted their hands and claws to themselves.

It was of no use. The Vikings fell on them.

Serena slashed throats with her claws and fought like she was possessed by a wild beast and took two men at a time.

Georgette realized just how dangerous a siren could be.

Then she remembered who she was and that she had strength and power too. She picked up a dropped knife and buried it into the chest of an oncoming Viking. His eyes glazed over as she twisted the knife in his chest, and when she withdrew it, his blood drenched her hand.

Captain Stone roared like a dragon as he waded through their enemies, cutting them down with Hakon's axe.

"To the portal!" Serena shouted as more Vikings emerged from the trees.

With their endless numbers, they swarmed them.

The four of them fought together as they backed away.

A woman slashed Serena's thigh with a jagged knife, which sent Prince Edward into a blind fit of rage.

He tore the woman's head clean off by grabbing her black braid. He moved to the next woman and smashed his fist through her chest.

"Edward, stop. We have to go!" Georgette called over the commotion.

She kicked and stabbed anyone who got too close to her, while Captain Stone cleared a path to the swirling portal and littered the ground in bloodied limbs.

It became impossible to know what happened as the mass of Vikings turned primal at how brutal their sacrificial lambs had become.

Blood sprayed like rain and splattered Georgette.

She spat out the metallic taste in her mouth and grabbed Serena, who had slumped to the ground. "Edward, stop. We need to…" She spoke through pants as she pulled Serena to the portal.

Captain Stone nodded back to her. "Take Serena. I'll get Edward," he said.

Georgette yanked Serena who had gone pale and clammy.

Her eyes rolled backward, and Georgette had to pick her up entirely to carry her to the portal.

With her sister in her arms, she stumbled through it.

The screams and clang of metal on metal rang in Georgette's ears until a heavy silence blotted it all out. The contrast made her shudder inside.

She stepped out into a dark cave illuminated by

crystals and ethereal blue light. It looked entirely foreign to Georgette, but she had no time to think about it.

Blood soaked Serena. But Serena's thoughts surprised Georgette the most. *"I can't believe this. How can I be this weak?"*

"You are not weak," she said aloud, giving her sister a firm look.

Serena blinked at her several times. She gave her a smile, and her eyes finally fluttered closed and didn't open again.

Georgette looked at the portal, wondering why Captain Stone and Prince Edward hadn't made it through yet. Did they die? Were they captured?

Would Serena die and leave Georgette all alone in a strange land?

"I'm not going to die, stupid. I just need time to heal." Serena's thoughts broke Georgette's worries.

Georgette set to work; she tore off a strip of her shirt and wound it tightly around Serena's thigh. Then she pressed on the wound with both hands, praying to all the gods she knew of to save her sister.

Finally, Captain Stone and Prince Edward fell through the portal, and as soon as they did, it vanished in a wisp.

"Thank the gods you are both alive." Georgette's chest heaved as relief flooded her.

Captain Stone gave her a grim look as he watched Serena bleeding on the ground. "Is she going to be all right?"

Serena's eyes shot open, and she glared at him. "It'll take more than a little cut to put me down." She waved her hand over her leg, supposedly in a bid to heal the wound but then she frowned.

Captain Stone did not seem to notice, and he smiled. "Good. Now we are all...Edward?" He turned to his brother.

Georgette followed his line of sight to see Prince Edward staring straight ahead, his face pale as he gaped at nothing.

"She'll be fine, Edward. Serena is strong." Georgette tried to reassure him despite the nagging feeling that something was very wrong.

The bandage on Serena's thigh reddened. Her wound still bled, and Georgette wondered why her sister couldn't heal herself.

Prince Edward moved his gaze to Georgette. "Serena is not who I'm concerned about." Slowly, he raised his hand and grabbed something from behind his neck.

"What the—" Captain Stone began as Prince

Edward pulled out a bone splinter with an inky black tip.

Black streaks grew around his neck and bulged. Then he sank to his knees.

"Edward, Edward! No! What have they done?" Serena cried, but her voice grew weaker with each syllable.

Captain Stone and Georgette looked on helpless and in horror as Serena and Prince Edward shared one final look and simultaneously passed out.

HERCULES

*H*ercules frowned as he watched Ava. She looked different from the feisty siren who bewitched him in the cave.

Before she left with Hades, she had been wide-eyed and hopeful. Now, her face twisted into a permanent scowl, and she hugged herself as if to brace against a chill.

But if anything, the cell felt too warm for comfort —at least, to Hercules. Sweat clung to Ava's temples, and a little vein stuck out of her left one.

Hercules did not know exactly what happened to cause Ava's change in personality, but he could connect enough dots to see that Ava had been traumatized.

And that troubled him more than he'd care to

admit. "Do you want to talk to me about it?" He tilted his head as he surveyed her.

Ava's watery blue eyes shot up to meet his, and she flinched. "No." She shifted and looked down again.

Hercules shuffled closer. "You told me you've been alive for over one hundred years... do not tell me this is the first time you've seen a man die?"

Ava averted her gaze with a sound that reminded Hercules of an angry kitten.

Before he could stop himself, he smiled.

But then her next words wiped the smile from his face.

"Hades lied to me, and I was foolish enough to believe him. Now an innocent man is dead, and there's a woman imprisoned here. All because of my foolishness."

Hercules frowned. "A woman? She's not called Persephone per chance?"

Ava's gaze burned Hercules as she met him with a piercing stare. "You've heard of her?"

Hercules scratched the back of his neck and snorted at the question.

Yes, he had heard of her. The question was, how had she not. But too much ugliness had happened to discuss, which would raise more uncomfortable questions.

He gave her a hard look and tried to steer the conversation away from Persephone.

"You cannot hold yourself responsible for Hades's actions."

His words seemed to hit her harder than he intended.

Ava buried her face in her hands and wept.

Hercules thought about reaching out and putting a hand on her shoulder but couldn't bring himself to do it. Ava seemed so fragile that he wasn't sure if his act of compassion would make her cry even more or break her entirely.

He was ill-prepared to handle either reaction.

After all, he had attempted to console her with words, but they only worsened her mood.

He opted for a distraction instead. "Well, let's focus on how we're going to escape."

Ava lifted her head and gave him a resolute nod. "We might be his prisoners, but I'm certain he will send someone to bring food and water. When they do, I'll slash their throat, and…"

"No," Hercules said, firm. "We are in the Underworld. Anyone working for Hades cannot be defeated like a pathetic human."

Ava shut her mouth and scowled again. "Of course. We need someone with the power of... a god."

Hercules nodded, grateful that she was quick-witted enough to follow his train of thought.

He pointed at the glowing jewel by the door. "When they come in, I'll distract them while you will take that wretched thing and throw it out of the door." He stared at the jewel with hatred swirling in his soul. "Then I'll wait for them to leave and break us out of this hell hole."

Ava looked at the jewel and hummed. "All right."

*S*omething about the Underworld twisted the mind. The damp, dark air seeped through the walls and right into the bone.

Morning and night, magic replaced the bucket in the corner of the cell with a new one. And a hooded figure gave them a cup of stale water and a piece of dry bread.

The figure who came in had glowing red eyes and a stench that clung to the back of Hercules's throat and burned his nostrils.

When he tried to shout to the stranger or distract them, the figure remained totally impassive and moved like the speed of light.

The basic food and water were just enough to keep them alive, but not enough sustenance to strengthen them.

A part of Hercules wondered if this was all part of an elaborate plan.

Hades was cunning and mischievous, and it would not be the first time he attempted to break Hercules down before he molded him into the man he wanted his nephew to be.

As days rolled by and no one else came, Hercules's heart weighed heavy with guilt and shame. After all, his arrogance thrust them into this perilous situation.

Ava had just been a naive siren, who had no idea what she had gotten herself into.

He knew better.

He should have known that Hades would play dirty. His wretched deals were never fair. He acted as trust-worthy as a tom in an alley full of cats in heat.

But Hercules needed his mace. It had become a part of his being, and without it, he could not hope to face the monsters that awaited them on their mission.

Now that Ava had seen what it could do, perhaps she understood.

Most days, he could barely glance at her. He thought of how he must look pathetic and weak. A far cry from the powerful demigod he had been born to be. He felt certain that her desire to be his wife had diminished.

He did feel uncertain, however, if that was a good thing or not as he knew he would never be able to fully give himself. To her or anyone else.

When Ava slept, though, he couldn't take his eyes off her. By the fourth night, she developed a permanent worry line between her brows. Time passed differently in the Underworld. Almost like a dream. Days passed like hours. But sometimes seconds stretched into days. There was no telling how much time passed in the world above. But Hercules found solace in watching over Ava. She mumbled in her sleep and some nights she cried—from nightmares, he assumed.

He didn't know exactly what transpired with Hades, but the guilt over what he made her do ate her up inside.

Watching the woman suffer like this made his heart burn. Day and night, he pictured crashing through the door and getting them both out.

But the glowing maroon jewel served as a reminder that he was no stronger than a mere mortal. And he would not be able to get them out until Hades wanted them out.

Hercules knew of only one way to play this depressing game: wait for Hades to make a move.

As time went on, the cell grew filthy and suffocating, and he kept to his corner, wishing he could find a way to melt into the walls and disappear.

He felt certain that by the sixth day, Ava found him utterly repulsive.

Every now and again, she gave him a furtive look, but then she'd curl up like a cat in the opposite corner of the cell. Her hair fanned out over her shoulders like a golden river.

No matter their filthy surroundings, she maintained a beauty that Hercules had not beheld for over a thousand years.

He wondered how this woman could maintain such beauty in such an ugly setting.

Sometimes, when she slept, he would just watch for his own benefit. Like looking into the flames in a campfire, seeing her healed his soul. Though Hercules could not work out why.

For so long, the presence of a woman ripped open old wounds and scorched his soul. But Ava soothed him, and she became the only reason he did not spiral completely into oblivion.

Finally, three young men entered the cell and tossed in a tiny bed with a scratchy blanket barely big enough for one person.

Ava looked at it hopefully. Her teeth nipped her bottom lip for a moment.

She looked over to Hercules and inclined her head. "You barely sleep," she said. "You should take the bed."

Hercules shook his head. "I don't want it."

Ava opened her mouth, likely to argue, but seemed to change her mind because she closed her mouth and crawled into it.

She fell asleep, and within moments, her slender body melted into the bedding, and Hercules matched his breaths with hers. For hours, he watched her, entranced.

He wished he could join her in whatever dream she was in. Especially the ones that turned into nightmares and had her weeping. He would jump in and destroy every imaginary beast that dared to frighten her.

As another week rolled on, Hercules grew curious about the mysterious siren who accompanied his cell and why he grew more protective of her.

Unlike many women he had encountered in his lifetime, she did not talk very much. Yet, her eyes lit up the dim cell like two glowing orbs and captivated him. Her face painted a picture that spoke a thousand words.

Every time the door opened, Ava did her best to sneak over to the jewel, but her chains were too restrictive and noisy to go unnoticed.

On the seventeenth day, she grew impatient and tried to claw at the next person to enter the cell. But instead of tearing human skin, her nails did nothing but slide harmlessly.

"What are you?" she asked in horror and disgust.

The hooded figure turned, and his face grew disfigured in the shadows. With a wild laugh, he said, "Your worst nightmare."

"Get your hands off her," Hercules roared, jumping to his feet. The cell walls seemed to rumble from his voice, and the hooded figure shrank back for a moment.

But then two glowing red eyes beamed at him, and an evil laugh sickened him.

"This must be killing you. The great Hercules, chained up like a beaten dog." He jabbed his thumb to the red jewel on the wall. "At least dogs don't whimper over glowing rocks. You're pathetic."

Hercules swiped the air with his broad hands, visualizing himself snapping the Devil Man's neck. But he moved too fast and flew out of the cell, the iron door slamming shut behind him.

Hercules lost track of the days they stayed in the cell, until finally, Hades decided to pay them another visit.

When the door swung open, he stood in the doorway and held his nose. "Good grief. You two stink," he said.

"Well, you have kept us in this wretched cell with no water to bathe, so what do you expect?" Ava hissed. Her eyes blazed with fury, and it did something funny to Hercules's stomach.

Hades was wrong. *They* did not stink. She couldn't. But he did, and he would have sold his own soul just to have a dip in a cold lake.

"Have you come to your senses, Uncle, and decided to let us go after all?" he asked, hoping that if he reminded Hades that he was family, it would stir up some loyalty and a sense of obligation to do the right thing.

But alas, Hades did not have an honest bone in his body and cared little about obligation.

"I need you to do something for me." Hades fixed his gaze firmly on Ava. "But you are no use to me in this condition. I shall have you escorted to the hot springs, so you can bathe."

Hercules shook his head. "Uncle. Do not be unreasonable. After all I have done for you, after what Ava has done… imagine how Persephone might react if she knew about this."

The name made Hades's eyes flash dangerously as he glared at Hercules for a moment. But then a new emotion washed over the god of the Underworld, one that Hercules could not quite read. Was it fury? Devastation? Hercules could not be sure.

After a tense moment, Hades smiled and tilted his head. "Oh, that's right. Ava's your wife, now." Hades spoke the words in a sickly polite tone. "I suppose it would be terrible of me to let Ava bathe alone in the hot springs with so many of my Devil Men about… watching."

Hercules stiffened. He did not take lightly to being teased at the best of times, but the depressing Underworld had made him even less tolerant.

The very thought of prying eyes watching Ava made a ripple of fury rush over him.

The Devil Men were lustful, inhumane beings, who would love nothing more than to take an innocent woman like Ava and defile her in every way.

Hercules puffed out his chest. "She must stay with me."

Hades hummed in thought as he surveyed Hercules for a moment. Then his eyes glinted, and Hercules wondered what went through Hades's mind.

"Very well. I shall have a bath brought into the cell." He stepped toward Hercules. "And you shall ensure that every inch of Ava is perfectly clean. I need her fresh for her next mission."

"I'm never doing anything for you again," Ava snapped, crossing her arms.

Hades turned to her and blinked. "Are you sure? Because if I find no more use for you, I may just decide to snap my fingers, and..." He leaned near her and drew a line across Ava's neck with his index finger.

"She'll be ready." Anger pulsed through Hercules's veins as he watched Hades taunt Ava.

But Ava looked at Hercules like he'd slapped her. "How dare you..." she whispered.

Hercules couldn't make sense of her reaction. Did she not know what fate she faced if Hades sent her to the hot springs alone? Had she really no idea what Hercules had done to save her?

"Good." Hades clapped. "Now, I shall unshackle

you both and have a bath brought in. But there is one rule…"

His eyes glinted as he let out a dark chuckle.

"You must wash each other…leaving no part untouched." He winked at Hercules as he unlocked his shackles. "Call it a consolation prize."

When Hades released Ava, she spat in his face.

But Hades appeared undeterred as a smile stayed fixed on his face.

Ava and Hercules shouted obscenities as Hades walked out, and they didn't stop until the door slammed shut.

Ava turned to Hercules, and her eyes narrowed into slits. "What makes you think you can speak for me?" Her body was nearly vibrating, and her nails elongated. It had been a long time since he saw this side of her, and it made his blood travel south.

"Because you're too stupid to speak for yourself," he shot back.

Ava's face turned crimson, and she opened and closed her mouth. "How dare you! I am not stupid…"

Hercules rubbed his wrists; they felt light without the heavy chains. "Yes. You are. And you're naive."

Though his words sounded harsh, they had such an effect on Ava, it looked as if he had stoked a fire.

Her eyes blazed, and she hissed at him. Fighting with her was the most pleasure he had experienced since they got to the Underworld.

He made a silent vow to keep insulting the siren, pushing her buttons, until his dying day.

If he could make her rage, he could awaken her powers, and they might just be the key to their escape.

Of course, the more incensed Ava became, the more aroused Hercules became.

She threw angry words at him, but he couldn't hear them, for he was transfixed on her pink and dry lips. He resisted the urge to wet them with his tongue.

"I'm not letting you touch me," Ava snapped, pulling him out of his head.

He took a deep breath and stepped closer. The cell suddenly did not smell so bad as the heat of arousal flooded the space.

The thought of Hades's consolation prize did not seem so bad.

"Do you know what the Devil Men do to innocent women like you?" He gently brushed locks of her hair away from her shoulder.

Ava held her breath, and her eyes flashed dangerously at him, so he continued. "They do not care about decency or respect. They do not ask for permission. They will be able to smell you from across the Underworld, and they will eat you, tear your flesh, and suck your blood. They are Devil Men, Hades's most dastardly souls."

Ava sucked in a breath, but she raised her chin in defiance. "I will not let them near me." She crossed her arms.

Hercules moved around her, and she shivered when he dragged his thumb over her hip. "They will bind you so you cannot escape. And they come from the shadows, quicker than lightning. You will be devoured for days, weeks, even years. Until there's nothing left. Not even a soul."

Ava shut her mouth, and for the first time, her face paled, and fear took over her defiant smile. She dropped her arms. "But Hades wanted me to do something for him…"

Hercules tapped her nose. "Exactly. And you decided to drop an ultimatum and tell him you'll never work for him again. You think he'll offer any protection when you're no use to him?"

Ava scowled and averted her gaze.

Hercules couldn't tell if she felt furious by the situation or just frustrated by her own naivety.

Finally, she met his gaze again.

Hercules picked up her hand. "After all, Isis gave

you to me. You are my wife, are you not? Or have you changed your mind?"

Ava's cheeks reddened as he brushed her knuckles with his thumb.

He loved to see how she responded to him. Even the slightest touch nearly made her pass out.

"No-no, I haven't," Ava whispered. "I only hoped…"

"That the first time I claimed you was not in a dirty cell at the bottom of the Underworld?" Hercules offered.

Ava looked down. Her shoulders slumped.

But when Hercules cupped her face, she met his eyes with a terrified stare.

Hercules smiled. "Then it is a good thing I have no plans to defile you here."

"You don't?" Ava's voice sounded equally hopeful and disappointed.

Hercules stepped back and let her go. Then he lowered to his knees before her. "I vow to you, Ava, daughter of Poseidon and Isis, I shall protect you with my life and see that no one defiles you. Not even me. Until you want me to."

Finally, Ava smiled.

HERCULES

A short while later, the hooded figure carried in a tub that almost filled the entire cell, handed Ava and Hercules a towel and a rag, and sat one lowly bar of soap on the floor.

After the door closed, Ava and Hercules looked at each other for long moments.

"I suppose now you finally get what you've wanted," Hercules muttered, rubbing his wrists. It relieved him to no longer have heavy manacles on his skin, and his wounds had scarred.

But now that he had a new mission, he wished he still had them on.

Once again, Hades played a game. Not only did he make shady deals, but he greatly enjoyed putting people in uncomfortable situations.

After a fleeting moment of temptation, dread settled on him.

Hades had just forced him into a scenario that he had spent over one thousand years trying to avoid. Bathing alone with a woman.

"Who should go first?" Ava asked, snapping Hercules out of his thoughts.

He looked at her, holding up the soap and rag. His gaze fell to the gaping neckline of her dirty dress, and he got an eyeful of her cleavage for the first time. His stomach tightened.

"You can wash me," he said, thinking it would at least buy him time.

Ava's eyes widened, and she looked at him like an owl. "All right. Do you need help taking your—"

"—clothes off?" Hercules finished for her, with mild surprise. "No. You may be surprised to hear this, but I've been quite proficient at removing my own clothes for over a thousand years."

Ava's forehead reddened. "Of course."

Hercules did not have many clothes to remove. And yet, when he removed his shorts and stood entirely bare for Ava, her eyes almost bulged.

He felt certain this was not the first time she had seen a naked man. But the way her gaze fixated on his manhood made him wonder if his sheer size intimidated her.

Slowly, he stepped into the bath. The water sloshed around as he lowered to a seated position, and he shut his eyes with a deep exhale. The hot water soothed his aching muscles.

He scooted back. "Your turn." He nodded to the empty space on the other side of the bath.

Ava opened her mouth to protest, but Hercules shot her down with a look. "You do not want to wait for the water to turn foul. Come in while it's fresh and hot."

Ava sucked in a nervous breath and slowly rose to a stand. "Close your eyes," she said.

"Why?" Hercules shot back.

Ava gaped at him. "Why? Because I'm going to take my dress off."

"And?" Hercules asked.

Ava opened and closed her mouth silently like a fish out of water, and seeing her squirm eased all of his tension.

For the first time in a long time, he grinned. "You are my wife," he reminded her. "Is that not what you said? That you are my gift from Isis. Now I would like to see my gift unwrapped."

Ava's cheeks turned beet red now. "I thought that

after what happened with Adonis..." She looked down. "And how disgusting I am..."

Hercules lurched forward and grabbed Ava's wrist. "There is *nothing* disgusting about you," he growled.

She could be covered in a millennium-worth of filth, and she'd shine with beauty and have him begging to devour her.

Ava's eyes lit up at his words, and her reaction made him drop her wrist and slide backward again.

Guilt encircled his heart, and it throbbed with every beat. He could not bear the thought of her feeling undesirable.

But at the same time, he did not want to excite her too much. He felt much happier when she was furious with him.

"Fine. I shall take off my dress, and you shall watch," Ava said, sounding resolute.

She puffed out her chest and maintained eye contact with Hercules as she picked up the skirt of her dress and lifted it up to her thighs.

Hercules reclined in the bath and breathed long and slow as he watched Ava strip to nothing.

Then she stood bold and confident, her long, golden locks flowing over her breasts and resting at her navel. She looked like a goddess, slender and curvaceous in all of the right places. Her naked form burned in his memory, and he shut his eyes to revel in the memory of seeing such beauty.

Then she climbed into the bath and settled on the opposite side.

"Are you happy now?" She crossed her arms.

In truth, for a fleeting moment, Hercules felt happy. After all, he was in a warm bath with a beautiful, naked woman. What more could a man want in life?

But as always, a sickly sense of guilt nipped at his insides as Ava's face disappeared, and she turned into the woman who haunted his dreams.

His heart bled.

"We have to wash each other," he grunted. Avoiding Ava's question and forcing the mental image to disappear, he picked up the soap.

Ava shrugged. "How could anyone know what happens in here?" She looked around the cell walls. "It is not as if there are any windows in here."

Hades's voice flooded the cell. "The walls are merely an illusion, Ava. I have eyes and ears everywhere in the Underworld. Follow my commands, or I'll send you to the Hot Springs."

Hercules resisted the urge to roll his eyes while Ava jumped and hugged her knees.

"Oh," came her only response.

Hercules picked up the rag and lathered the soap on it. "Stand up."

It had become time to get the awkward situation over with.

A cascade of water fell as Ava rose to a stand, and droplets clung to her pale skin like gemstones.

Hercules tried to think about all of the ugly things he had seen in the world as he moved the rag over her body. But nothing could stop his body from reacting to the delightful sight.

Ava spread her legs and let him wash her inner thighs, and she squeaked when he cupped her.

He slid his fingers through the folds of her skin, rubbing and circling until he felt sure he had cleaned her. Ava let out a shuddering breath; she seemed to be enjoying the experience far too much.

Then she turned around, and he washed the rest of her body.

He stood and removed every last speck of grime on her neck and shoulders.

The soap had been infused with lavender and left a pleasant smell in its wake.

He moved her hair away from her neck and leaned in to inhale the aroma. Then he squeezed the rag, letting water trail down her front. More droplets settled on the soft peaks of her breasts, and Hercules licked his lips.

Ava gasped and stiffened, and Hercules realized that his growing arousal had pressed against her.

"What is that?" She skipped forward a step.

"Nothing to be concerned about," Hercules said. "Now, turn around and let me wash your face."

Ava did as he told her, and her gaze dropped downward. She let out another gasp.

Hercules grabbed her chin and lifted her head, forcing her to meet his stare. "I told you…" He rubbed the cloth over her collarbone and traced a line down to her navel. "It's nothing to be concerned about."

"But you're so…" Ava began.

Hercules fisted her hair and yanked on it, stopping her from looking down again. "Filthy. That's right," he growled in her ear.

She shuddered, and the tips of her nipples tickled his muscular chest.

"Now, take this soap. It's your turn to wash me."

CAPTAIN STONE

*I*n the heart of the Underworld, Captain Stone stood, and his gaze swept across the cavernous expanse bathed in an ethereal dark blue light.

Shadows danced on the jagged walls, intertwining with the eerie whispers that filled the air, whispers that seemed to carry the secrets of ages past. The atmosphere charged with palpable tension, the kind that sank deep into one's bones and refused to let go.

Beside him, Serena lay unconscious. Her chest rose and fell in a shallow, uneven rhythm.

A few feet away, Prince Edward groaned. The poison from the dart coursing through his veins painted his face with a ghastly pallor.

Georgette paced back and forth, her movements erratic, a stark contrast to the stillness of their surroundings.

"Can't you cry, Georgette? Your tears will heal them," Captain Stone suggested, his voice meant to be a steady anchor in the midst of chaos.

Georgette's eyes, usually as vibrant as the ocean during a storm, dulled and widened with a sort of wild, feral look to them.

She shook her head. "I can't, I just can't. Not a single tear—it's like they've dried up."

Her gaze flitted over Serena and Prince Edward, and she swallowed deeply.

Captain Stone's chest ached at the sight of his brother so weak and vulnerable.

"We need to get out of here, now." Georgette's voice gained a frantic edge.

Captain Stone wrapped his arms around her, drawing her into a comforting embrace. "We will, love. We will," he murmured, hoping that his voice became a soothing balm to her.

But their moment of solace was shattered by Prince Edward's pained groan, a stark reminder of their dire situation.

Captain Stone's mind raced, formulating a plan

amidst the uncertainty. "We need to find Hades. He might be our only hope now."

Georgette's breath hitched. The idea of seeking out such a powerful and unpredictable deity felt daunting, yet they seemed to have no other option.

"But how do we even begin to look for him in this labyrinth?" She stared at Captain Stone, and worry laced her voice.

He took a deep breath, and his mind worked overtime. "We follow the whispers. They seem to carry the essence of this place. Perhaps they'll lead us to him."

Georgette nodded, and a newfound determination lit up her eyes.

With a resolute stride, Captain Stone hoisted Prince Edward's limp form onto his broad shoulders. The prince, usually so regal and poised, now seemed as fragile as a fallen leaf in the captain's sturdy grasp.

Georgette, with equal determination, gently lifted Serena into her arms, cradling her sister.

Together, they turned their attention to the whispering winds, letting the haunting melodies guide them through the winding passages of the Underworld.

The path was treacherous, the uncertainty of

what lay ahead weighing heavily on their minds. But with each step, they moved closer to a potential ally in this realm of shadows and secrets, their hearts beating in unison against the odds.

Oppressive silence between them, the kind that echoed louder than any sound, marked their journey through the Underworld's tunnels. The air felt thick and damp, clinging to their skin like a suffocating veil.

They moved through the darkness, guided only by the whispers and the faint, otherworldly light that seemed to emanate from the very stones of the cavern.

After what felt like an eternity, the twisting, serpentine tunnels gave way to a vast throne room. It looked like a grand, yet foreboding space, adorned with sculptures and reliefs that depicted scenes of ancient myths and forgotten tales. The throne itself stood as a masterpiece of eerie beauty of bones, carved from what appeared to be black obsidian, and it sat empty, casting a long, ominous shadow across the room.

As they stepped into the throne room, a chilling sensation crept up Captain Stone's spine.

Hooded, ghostly figures surrounded them, their forms barely more than wisps of smoke and shadow.

These specters moved with an otherworldly grace, encircling them with a quiet malevolence.

"We demand to see Hades." Captain Stone's voice echoed through the cavernous space, imbued with a bravery he did not feel.

The hooded figures seemed to hesitate. Their ghostly forms swirled as if stirred by an unseen wind.

For a moment, it appeared as though they would attack; their ethereal hands reached out with a chilling intent.

But before they could reach them, a deep and resonant voice filled the room. "Well, this is a surprise."

At that moment, Hades emerged from the shadows like a creature born of the night. His presence felt commanding and undeniably powerful.

His eyes, dark as the abyss, held within them the wisdom of ages and the weight of countless souls. His cloak billowed around him, creating an aura of both majesty and dread.

Captain Stone tightened his grip on Prince Edward, ready to defend his brother against whatever might come.

Georgette, holding Serena close, gazed at the god with a mixture of awe and fear.

Hades's gaze swept over them, piercing and discerning, as if he could see into the very depths of their souls. "I see you have journeyed far and braved the shadows of my domain," he began. "Speak, mortals. What brings you to the throne of Hades?"

Serena grumbled and stirred in Georgette's arms, while Captain Stone put Prince Edward down.

When he did, he noticed the patch of crimson staining the rock floor by Georgette. Then he lifted his gaze to follow the trail of blood up Serena's leg to the sodden bandage around her thigh.

"My name is Mannington Stone, and this is my wife, Georgette. We are friends of your nephew," he said, with a respectful bow. "We come seeking your aid."

He gestured to his sister-in-law. "Georgette's sister has been stabbed, and my brother had this buried in his neck." He pulled out the bone splinter which had feathers tied to one end. The tip had been stained black, and Captain Stone carefully avoided letting it touch his fingers as he held it out for Hades to inspect.

Hades stepped forward and held it close to his eyes. He hummed low and soft. At last, he surveyed Prince Edward on the ground and Serena bleeding in

Georgette's arms. "You are friends of my nephew, you say?" he asked.

"Yes, Hercules should be here with his wife, Ava…" Georgette said, her voice hopeful.

Something flashed across Hades's eyes, but he turned impassive. "Of course. Any friend of Hercules is a friend of mine." He snapped his fingers, and two hooded figures appeared at his sides. "Take these wounded mortals to the healing waters and ensure they are restored to their full health."

Georgette hesitated when one of them reached out for Serena. Her eyes narrowed on Hades as though she did not entirely trust these strangers.

But Hades raised a palm. "It's all right. They will come to no harm; you have my word." He held a hand over his chest.

Georgette looked at Captain Stone who nodded to her. "We have no choice but to let them help us," he murmured to her.

Finally, she handed Serena over, and Captain Stone watched the two figures disappear with Prince Edward and Serena in their arms.

For reasons unknown to Captain Stone, the hairs on the back of his neck stood on end, and he felt a sense of foreboding.

Perhaps the ghastly setting had him on edge, or

the fact that he had to give up all sense of control and relied solely on the god of the Underworld to save his family.

His eyes prickled at the word. It was the first time he consciously thought of his brother and Serena as family. But in the time they spent crossing the seas, encountering all manner of enemies, he had grown fond of them.

Even if Serena acted particularly moody, and Prince Edward behaved annoyingly.

He found Georgette's hand and squeezed it, and he felt unsure if it had been for her benefit or his own.

Hades's gaze lowered to their intertwined hands for a moment, and he smiled at them both. "It is clear you are both weary from your...adventures. And I'm certain you have a great story to tell. Allow me to take you to my finest guest chamber." Hades marched away.

Captain Stone followed, and Georgette rushed to keep up. But then they all halted when she asked an innocent question. "Is Hercules still here?"

Hades's shoulders rose, and he stood silent for a moment as though he was choosing his words carefully.

He slowly turned and gave a smile that felt as if it

covered them in ice cold water. "My nephew is otherwise engaged at this time… for now, I want you both to rest. There is much to talk about."

Captain Stone glanced at Georgette, and her expression matched the sense of unease in the pit of his stomach. Something did not feel right.

"And what of his wife, Ava?" Georgette asked.

Hades ignored the question and led them through the winding, endless maze of tunnels.

He stopped outside of an ornate door made of obsidian. The brass handle glowed in the blue glow of the Underworld.

Hades ushered Captain Stone and Georgette into a room that seemed a world away from the dank tunnels of the Underworld.

Greek architecture adorned the space, and elegant columns lined the walls with intricate frescoes that depicted scenes of ancient glory. Luxurious tapestries hung from the walls, and their threads shimmered in the ethereal blue light, weaving stories of gods and heroes.

In the center of the room stood a large, steaming bath, its waters inviting and fragrant. An ornate armoire, its wood polished to a mirror-like sheen, promised garments far more comfortable than their travel-worn clothes.

"You'll find fresh attire in the wardrobe," Hades said, a hint of hospitality in his otherwise stern demeanor. "And the bath is prepared for your comfort."

Captain Stone, his brow furrowed with concern, seized the moment. "You didn't answer my wife's question, Hades. Where is Ava?"

Hades's nostrils flared, and a brief flash of annoyance crossed his otherwise composed face. He laughed it off, a sound that seemed to reverberate off the ancient stones. "All in good time," he said, his voice smooth yet foreboding. Then, with a swirl of his cloak, he departed, leaving them alone.

Captain Stone and Georgette stood in stunned silence. The click of the door's lock snapped them back to reality.

Georgette rushed to the door, but her attempts to open it were futile. "He locked us in?" she asked, disbelief lacing her voice.

Captain Stone began to pace, his mind racing with possibilities. "What happened to Hercules and Ava? Are they still in the Underworld? On some perilous mission, or worse, imprisoned like us?" He looked at Georgette, and her eyes reflected the gravity of their situation. "I don't think any of us are safe here. We need to get to the others. Can you conjure a portal?"

Georgette dragged her hands through her hair in a gesture of frustration. "No, that was Serena's power. I can't do anything except... accidentally heal people when I cry."

In any other circumstance, Captain Stone would have taken the time to reassure her, to remind her of the strength he saw in her every day. But the urgency of the moment left no room for gentle words. "Can you try? You might surprise yourself."

Georgette's expression shifted as she absorbed the severity of their plight. She muttered something under her breath and swept her hand in an oval shape, mirroring the motions she had seen Serena perform countless times. But nothing happened. No shimmering portal appeared; no escape offered itself to them.

Frustrated and desperate, Captain Stone threw his shoulder against the door, but it stood unyielding, as immovable as the fate they seemed to be facing.

Tears welled in Georgette's eyes. "Serena... Edward... What have we done?"

The weight of their predicament hung like a dark cloud in the room.

Only the soft crackle of the torches on the walls punctuated the silence.

Captain Stone took a deep breath, trying to quell the rising tide of panic.

The god of the Underworld had trapped them in his domain at his mercy, with their friends' fates unknown and their own future uncertain.

*A*va struggled to catch her breath as she licked her lips and focused on the task at hand.

Hercules was a beast of a man. Big, broad shoulders, hard pectorals, and defined abs that rippled under her touch.

She stole another glance at the enormous shaft pointing at her. Too big to go anywhere, she reasoned.

She swallowed and worked on the demigod, trying not to let her mind wander.

After seeing the sheer size of her new husband, Ava began to wonder if she should have taken her chances with the Devil Men.

After all, someday, Hercules would want to claim

his bride. It was only natural. And when that day came, she felt certain he would split her in two.

She took her time, washing his face, his hair, his back. She worked on his legs, and she dragged her fingers over the bulging veins on his arms.

He breathed hard and slowly, like a sleeping dragon.

All the while he maintained an erection.

When he had nowhere left to clean, she held her breath and shut her eyes as she dragged the cloth over his manhood.

She squeaked as it pulsed under her touch, as if it had a mind of its own.

When she pushed it down, it sprung upward, pointing to her face again.

When she cupped him, it surprised her how heavy his testicles felt in her palm.

He grunted slightly as she moved the rag over every sensitive part of him.

How his body reacted to her touch surprised her the most.

Her core ached and throbbed in a way she'd never experienced. It took all of her resolve to resist the magnetic pull to gently press her body to his.

She reasoned that they were husband and wife. It would be perfectly appropriate to connect with him, and she had yearned for it ever since she had matured.

After spending such a long time in a cell, she wanted his warmth to envelope her body. Even if he only hugged her. Just feeling his big arms around her body would be enough to satisfy her longing.

She remembered the soft oohs and ahhs from the cabins as Captain Stone and Prince Edward made love to her sisters. It did not sound like an act that she should fear. And curiosity had her mind racing, conjuring all kinds of forbidden thoughts.

"I think that's everything," Hercules said, snapping her out of her thoughts.

She stood and met his gaze. "Are you sure?" she asked. "Perhaps you missed a spot on me..." she whispered.

It was a bold move, but her brain failed to tell her before she took his hand and placed it over her heart. She edged closer, letting the tip of his erection heat the space between her thighs.

Hercules's eyes darkened, and his breaths grew shallow.

She may have been naive to many things, but one thing was clear: he wanted her.

And despite their surroundings, she wanted him to have her, right there in the bath.

She hovered near his mouth, but just as her lips brushed his, he jolted backward and staggered out of the bath.

"Look, Hades left us fresh clothes." His voice sounded too high to be natural.

Ava hugged herself as a shiver rushed over her.

He tossed her a towel and a gray, cotton dress. "Get dressed." He pulled on a fresh pair of shorts. "We need to find out what Hades wants you to do."

Ava's heart sank. She waved her hand over herself in a vain attempt to magically dry herself, but as usual, her powers were useless in the Underworld.

She toweled off and put on the simple dress instead.

Her long, damp hair hung over her shoulders, wetting the cotton.

She pulled on her undergarment, avoiding eye contact with Hercules.

Foolishness washed over her along with humiliation at Hercules's rejection. She could not understand why he didn't take her; his body wanted to. That had been obvious. But there seemed to be something holding him back.

She needed to know what. Because until she did, he wouldn't touch her the way she wanted him to. After waiting one hundred years, she did not want to be stuck in a cold marriage for all of eternity. She could think of nothing more torturous.

No. She would have to take matters into her own hands.

Her mind moved to her spirited baby sister, Serena. She had managed to seduce the prince even after he had given his heart to Georgette. Now, they seemed happy together.

Although, one distinct difference existed between Serena and Ava.

Serena was comfortable with her sexual desires and had no problem expressing what she wanted.

Ava, on the other hand, spent her whole life suppressing her own needs in order to please her mother.

One thing became clear: staying locked up in the Underworld would not solve anything. They needed to escape, and perhaps doing one last task for Hades would be the key.

*S*ure enough, as soon as they dressed, Hades appeared in the room.

He smiled in a way that she was sure he meant to

look comforting but only made Ava feel more anxious.

He gestured to the open door. "Come."

Ava exchanged a nervous glance with Hercules and crossed her arms. "I am not going anywhere without my husband." She glared at Hades in the eye.

Hades's brows lifted a fraction, but his face broke into a knowing grin. "Very well."

He snapped his fingers. A heavy pair of shackles appeared at Hercules's wrists, lined with red jewels, and Hercules let out a groan. "Are these necessary?" he asked.

Hades winked at him. "Just a precaution, nephew. I can't have you trying to escape."

Hercules put on the shackles. He and Ava followed Hades down the maze of corridors, passing all manner of ugly creatures, including hooded Devil Men, who stood immobile and quiet, like deadly monoliths.

Soon, Ava stood before Persephone, but her powers dwindled in the grip of the Underworld.

The attempt to hypnotize the Queen, to unearth her buried memories of being Hades's consort, felt like grasping at smoke.

Persephone's gaze looked distant, lost in a fog woven by Adonis's deceit.

Hades, ever the enigmatic ruler, explained with simmering anger. "Adonis has played his hand well, keeping my queen in a stupor, far from her throne." His words tinged with an unexpected vulnerability.

Persephone, however, shook her head and scoffed. "My husband, you? That's the stuff of nightmares, not memories."

Hades turned to Ava. "Take her to the real world. There, perhaps, her memories will return." He eyed Hercules, probably weighing the risks. "And yes, your husband may accompany you."

As they prepared to leave, their path crossed a door from which a faint, familiar voice emanated.

Ava, driven by curiosity and a sense of recognition, pressed her ear to the door. "I hear voices… and I think we know who they belong to."

Hercules, sensing the urgency, quickly created a portal.

But Ava turned to Hercules in shock. "Why couldn't you do that in the cell?"

He gave her a pointed look, "you think Hades would be foolish enough to lock us in a cell that I can escape? Come on."

They ran into the portal and ended up on the other side of the door.

Inside, they found Georgette and Captain Stone,

their expressions etched with worry and despair. The sudden appearance of Hercules and Ava, along with Persephone, added to their confusion.

"What are you doing here?" they all exclaimed in unison. The absurdity of the situation momentarily lightened the mood.

Georgette, her voice a flurry of words, recounted their bizarre experiences, and it made Ava's mind spin.

"Vikings... new prophecies... It's all so surreal," Ava said, unable to grasp the reality of her story.

"Serena was stabbed, and she's not healing..." Captain Stone added, his voice heavy with concern.

Ava frowned, and her mind raced to piece together the puzzle. "But Serena's a siren. Since her binding with Edward, she shouldn't be vulnerable to steel."

Georgette closed her eyes. "I thought so too, but the Vikings didn't just use steel. Their weapons were different. They used splintered bones, possibly dipped in poison. Edward was hit by a dart, and it turned his veins black."

Persephone's eyes widened in recognition. "I know what that is." Her voice had a mix of fear and understanding.

Everyone turned to her, and Ava realized they

had no idea who she was. "Sorry, this is Persephone... long story."

Persephone hugged herself and kept her voice barely above a whisper. Everyone huddled closer to listen as she spoke.

"My mother taught me about every flower in the world. There's a rare one that grows in the coldest parts of Norway, blooming under the moonlight. Its nectar is as deadly as a viper's venom. It kills within moments."

Captain Stone's expression turned grave. "They were injured several hours ago."

Persephone's brow furrowed in confusion. "But that's impossible. The poison should have killed them."

"The only reason they are alive is because of what they are," Hercules said. He grabbed Captain Stone's arm and gave him a piercing look. "Tell me, where are they now?"

Georgette frowned. "I think Hades sent them to the Healing Waters to be healed."

Hercules frowned. "You mean The Hot Springs."

Ava and Hercules exchanged looks with a gasp. "Oh no," Ava groaned.

The room fell into a tense silence as they grappled with the implications.

The poison, the Vikings, Captain Stone and Georgette's unexpected capture, and now Persephone's revelations—it all seemed to be part of a puzzle that grew more complex by the minute.

Without saying a word, Hercules created a new portal. "Hurry, your friends are in grave danger."

HERCULES

*J*n the heart of the Underworld, a plan as daring as it was desperate began to unfold.

Persephone, her resolve hardened by Hades's manipulation, offered to play the deceiver.

The goal was simple yet fraught with peril: Ava would steal the keys to Hercules's shackles, setting the stage for an ambush against Hades.

Hercules waited in the shadows for the right moment.

"Hades!" Persephone cried, running into the throne room.

Ava stood across the room, peeking out from a gargoyle statue.

Hercules nodded to her, and she nodded back.

When Hades strode into the room, his cloak billowing out in his wake, he did not see them. After all, he only had eyes for Persephone, who sat on his throne.

"I thought you went with the others to the surface?" He kept his tone measured, but Hercules sensed a spark of curiosity in his voice.

Persephone perched on the edge of the throne with her back straight as she gripped the sides. Her strawberry blonde waves fanned out like rays of sunset.

Hades already transfixed on her.

"I believe I had a flicker of a memory." Persephone's voice filled with power and authority. She looked so poised and powerful that it took Hercules aback.

For a moment, he forgot that she acted, and she even convinced him that the old Persephone had returned.

"A memory that makes you dare to sit on my throne?" Hades asked, stepping closer.

A flurry of movement across the room told Hercules that Ava slipped into position.

The ring of keys jingled at Hades's belt as he walked.

But Ava moved silently, like a cat.

Hercules edged closer, careful to stay hidden.

Persephone laughed, and it sent a chill down Hercules's spine.

It formed an echo of the past that he had long forgotten.

Centuries ago, Queen Persephone had been ruthless. Even as cold and manipulative as Hades.

They made a formidable couple, and when Hercules had heard that Adonis stole her away, he thought for a long time that it had been for the better.

The sound of her dark laugh made Hades wobble, as though he would fall to his knees.

Hercules smirked.

Hades was unstoppable, yet even now, Persephone had him in the palm of her hand.

She lifted her chin and gave him a sly grin. "I remember sitting on this throne…and you bowing to me."

Hades paused. "You do?" he asked, though he did not sound the slightest bit convinced.

Persephone leaned forward and uncrossed her legs.

The neckline of her gown gaped open, and Hades must have seen something he liked, because when she purred, "Yes," to him, he promptly sank to the floor.

She lifted her skirt to her pale thighs and spread her legs wider, and an audible groan from Hades echoed around the vast room.

For a moment, Hercules felt pity for Hades, knowing that soon, Persephone would crush him.

After all, he reacted as a man starved of love. Hercules knew all about that.

And he felt sure that Hades longed to believe Persephone's act.

"I remember your hand caressing me, right here…" Persephone touched her left thigh.

Hades crawled to her and dragged his palms over her legs.

She threw back her head and let out a shuddering breath.

Ava appeared to the right, waiting. Her eyes glowed as she watched in anticipation while Persephone seduced Hades.

"Then you touched me…here." Persephone took Hades's hands and placed them on her breasts.

Hades panted, and it took every part of Hercules's resolve not to dry heave.

He found it laughable that a woman could so easily manipulate the great and powerful Hades.

Of course, to Hades, Persephone was not just a woman. She was the *only* woman.

Hades reached for her neck, and she let him kiss her.

"Persephone." He whispered her name like a prayer when they broke apart.

Persephone fumbled with his belt and tossed it to the side where it landed at Ava's feet—with the keys still attached.

"If you want your throne back…" Persephone's voice stayed low and teasing. "Then you'll have to take it from me."

Hades pinned Persephone's wrists above her head against the throne, and the two of them began to moan like a pair of lovers on their wedding night.

Meanwhile, Hercules tip toed to the other side of the throne room and held out his shackled wrists to Ava.

She carefully unfastened the keys from Hades's belt and tried them in the lock.

"Oh, yes!" Persephone cried out, and Hercules thought the woman deserved an award for her art of deception.

Then the lock clicked, and Hercules's hands sprung free.

Ava smiled at him with another nod and hurried away, throwing the red jewels as far from him as possible.

Already, Hercules felt the godlike strength pulsing through his veins. He took a deep inhale, strode out of the shadows, and landed a hard punch right on the side of Hades's head.

He fell sideways, and Persephone scrambled out of the way, adjusting her dress.

Hades shook himself as though dazed and rose to his feet. His eyes flashed with rage as he looked upon Hercules.

The confrontation, when it came, was nothing short of epic.

Hades, lord of the Underworld, faced off against Hercules, a hero of legend.

"What games are you playing?" Hercules spat as he landed another punch to Hades's gut.

Hades grabbed Hercules's fist and threw him back with one mighty shove.

Hercules's boots squeaked across the stone floor as he slid backward.

Hades squared his shoulders and summoned a sword in his right hand. "Forgive me, nephew. For I do not understand what you mean." He conjured another sword at Hercules's feet.

Hercules picked it up and held it up in front of him, ready.

"I let you go. I even let you leave with my most

precious treasure… and yet you come back and have the audacity to strike me from behind… like the coward that you are." Hades laughed. "I suppose that is the only way you can ever defeat me."

Hercules tightened his grip on the hilt of the sword in his hand. "First, you send Ava on a dastardly mission, while taking my strength and locking me up in your pitiful dungeon," he growled. "Then you leave us like rats to fester and rot for weeks."

"Nonsense. I believe you two had a very comfortable bath," Hades argued, and his teeth flashed in the dark room.

The thought that he spied on them sent blind rage through Hercules.

"Then you lock up two of our friends… and send the others to the Hot Springs…"

"To be healed." Hades held up his index finger.

Hercules paced like a lion, panting through his nostrils. "You and I both know what lurks within the Hot Springs."

Hades shrugged. "What did you expect?" He tilted his head to the side. "Or did you forget, dear nephew? I am the god of the dead, not the living."

"Then I shall send you to be with your people in the river you love so much," Hercules hissed, charging forward with his sword raised.

Their clash formed a dance of power and fury, and the air crackled with each blow and parry.

Hercules, in his unparalleled strength, seemed to have the upper hand.

His blows clashed like thunder, and each strike echoed through the cavernous depths of the Underworld.

Ava and Persephone watched from the side, like two frozen statues.

Knowing that Ava watched fueled Hercules with a type of determination and strength that he had not known in a lifetime.

But Hades was no ordinary foe.

As they battled, his words cut deeper than any physical wound. He taunted Hercules, dredging up the darkest moments of his past. "Megara... you couldn't save her, could you? A thousand years, and her screams still haunt your dreams."

Hercules's resolve faltered. The weight of his failures and guilt bore down on him like an elephant on his chest.

Hades's words cut him so deeply, he felt certain his heart would hemorrhage, and the anguish alone would be his undoing.

He slumped over while Hades lowered his sword and bent down to hiss into his ear like a King Cobra.

"Even after all this time, you still can't move on. And here I was trying to help you…"

He grabbed Hercules by the chin and directed his gaze toward Ava. "I locked you up with a beautiful siren. Someone you called your wife. Yet, you did nothing. And even when I presented her to you naked, you still couldn't get it up for her…"

"Stop that!" Ava shouted.

Hades looked at her and grinned at Hercules. "Are you not at all ashamed about how poorly you've treated this woman? Does she know you will never love her, that you will never be capable while your heart is still within the clutches of a corpse?"

The mighty Hercules, brought low not by physical force but by the ghosts of his past, sank to his knees.

The ghost of Megara's beautiful face appeared before him in a vision, and once again, he silently begged for her forgiveness.

Tears streamed down his face. The pain of Megara's loss, the guilt of not being able to save her, drowned him in a tsunami of grief.

He turned his face away, unable to bear the sight of Ava, and his heart felt heavy with shame.

Hades was right. Even after a millennium of time, he still could not let Megara go. Ava deserved better.

Meanwhile, Persephone, her own heart a storm

of conflicting emotions, took a knife in her hand and held it to her own throat. "Let him go, Hades," she demanded, her voice trembling but resolute. "Or I'll end this charade once and for all."

The Underworld stood still, and the air thickened with the gravity of her threat.

Hades, his face a mask of shock and fury, realized the tides had turned. The woman he thought he controlled was now the arbiter of his fate.

"Persephone... you're with them?" Hades dropped his sword, and it fell with a clatter.

Persephone gave him a stern look, but kept her blade pressed to her neck. "You call Hercules your nephew. Yet, you torment him? Anyone with eyes can see he has a broken heart. Perhaps losing me for good will help you to know what it is like..."

"Enough," Hades finally said, his voice a low growl. But his eyes looked misty and dark.

He scowled at Hercules and Ava. "Leave, both of you. But remember, Hercules, the shadows of your past will always be a part of you. I have tried to make you see the light, but sooner or later, you need to move on from the darkness or it will one day consume you."

Ava ran to Hercules's side and yanked on his arm, pulling him to his feet.

He looked up just as Persephone lowered the knife from her neck and gave him a resolute nod. "Go and save your friends," she said.

"What about your memories?" Ava looked from Persephone to Hades. "Are we not to take her to the surface?"

Hades glared at the floor, silent.

Persephone answered in an emboldened and confident voice. "Find your friends, then I shall join you to the surface."

Hercules inhaled a deep breath.

The battle may have been won, but the war within him raged on.

Ava walked beside him, and her presence became a silent support.

The group moved through the Underworld's labyrinthine paths.

Each step brought them closer to the Hot Springs, so they picked up their pace and hoped that they did not arrive too late.

*A*va's heart ached with a mix of compassion and longing as she watched Hercules from the corner of her eye.

His silent suffering, the weight of a thousand years of guilt and loss, hung over him like a black cloud.

In all her existence, she had never seen a man so burdened, so broken.

He became a fortress of sorrow, and every instinct in Ava screamed to breach those walls, to offer solace.

She longed to reach out, to squeeze his hand in silent encouragement, recognizing her own weakness for healing wounded souls.

Silently, she made a vow: once their friends were safe, she would devote herself to mending Hercules, no matter how long it took. She had set her heart; she would be there for him, whether it took another thousand years or more. Everyone deserved love, and Hercules, with his deep capacity for love and loss, held her heart captive.

A piercing sound tore through the silence and abruptly shattered her thoughts. She clutched her head in pain, and Hercules grasped her arm.

"We're getting close. Come on." His voice sounded like a blend of worry and determination.

They emerged into a cavern nothing short of otherworldly.

The Hot Springs of the Underworld lay before them, and their waters swirled like galaxies in motion.

The steam rose in graceful spirals, carrying with it the scent of salt and water lilies, a fragrance both soothing and haunting.

The water reflected like a myriad of stars on the cave walls, casting the cavern in a surreal, celestial light. But the beauty of the scene marred by what lay at its heart.

Serena and Prince Edward's motionless forms lay stretched upon an altar with serene faces that looked unnaturally pale.

Figures clad in black cloaks surrounding them—the Devil Men of the Underworld. Their presence felt ominous, a stark contrast to the ethereal beauty of the springs.

They clearly prepared for some dark ritual as they moved in precise and ritualistic stances.

Just as the tension reached its peak, Georgette and Captain Stone burst into the cavern from another side, their arrival like a storm breaking the calm.

They lunged at the cloaked figures, their movements a dance of desperation and fury.

Each strike and parry became a fight not just for their own lives but for the souls of their companions.

Ava and Hercules joined the fray. Their own battles fueled by love and the unyielding desire to protect their friends.

The cavern echoed with the sounds of combat: the clashing of metal against metal, the grunts of exertion, and the hiss of the steaming springs.

The fight was chaotic, a whirlwind of motion and emotion.

Ava moved with a grace that belied her urgency, her every strike aimed with precision.

Hercules, his strength a force of nature, was a whirlwind of destruction, his every blow sending Devil Men staggering.

The battle raged on, and the fate of Serena and Prince Edward hung in the balance.

The air filled with the electric energy of the fight as the stakes rose higher than ever.

In this moment, in this fight, they became more than just a group of individuals; they formed a unit, bound together by a shared purpose, fighting against the darkness that threatened to consume them all.

As the battle raged on, Captain Stone, in a swift motion, tore off the hood of one of the Devil Men.

The revelation beneath took the group aback: not the grotesque face of a demon, but the rugged, handsome features of a warrior. It jarringly contrasted the sinister aura that surrounded the beings.

The Devil Men moved with an unsettling, unnatural agility; they moved both awkwardly and swiftly.

But Ava and Georgette matched their pace with graceful and precise movements of their own.

They darted and weaved through their attackers, evading their grasps with an almost ethereal nimbleness.

Amidst the chaos, Ava and Georgette unleashed their fury, their claws extended, slicing through the air with deadly accuracy.

One by one, the Devil Men fell, their throats slashed in swift, clean cuts. They dropped to their knees and life faded from their eyes, only to be replaced by more of their kind, emerging from the shadows like a relentless tide.

However, the tide of battle abruptly turned.

Devil Men slipped behind Captain Stone and Ava while they fought and gripped both in their strong hands.

The situation grew dire, the air thick with the scent of impending doom.

It seemed as if all hope was slipping away, the victory they had fought so hard for about to be snatched from their grasp.

Then, Hades emerged from the shadows like a ghost. With a commanding presence and dark authority emanating from him. "Stand down." His voice echoed through the cavern and carried the weight of absolute power.

At his words, the Devil Men ceased their assault. They bowed low and vanished into thin air as if they had never been there in the first place.

The abrupt end to the conflict left the group stunned, their hearts still racing from the adrenaline of battle.

The cavern, now devoid of the Devil Men, became silent except for the gentle hiss of the steaming springs.

Ava looked at her friends, and each held mixed expressions of relief, confusion, and wariness.

Hades's intervention had saved them, but the reason behind his sudden change of heart remained a mystery.

"Why are you helping us?" Georgette asked the question in all of their minds.

But Hades did not reply. Instead, Persephone stepped into the light and rested her hand in the crook on Hades's arm. "Because I commanded it."

Hercules could not be certain whether this was still an act, or if Persephone had actually regained her memories. But Persephone stood powerful and strong, a perfect equal to Hades.

"But… you saw what he did to Adonis…" Ava said, aghast.

Persephone's cold stare moved to Ava. But then the corner of her mouth twitched, and Hercules got his answer.

"I will not accompany you on your journey," Persephone said. "I wish to stay here, with my husband." She smiled up at Hades, who grinned, his face radiant with joy.

But then she pointed at the altar. "If your friends have been poisoned with Moonviper venom, there is a cure."

"What is it? Where is it?" Captain Stone's eyes widened as his voice rose.

Hercules rested his hands on his hips, thinking about it.

"Venom?" He turned to Persephone.

She nodded to him.

"But venom will surely kill them?" Georgette argued.

Ava shook her head. "No. Our blood grows stronger with venom."

Hercules looked around everyone, strode over to the altar, picked up Serena and Prince Edward, and draped them over his shoulders.

Meanwhile, Hades created a new portal that hovered in the air like a magical mirror.

"Good," grunted Hercules. "We shall be on our way…" But then he turned to Hades and lifted his brow. "One more thing…Uncle."

Hades sighed and walked forward. "Very well. I suppose I no longer have any need for this anyway." He conjured the golden mace in his hands.

"Ava, do you mind?" Hercules jerked his head to her. As though it was not obvious that he had his hands full.

Ava hurried forward and took the mace. She rolled it between her palms, and the golden staff twinkled like a golden ray of sunshine. The deadly spikes sparkled without so much as a spec of blood.

Yet, the sight still made her stomach churn.

"Go and save your friends," Persephone said as everyone took their position in front of the swirling portal.

"How do we know this isn't another one of your tricks, Hades?" Captain Stone narrowed his eyes at him.

A part of Ava agreed with him. It was hard not to be skeptical after everything that had happened.

Hades laughed and wrapped his arm around Persephone's shoulders. "I suppose you shall just have to trust me."

When no one replied, he waved his hand to shoo them. "Go on. None of you are welcome in the Underworld anymore. I do not expect to see any of you for a very long time." He turned to Hercules. "Most of all you, Hercules. Go. Live your life, love your woman, and next time I see you, I want to see a god of strength, not sorrow."

Ava's mouth dropped open when she sensed an emotion that did not belong to her.

It permeated like a warm beam over her when the side of Hades's jaw bulged as he gave Hercules a firm look, but in the corner of his eye, a tiny teardrop formed, barely noticeable.

Yet, the feeling felt unmistakable. Not malice, nor greed or anger. Even though he had just been fighting with Hercules.

No. Ava only found one word for the emotions that swam inside her from Hades's soul, a word that Ava had never in a million years dreamed to connect with the god of Death: Love.

GEORGETTE

$\mathcal{T}$he transition from the Underworld to the Land of the Living came abruptly and disoriented them all.

Georgette, along with the rest of the group, stumbled through the portal, emerging into a world that starkly contrasted the dark, oppressive realm they had left behind.

They found themselves in a foreign land, under the cloak of night. The moon stood as a silver sentinel in the sky.

The air felt crisp and cool, a refreshing change from the stifling atmosphere of the Underworld.

Georgette took a deep breath as air fill her lungs, so cold it almost felt like they froze.

The smells and sounds of the forest enveloped them—the earthy scent of rain-soaked soil, the distant calls of nocturnal wildlife, and the gentle rustle of leaves in the breeze.

Captain Stone looked around, and his eyes scanned the land. "I do not recognize this place," he admitted, "but it is a relief to be breathing fresh air once more."

"We are in Peru," Hercules said.

Georgette wrapped her arms around herself. The chill of the night seeped into her bones. "I only wish Hades sent us somewhere warmer." Her breath formed small clouds in the cool air. "Hercules, can you make another portal? Perhaps we should go back to your island."

Hercules, his face a mask of concentration as he gently lowered Serena and Prince Edward to the ground, turned sharply at her suggestion. "No," he barked, his voice firm and resolute.

The intensity in his eyes spoke of a determination that went beyond mere physical strength. He had such a presence about him that made Georgette step back.

He seemed to notice her reaction because his gaze softened. "Your friends will be dead by morning if we do not treat their wounds."

"They're not friends." Georgette curled her fingers and dug her nails into her palms. "They're family."

"Serena," Ava whispered, rushing to her sister's side.

Serena began to stir; her face sickly pale.

"Has anyone got any water?" Ava lifted Serena's head and rested it on her lap.

Captain Stone handed her a sheepskin flask. "It's a little stale."

Ava carefully moistened Serena's lips and stroked her hair with tenderness. "My sweet baby sister," she whispered as her tears began to flow freely. They fell on Serena's brow and seeped into her pours.

Georgette watched with bated breath, wondering if anything miraculous might happen.

But Serena only moaned and fell asleep once more.

Prince Edward, however, lay eerily still. His chest hardly rose and fell.

"Right." Captain Stone withdrew his knife, looking at Hercules. "Do we need a snake in partic-ular or will any do?"

"The one standing behind you will do just fine," Hercules said mildly.

Everyone froze and looked where Hercules

pointed, and sure enough, a small black snake hissed at Captain Stone. It raised its head a foot off the ground.

"A pit viper—how fitting," Captain Stone said.

"Don't fear it," Georgette reminded him. "Remember, its bite will only make you stronger."

"Good." Captain Stone grunted and promptly grabbed the snake in one hand and lifted it to his arm. The snake lashed out and sank its fangs into him. Then it drew back, leaving two small pin pricks.

Georgette held her breath. "Do you feel anything?"

Captain Stone shrugged. "A slight pinch, not a dull ache."

Hercules knelt beside Prince Edward and lifted an eyelid with his thumb before he hummed.

"You should try it on this guy first. It might already be too late for him."

Captain Stone took the snake and forced it near Prince Edward's neck.

The snake appeared to consider him for a moment but hesitated and refused to strike.

"Come on, you blasted snake, bite!" Captain Stone growled.

The snake turned to him and seemed to frown, its little eyes narrowing.

Georgette knelt beside him and flicked her fingers by the snake, prompting it to lunge at her. But she withdrew her fingers at the last second, revealing Prince Edward's neck.

Hercules hummed again, rose to his feet, and walked away.

"Where are you going?" Ava called out.

"We need more venom. A lot more. Stone. Are you coming?" he called over his shoulder as he swaggered into the forest.

Captain Stone handed Georgette the snake and kissed her on the forehead. "I'll return as quickly as I can," he whispered.

When the men left, just Ava and Georgette knelt beside their fallen companions.

The peaceful night belied the turmoil that had brought them here.

Georgette looked around, taking in the lush greenery that surrounded them and the silhouettes of the mountains visible against the starlit sky. She could not deny the beauty of this place, a stark contrast to the dangers they had just faced.

Yet, despite the serene setting, a sense of unease lingered in the air.

Ava continued to stroke Serena's hair, while Georgette watched Prince Edward for any signs of change.

His cracked lips looked dry, and his sunken-in eyes made her heart ache. Deep black veins bulged from his neck and temples.

Hercules's words echoed in her mind. *"It may already be too late for him."*

"He is not going to die. He will not. There is more for him to do here."

Georgette jumped at the voice in her mind, looking at Serena who lay in Ava's lap with her eyes closed. Then her gaze met Ava's.

"Ava?"

Ava jumped back. "You heard my thoughts?"

Georgette forced a smile, despite the dread that dragged her down.

She looked at Serena again. *"It is a new ability. At first, I could only hear Serena. But I suppose I can hear you too, now."*

Ava smiled at her. *"Your siren powers are awakening. That's exciting."*

But then Georgette glared at Ava. "Exciting? I hardly think any of this is exciting. We're no closer to finding Osiris's bones, our group is dropping like flies, and we've barely escaped the Underworld."

Ava's eyes flashed. "You were hardly there," she snapped. "Hercules and I were chained like dogs and left for months in a filthy old dungeon. So, don't lecture me about finding something to be excited about."

Georgette clenched her jaw. "Months? It's hardly been over a fortnight. And it's not like we were enjoying the sun and the beach as we waited for you two. We were almost sacrificed by Vikings…"

"It might have been two weeks out there, but time here passes differently--Wait. Did you say Vikings?"

Ava scoffed. "Vikings."

Anger rushed through Georgette's veins. "Do you think I am lying?"

"Yes," Ava thought. "No," Ava said aloud.

Georgette dragged a hand over her face. "I heard that."

Ava's lips turned into a thin line when she pulled them inward. *"If you can hear me, then listen. Vikings have not existed since long before my birth. I do not know who these barbarians are, but they're not Vikings."*

Georgette's heart pounded as she watched Captain Stone and Hercules return, their arms laden with writhing pit vipers.

The urgency of the situation eclipsed the tension between her and Ava. "Hurry!" she called out, her voice laced with desperation.

The immediate need to save Prince Edward and Serena pushed all other concerns aside.

Hercules and Captain Stone carefully placed the ominous yet strangely majestic snakes on the couple. The creatures moved with a certain deliberateness.

Their fangs sank into the skin, delivering the potentially life-saving venom.

Georgette could hardly bear to watch as the snakes peppered bite marks all over their arms.

Time seemed to crawl, and each minute stretched into what felt like an eternity.

They all watched, holding their breath, praying for a sign of recovery.

The night air, filled with the sounds of the Peruvian wilderness, seemed to be holding its breath too.

Captain Stone approached Georgette. He spoke in a soft voice, tinged with concern. "Georgette, can you not cry?"

Georgette stiffened at his words, and her frustration at her own helplessness surfaced. "Do not mistake me, I have tried countless times. Yet, I cannot."

Bitterness tainted her tone. The inability to summon tears, a siren's healing gift, weighed heavily on her.

"Not even a single tear for your own sister?"

Everyone jumped at the sound of Serena's weak voice.

To Georgette, it was the most beautiful sound she had heard in a long time. A wave of relief washed over her, cleansing away the tension and fear that had gripped her heart.

Serena blinked slowly, and her eyes focused as she gradually sat up. The bite marks on her skin faded as if being erased by an invisible hand.

Georgette's eyes widened in disbelief and joy. Her sister healed right before her eyes.

A hush fell over the group as they witnessed the miracle unfolding. The sight of Serena's recovery brought a sense of hope, a light in the darkness they had been traversing.

Georgette's heart swelled with gratitude and love, and the fear and uncertainty that plagued her slowly dissipated.

The night air, once heavy with the weight of impending loss, now sang with a quiet triumph.

The healing power of the snakes, combined with the strength and resilience of their group, had turned the tide.

In that moment, amidst the lush greenery and under the watchful eye of the moon, they were reminded of the power of unity and the unbreakable bonds of family and friendship.

"How do you feel?" Ava asked her.

Serena rubbed her arms and stood to her feet. "Like I've been trapped in a strange dream."

Her gaze landed on Prince Edward, and she fell to her knees by his side. "Why is he not awake yet?" Worry twisted Serena's face as her wide, desperate eyes searched Hercules for reassurance. "But he shall heal, yes?"

Hercules, with a solemn expression, nodded slowly. "He's been struck by a poison dart. It went straight to his bloodstream. It will take longer to heal." He reached out and gently patted Serena on the shoulder.

Georgette turned to Serena and looked into her desperate eyes. "Can you do anything? Remember at Imerta... you saved him."

Serena looked back at Georgette as though that was a memory from a lifetime ago.

Nodding, Serena waved her hand over him. But then she frowned. "It's not working." She shook her head, looking both horrified and troubled.

The revelation hit Georgette hard. She had always believed in the miraculous healing powers of her tears, but to see Serena struggle made her question everything.

Serena's eyes filled with tears as she looked up at Georgette, and her voice quivered. "Will you heal him? Please. I will do anything. Just do this one thing for me."

Georgette's heart tightened. "I've already tried," she murmured with her voice barely above a whisper.

"Well, you haven't tried enough," Serena insisted, her tone laced with both desperation and determination.

"I've seen you heal him before… on the beach in Imerta. Just by moving your hand," Georgette shot back. "Why are you putting me under this pressure?"

Serena's eyes turned to slits, and she seethed. It was evident that to admit a weakness was a form of torture. But she did not need to say it.

Instead, Ava jumped forward. "Serena needs to rest. She's still healing herself."

"Can't you heal?" Hercules asked Ava.

She flinched and looked at him with alarm. A flush of color rose to her face. "I can heal superficial wounds with tonics and herbal tinctures, but this is beyond my capabilities." She looked down.

Serena grabbed Georgette again. "Please. Help him."

Georgette's gaze drifted to Captain Stone.

Her mind raced through a myriad of sad memories: the lifeless body of her father in his study, the loss of their unborn child, and the heart-wrenching day Captain Stone died in her arms. Each memory became a sharp stab to her heart and threatened to overwhelm her.

Yet, as her eyes fell upon Prince Edward, a different memory surfaced.

A scene from her childhood emerged, a time of innocence and joy.

She recalled running through the palace in a playful game of chase with Prince Edward. Their laughter echoed through the halls.

It seemed a lifetime ago.

In that moment, a single tear broke free, rolling down her cheek. It shimmered in the moonlight as a tiny beacon of hope before it landed gently on Prince Edward's nose.

The group watched in silence, holding their breath.

Georgette's tear, a solitary droplet born of a mixture of sorrow and fond memories, seemed to hold the key to their salvation.

As the tear touched Prince Edward's skin, the air shifted.

Everyone's eyes fixed on him, waiting for a sign, any indication that the miracle they so desperately hoped for unfolded before them.

"Edward. My prince…" Serena whispered, holding his pale hand to her heart. She sobbed and stroked his face. "Fight. Come back to me."

Her tears flowed like rain drops and landed on his cheeks.

SERENA

*E*nergy pulsed through Serena's body, and when she shut her eyes, she sensed the venom in her blood purifying and strengthening her. Yet, her brain stayed foggy, and her hands had gone numb.

She had fallen in and out of consciousness after she had been wounded on Viking Island, and now that she had awoken again, she felt detached from the world.

Even so, she had heard every exchange that happened while she had fallen unconscious.

A woman said she had been poisoned by Moonviper.

Captain Stone and Hercules had forced pit vipers to bite her and Edward as snake venom made sirens more powerful.

She looked at the love of her life, who lay so still, and wondered if she might still be trapped in a space between waking and sleeping.

She peeled away the damp bandage on her leg and found nothing but a silver scar where the jagged wound once was. Soon, even that would fade, and it would be as if nothing happened.

She bit her lip and reached for Prince Edward's hand again.

It felt cool in hers—too cool.

The rest of the group stood in a circle around them, silent as they casted shadows over her.

In Serena's world, everything came to a screeching halt while she waited for the venom to heal Prince Edward like it had healed her. Or for Georgette's tears to awaken him.

She waved her hand over him again, willing every molecule in his blood to be healed. But her hand felt heavy, lacking the vibration she usually felt whenever she performed healing magic.

"My powers…" She looked at her hands like they did not belong to her.

Ava stepped forward and touched her arm. "They are blocked by emotion. And you need to rest."

The air thickened, made heavy with the weight of dread.

Prince Edward's breath, once ragged and strained, ceased abruptly, leaving a haunting silence in its wake.

She clutched at his cheeks, her fingers numb, her mind refusing to accept the reality unfolding before her. "No. No. This is not happening. Edward." Her voice was a ghost of its usual strength.

"Serena..." Ava's voice felt like a soft caress.

But Serena recoiled, and her body and soul rejected any form of comfort.

Her heart thundered against her ribcage. Its frantic beats drowned out the sounds of the night.

The world blurred, and colors and shapes melded into an indistinct haze.

"Why can't I heal him? Why?" The question tore from her throat, a raw, anguished cry that resonated with the despair that consumed her.

And then, as if her body could no longer contain the storm within, Serena clutched at her stomach and let out a scream. So primal, so filled with pain, that it caused everyone around her to flinch, to recoil from the raw intensity of her sorrow.

In a frenzy of grief, Serena lashed out at

Hercules. Her fists pounded against him, and her sobs became a torrent of unbridled anguish.

Ava reached out, trying to offer some semblance of support, but Serena was beyond reach.

She threw Ava off with a force born of despair, releasing a howl that seemed to tear at the very fabric of the night.

She simultaneously pleaded with and cursed all the gods.

Even with snake venom magnifying her powers, nothing gave her the strength to carry the grief of losing Prince Edward--*her* prince. And now she had been robbed of him.

Georgette turned to Captain Stone. He stood beside her with an ashen face and hollow eyes. It was the look of a man who had just witnessed the death of his brother, a sight that would haunt him for all his days.

But Serena could not bring herself to summon any ounce of compassion.

The man had abandoned his brother, after all. For years, they had been enemies. He did not have the right to mourn.

The air around them was thick with disbelief, with a despair so profound it seemed to suffocate all hope.

Serena thrashed and wailed. "Why didn't the venom work? Why can we not heal him?" She cried out again, and her voice broke.

Then she gasped and whispered one word to herself. "Resurrection." She ran to Georgette and gripped her by the upper arms. "I know you do not care for me, but I implore you. For Edward's sake… for your husband's happiness… resurrect him. You're the only siren other than Isis to do it."

Serena was not one to beg, but she had nothing else to try. Her twin sister was her last hope.

Georgette's dam of composure finally burst. Tears streamed down her face as she shook her head and choked on her tears. "I tried to help. I'm so sorry, but it's too late," she said.

Serena looked to Captain Stone, hoping he might persuade Georgette to try again, but he remained motionless, perhaps rooted in shock, or lost in his own chasm of despair.

But then, amidst the cacophony of grief, a strange noise pierced the night.

Faint at first, almost imperceptible, but it grew steadily and drew their attention.

"Do you see that?" Captain Stone whispered, looking over to Hercules.

Everyone watched Prince Edward with concentration, waiting for any sign of life.

And then, as if by some miracle, Prince Edward inhaled sharply, a dramatic and life-affirming gasp that filled the air with the sweet promise of hope.

The black veins faded from his neck and a soft pink blush appeared on his cheeks.

Slowly, he opened his eyes and blinked as though he had just come out of a vivid dream.

Serena fell upon him in an instant. Her kisses rained down upon his face, and each one became a testament to her relief, her love, and her unspoken vows.

"Never scare me like that again. Never. Never ever. Or I shall kill you myself," she admonished between kisses.

Prince Edward lifted an arm and rested his hand on Serena's cheek. His hand held some warmth to it, and Serena sensed the steady rhythm of his heartbeat.

She clung to his hand, holding it to her face as she continued to cry.

"I could never leave you," he whispered. "Never."

HERCULES

The group made camp and decided to rest for the next couple of days and regain their strength. So much had transpired since they last united on the beach.

Hercules could not take his eyes off Ava as they walked side by side through the forest.

It came their turn to hunt, and it was the first time Hercules had her to himself since they had been captured in the Underworld.

It felt like an unusual type of torture to watch Serena and Prince Edward cozy up by the fire, with Georgette and Captain Stone snuggled up on the other side of the camp.

It forced Ava and Hercules to witness more than their desired share of swooning couples.

Captain Stone did not even try to hide the fact his hand stayed permanently inside Georgette's shirt. He'd murmur sweet nothings in her ear while planting kisses down her neck.

Serena would not take her hands off Prince Edward, and she stole a kiss every moment she could. He propped himself up against a fallen tree and held her in his arms with a lazy smile on his face.

Hercules welcomed the relief to be away from the couples and breathe fresh air.

Ava's presence brought a surprising comfort to him. Her ash blonde hair fell in waves to the small of her back, and her silver dress flowed like a river as she walked with such grace and elegance.

She caught him staring at her and offered a small smile but averted her gaze. "You will not find anything to shoot if you spend the entire time looking at me," she quipped.

Hercules found himself smiling at the comment.

"You make a good argument." He pulled out his knife and scanned the ground for tracks.

He glanced at Ava one more time. "I am just curious to know if you can hear anything…"

Ava stopped and placed her hands on her hips. Then she shut her eyes.

"There's a sloth in a tree somewhere ahead. A lot

of frogs, but there's hardly any meat on their bones. A family of Howler Monkeys swing in the trees to the right of us. Or we could follow the birdsong and try to catch a Toucan perched near a waterfall."

Hercules's smile widened. "I'm impressed. You can identify nearby creatures just by listening to them?"

Ava climbed over a log and pushed her way through the dense foliage to the left, heading for the birds. "I grew up on an island with forests like this one," she said over her shoulder.

Hercules followed her. "It appears there is a lot that I do not know about you."

"What do you want to know? I have no secrets."

"What's your favorite color?" Hercules watched as Ava thought for a moment.

"Rose." She replied with a softness in her voice that hinted at a deeper sentimentality.

"Sunrise or sunset?"

"Sunset. There's something about the end of a day that feels like a promise of renewal."

Hercules nodded, understanding her perspective. "Land or sea?"

"Sea, without a doubt." Her eyes lit up. "The ocean has always been a part of me."

Their conversation flowed easily, each question and answer revealing new layers to Ava's character.

Hercules found himself both fascinated and troubled by how much he enjoyed her company. It was a feeling he hadn't experienced in a long time, and it scared him just as much as it intrigued him.

"What may I know about you, Hercules?" Ava gave him a grin. "You're a demigod shrouded in mystery. All I know is that you love that golden mace more than anything in the world, and you have a toxic relationship with your uncle, who is the god of the Underworld."

But before Hercules could respond to the question, Ava stumbled over a hidden tree root.

Instinctively, Hercules reached out, catching her in his arms.

For a moment, they locked gazes, and the world around them faded away.

"You may not speak the words, but your eyes tell me so much," Ava whispered, blinking at him. Her hand reached up to his cheek, a gesture so intimate that it took Hercules back to a time long gone.

The sun reached its highest point in the sky, and Hercules walked through a meadow, running his palms over the tall grass.

A woman with long brown hair ran ahead. Her laughter filled the air and sounded like the most beautiful symphony.

A soft breeze flowed over them and brought with it a fragrant scent that made Hercules smile like a fool.

Finally, the brunette turned, and her face beamed with happiness as she called out to Hercules. "You are walking so slow! You shall be left behind if you do not hurry!"

Then she turned and ran.

Hercules broke into a sprint, and when he caught up with the woman, they reached a slope of a hill, and he grabbed her by the waist as he tumbled to the grass.

They rolled down the hill. Their laughter mingled with birdsong.

It became the sweetest memory Hercules had. So sweet that it had been long forgotten as though his own mind had tried to protect him from the bittersweet emotions that came with it.

Then he returned to the present. In that instant, Ava's face morphed into Megara's in his mind. The pain of the past surged through him, overwhelming the moment.

He jerked back abruptly, releasing Ava as if burnt by her touch. The ghosts of his past felt too strong, too painful. And the memory had been more vivid than any dream.

"What did you do?" He eyed her with suspicion. "What witchcraft is this?"

Ava looked at him with horror. "I'm sorry, I cannot always control it. But I will admit I've been curious…"

"Curious?" Hercules repeated, dragging a hand through his hair and willing Megara's image to evaporate from his mind. But alas, her beautiful, angular features burned inside his brain. His attempts to wipe her from his memory were futile.

"Yes, well, Hades would so often bring up Megara—"

"Don't say her name," Hercules snapped.

Ava looked at him like he'd slapped her.

He released a breath to ease some tension. "We should focus on the hunt."

His voice hid the turmoil inside. "The sun will be setting soon, and we need to find food."

Ava nodded. A hint of confusion and hurt flashed in her eyes, but she said nothing.

They continued their hunt in silence, the easy camaraderie of before replaced by a heavy weight.

Guilt nipped at Hercules. Once again, he pushed Ava away, when she only tried to understand his sorrow.

But she could never truly understand. After all,

his conflicting emotions were as much a mystery to him as they were to anyone.

To his dismay, he had been caught in a battle between the past he couldn't forget and a future he felt uncertain he deserved.

AVA

*A*va lay in her makeshift hammock, suspended between two sturdy trees, and gazed up at the star-studded sky. The celestial bodies shimmered like jewels strewn across the vast tapestry of the night, and their light pierced the dark veil of the world. The night's quiet beauty a stark contrast to the turmoil in her heart.

Her thoughts became a whirlpool of emotions. Each star above reflected a memory, a possibility, and a lost dream.

Her mind replayed the vision she had experienced when she touched Hercules's cheek, the image of Megara—so radiant and joyful.

The memory looked so vivid that it formed an imprint on her soul.

Ava could sense the depth of Hercules's love for her, a love so profound and all-consuming that it seemed to transcend time itself. Her heart ached with the weight of his loss.

Even after a millennium, his soul still yearned for Megara, like a lighthouse yearning for a long-lost ship in the tempestuous sea of eternity.

She pondered the fact that he had not moved on in more than one thousand years, and she wondered whether it would be wise to expect him to ever move on.

The idea loomed over her like a shadow, casting doubt and uncertainty on her path. Perhaps, she was destined to be with an emotionally unavailable man for the rest of her days, and the thought sent a shiver of loneliness through her.

The group had decided to resume their quest for Osiris's remains, which naturally shifted everyone's attention to Ava. Her role was pivotal, her visions a guiding light on their journey.

They expected her to lead the way, relying on her visions of the burial sites. But her memories faded, clouded by the distractions Hercules presented.

Now, she only had fragmented clues and vague recollections of locations. One of them seemed to be a secluded site in Peru, characterized by ancient, towering structures, partly reclaimed by the jungle, and their original grandeur had been obscured by time and nature.

The thought of venturing into such a mysterious and ancient place filled her with a mix of dread and excitement.

The night sounds soothed and lulled her into a state of calm reflection, but then a rustle in the foliage alerted her.

Georgette's figure barely looked discernible in the moonlight. The young woman moved with a hesitant grace, like a fawn stepping into a clearing, unsure of the safety it offered.

"I want to apologize for the way I spoke to you before," Georgette said, her voice carrying a hint of vulnerability. Her words floated in the air, mingling with the night breeze.

Ava shook her head gently. "There's no need for that. Emotions were high that day. We almost lost Edward." Her words sounded as calming as the night sky above.

Georgette shivered in the cold night air.

Ava, sensing her discomfort, shuffled over in the hammock. "Come here."

Georgette climbed in beside her, and Ava wrapped her arms around the younger woman, providing warmth and comfort. It was a rare moment of human connection, a fleeting respite from the loneliness that often accompanied their quest.

She resumed her contemplation of the sky and gazed at the stars that twinkled like distant beacons of hope. Each star seemed to hold a story, a secret, a promise of the unknown.

"Is this what it's like to have an older sister?" Georgette asked softly, her voice tinged with wonder and a hint of longing.

"I do not know," Ava replied honestly. "I have never had one." Her admission came out as a whisper, a truth spoken into the night.

They fell into a comfortable silence, and the stillness of the night enveloped them like a blanket. The air felt cool and crisp, carrying with it the scent of the forest and a mixture of earth and leaves and the indefinable essence of the wild.

Georgette broke the silence in a hesitant tone. "Do you know where the burial site is? And what beast is guarding it?" Her questions hung in the air, filled with the weight of their quest and the dangers they faced.

Ava closed her eyes, concentrating, trying to bring forth the elusive images from the depths of her mind. "I believe we are close to one of the sites. But as for what guards it... that remains a mystery. We'll need to be vigilant and prepare for anything." Her words were a blend of confidence and caution, a reflection of the uncertainties that lay ahead.

"We're all strong in our own way." Georgette nodded firmly as if determined. "I'm certain that we will make a formidable team."

Ava nodded, feeling a renewed sense of purpose. They would face whatever challenges lay ahead together and would remain united in their quest. Though the path would be uncertain and perilous, she believed in their strength and resilience.

The future formed an unwritten story, and they were its authors.

Ava's heart softened when Georgette fell asleep in her arms. She couldn't remember the last time, if ever, she had experienced such a close connection with a sister.

She had hundreds of sisters, and yet they acted cold and distant.

Many had been captured or slaughtered in the bloodthirsty war. The memory created a haunting echo in the quiet of the night.

But holding Georgette sent a sense of peace that cleared her mind and slowed her breathing. She relaxed into the hammock and closed her eyes, waiting for sleep to come.

The hammock swayed gently, like a cradle rocked by an unseen hand, and the rhythm felt soothing and hypnotic.

But instead of transcending into a world of dreams, her mind thrust her into a vision.

Images unfurled in startling clarity. A tapestry of sights, sounds, and scents weaved an otherworldly tableau.

A shimmering lake, surrounded by all manner of wildlife, showed her rising to a seated position. Her sudden movements jerked Georgette awake, who grumbled.

But Ava's heart pounded too loud to hear what she said.

The clear vision demanded her attention in a siren call to the unknown.

"I know where the burial site is."

PRINCE EDWARD

n the heart of the dense jungle, Prince Edward felt a vitality coursing through his veins, an unexpected gift from the snake venom that had once brought him from death's door. The sensation felt akin to a surge of adrenaline, a powerful and invigorating force that made him feel more alive than ever before.

Beside him, Captain Stone, who had also been bitten by the pit vipers, shared a similar sentiment. "I feel strong. I'm tempted to adopt a snake and keep it as a pet." The captain flexed his arms as if testing the newfound strength.

They both wondered, with a mix of curiosity and apprehension, how long these extraordinary effects would last.

However, amidst this newfound strength, a persistent shadow stayed with them—Serena's constant concern.

She hovered near Prince Edward, and her eyes filled with a protective fervor that, while born of genuine care, began to grate on his nerves.

Her constant inquiries about his well-being, though well-intentioned, made him feel coddled, almost weak.

In an effort to escape the confines of her watchful gaze, he concocted a plan. "Serena, let's walk to the river and fill our flasks. We need to prepare for the trip," he suggested, hoping the task would provide a respite from her overbearing concern.

She agreed, albeit with a hesitant nod, and they set off toward the river.

As they made their way through the jungle, the dense foliage parting as they walked, the sound of their footsteps mingled with the chorus of nature.

And Prince Edward's frustration simmered.

Finally, unable to contain it any longer, in a swift motion, he pinned Serena against a tree. His eyes locked onto hers with an intensity that silenced the world around them.

"Stop looking at me as though you expect me to

disappear," he said, his voice a mix of frustration and a plea for understanding.

The words hung in the air between them, heavy with unspoken emotions.

Serena, caught off guard, looked up at him with a mix of surprise and something deeper.

"You died, Edward," she whispered, looking up at him with deep soulful eyes. "And I cannot stop thinking about it. I suppose I keep fearing you're going to leave me."

The weight of her words hit him like a wave, washing away the frustration and leaving a raw, aching vulnerability in its wake.

In that moment, he saw the fear and love that had driven her concern, and he understood.

Without a word, he cradled her face and kissed her. A soft, tender kiss that lasted moments but seemed to stretch to all eternity.

As they parted, the world around them came back into focus—the sounds of the jungle, the distant murmur of the river, and the rustle of leaves in the gentle breeze.

He wrapped her up in his arms and kissed her atop the head. "I'm sorry, my love. I wish there was a magic that existed to remove the memory. But I promise you this—no matter what happens, I shall never leave you. And if I become lost, I will always find a way back to you."

He tightened his grip on her. After a few moments, he pulled back to inspect her face. "All right?" he asked.

Serena gave him a teary smile.

Then Prince Edward saw something in her eyes that he hadn't seen for a long time: trust.

HERCULES

*H*ercules trudged through the dense jungle as the group followed the relentless rush of the river beside them. The air thickened, laden with the scent of damp earth and lush greenery.

Ahead, Ava led with determination, and her ash blonde hair rippled like the ocean at dusk.

Every now and then, a breeze would waft past, bringing with it her floral scent.

Hercules caught himself admiring her form and quickly reprimanded himself for the distraction. His focus needed to be on the mission, not on the graceful way Ava moved through the underbrush.

"Are we getting close? We've been walking for

days." Georgette's voice cut through his thoughts, her tone laced with a mix of weariness and impatience.

"I can hear rushing water," Ava called back. "We are almost there."

"Of course, she hears rushing water," Serena grumbled to the others. "We're walking next to a river."

"She knows what she's doing," Prince Edward murmured. "Just focus on the beauty and think of better things."

"Better things than the mysterious monster that awaits us?" Georgette shot back with a laugh. But her words seemed to put everyone in a somber mood.

Hercules glanced over his shoulder to see everyone looking intently at the ground.

"I don't know… I think it'll be a pleasant change to fight a beast." He winked at Ava who looked back at him with her brows lifted.

Eventually, they reached a breathtaking waterfall. Its waters cascaded down with a thunderous roar, and mist sprayed their faces which offered them a brief respite from the jungle's humidity.

As they prepared to cross, a sudden, rhythmic drumming pierced the air, followed by a flurry of darts that zipped dangerously close.

"By the gods." Prince Edward drew his sword. "Vikings, here?"

"Seems we're not the only ones interested in Osiris." Serena narrowed her eyes.

"Vikings?" Ava shrieked in disbelief. "They're real?"

Before Georgette could reply with, "I told you so," another flurry of arrows sailed toward them.

They backed up and raised their weapons.

Hercules stepped forward, puffing out his muscular chest and brandished his golden mace. "Stay behind me," he growled over his shoulder.

The Vikings surged forward, and their shouts filled the air.

With each swing of his mace, Hercules sent them flying.

Their weapons clanged harmlessly against his skin, unable to penetrate it.

"His skin's like iron!" one of the Vikings exclaimed in disbelief.

"Watch out!" Serena's warning cry came as a dart narrowly missed Edward; it soared past his right ear.

"You can run, but we'll be here waiting for you," one of the Vikings shouted after them.

In a rush, their group sprinted for the waterfall.

But as they charged through, the ground beneath them crumbled and sent them sliding into an abyss.

In the chaotic tumble, Hercules lost time and track of everything as it became a maelstrom of shouts and limbs scrambling for purchase.

When they landed, the air around them felt cool and stale.

Hercules found himself in a dimly lit hidden crypt with walls adorned with ancient symbols and faded paintings. Ava tightly clutched in his arms.

"Are you all, right?" He scanned their new surroundings with a wary eye.

Ava, catching her breath, nodded. "But where are the others?"

"We've been separated." Hercules's voice echoed in the cavernous space. "We need to find them."

Ava's gaze swept the area, and a sense of caution became evident in her posture. "This place is ancient. There could be traps. We have to be careful."

Nodding, Hercules tightened his grip on his mace. "Stay close to me."

They proceeded with caution, and their footsteps softly echoed in the vast chamber.

The air felt heavy with history, and the dust of ages hung in the stillness.

A low growl reverberated through the chamber.

"Did you hear that?" Ava's eyes scanned the area for a weapon.

In the dim, eerie light of the crypt, a monstrous form emerged from the shadows.

The Hydra, a creature of nightmares, unfurled itself with menacing grace. Its scaly hide shimmered in the faint light, shades of green and black intertwining like the murky waters of a stagnant pond. Each of its heads looked like a grotesque masterpiece, with snapping jaws and razor-sharp teeth that dripped with venom. The stench of decay wafted from its maw, a foul, pungent aroma that filled the air and made Hercules and Ava recoil.

"Look at the size of that thing!" Ava gasped, her eyes wide with a mix of fear and awe.

Hercules, his protective instincts surging, stepped forward. "Get behind me," he ordered, his voice a deep rumble.

Ava bristled at the command. "I'm not weak," she retorted, her tone defiant. She quickly grabbed a rusty sword from a nearby statue with a worn yet menacing blade.

As the Hydra advanced, its many heads weaving a dance of death, Ava lunged forward with surprising agility.

She struck true, and her blade sliced through one of the Hydra's necks.

The beast let out a guttural howl as its head thudded to the ground, and dust and ancient debris billowed around Ava.

"Ha! Take that, you overgrown lizard!" she exclaimed triumphantly, standing amidst the cloud of dust.

But Hercules's face became a picture of horror. "Oh no. What have you done?" His eyes fixed on the Hydra's wound.

Ava, confused and still caught in her moment of victory, turned to him. "What do you mean?"

"Do you not know what a Hydra is...?" Dread oozed through Hercules's voice.

Before Ava could respond, a grotesque squelching sound echoed through the crypt.

They watched in disbelief as the severed stump began to move. Flesh and sinew twisted and grew, sprouting two new heads where one had fallen.

Each head looked more ferocious, and their eyes burned with a vengeful fire.

Ava's triumphant expression turned to horror. "A Hydra? Oh dear..." She eyed the regenerating beast.

Hercules, gripping his mace tightly, glanced at

Ava. "Cutting its heads off only makes it stronger," he barked.

"Well, you could have mentioned that sooner!" Ava's eyes darted between the snarling heads.

One of them lurched forward, baring its teeth. Hercules thrust the spikes of his mace up into the roof of its mouth, and it made an unearthly sound of pain. It made a strange high-pitched howl that ended with a screech and made Ava hold her ears.

"I thought you would know about these beasts..." Hercules said.

The Hydra, now more dangerous than ever, lunged at them with renewed fury.

Hercules and Ava leaped into action; their movements synchronized in a desperate dance of survival.

They dodged the snapping jaws, and their weapons blurred as they parried and struck, seeking a way to subdue the beast without triggering its terrifying ability.

"Any bright ideas, Hercules?" Ava called out, narrowly avoiding a bite.

"Just keep moving and cut as many times as you can. The only way to conquer it is to let it bleed out or pierce it directly into the heart." Hercules's mace crashed against the Hydra's scales with a resounding clang.

The battle raged on, and the crypt echoed with the sounds of their desperate struggle.

The heavy air grew clouded with the beast's putrid breath.

"Where are the others?" Ava shouted in frustration.

Hercules caught a glimpse of her reddened face, wisps of her hair clung to her temples, and she had a film of sweat across her bottom lip.

Hercules slid across the floor on his knees and raised his mace with both hands.

The Hydra howled and screeched again as the deadly spokes slashed one of the necks until he reached the beast's body.

Above him, the beast's heads thrashed wildly, but here, under its massive body, Hercules faced a different challenge—the Hydra's legs and claws.

The thick and powerful limbs were armored with scales that glistened like dark, wet stone.

Each claw was like a curved dagger, sharp and deadly, scraping against the stone floor of the crypt with a menacing hiss.

Hercules, his muscles tensed and ready, gripped his golden mace tightly.

Even he, as a warrior of immense strength, felt dwarfed by the monstrous creature looming over him.

The Hydra moved with terrifying agility, and its legs struck out like pistons, and each blow would be enough to crush stone.

As a clawed leg descended toward him, Hercules swung his mace with all his might.

The weapon connected with a resounding clang, and the impact sent shockwaves up his arms.

The Hydra let out a howl of anguish, a sound filled with pain and rage that echoed off the ancient walls.

Stunned but not defeated, the creature scrambled around, its movements reminiscent of an aggressive spider.

Hercules dodged nimbly, a feat of agility surprising for his size, as he sought an opening to strike again.

Another leg came crashing down, aiming to pin Hercules to the ground.

He rolled away just in time. The claw missed him by inches and shattered the stone floor where he had just been.

Hercules swung his mace again, smashing another of the beast's feet.

The beast recoiled with another scream, and its body writhed in fury.

The Hydra's movements became more frantic,

and its legs flailed in a frenzied attempt to hit the elusive Hercules. But as a warrior of both strength and cunning, he anticipated each strike and moved with a fluidity that belied his powerful build.

Each swing of his mace was precise and devastating.

Despite the danger, Hercules felt a surge of adrenaline.

He was in his element, facing a formidable opponent in a battle that tested his limits.

Every smash of his mace, every narrow escape from the beast's claws, became a testament to his skill and valor.

Above them, the heads of the Hydra continued their assault, but for now, Hercules singularly focused on the creature's underbelly.

Ava counted on him, and he would not let her down.

With a roar that matched the Hydra's own cries of rage, Hercules prepared to strike once more, and his golden mace blurred in the dim light of the crypt.

The battle was far from over, but Hercules felt determined to emerge victorious, no matter what it took.

CAPTAIN STONE

*C*aptain Stone, Georgette, and Serena fell into a small room.

All manner of ancient drawings painted its stone walls. They depicted a civilization that existed long ago, with runes and secrets in a language that Captain Stone could not read.

"Edward," Serena shouted, looking wildly around them.

The air thickened with dust upon their sudden arrival.

Coughing in the far corner sent Serena running at a full sprint toward another figure Captain Stone assumed to be his brother. "Thank the gods."

Georgette lit a torch by sparking two rocks. She held it up and peered at the drawings. Her eyes widened at the sight of them. "I wonder if this is a puzzle."

Serena replied quickly. "No, it's a warning."

Captain Stone turned to see Prince Edward and Serena emerging from a cloud of dust. "You can read this text?"

Serena shot him a filthy look, as though the question had mortally offended her. "Of course, I can. These markings are Atlantean."

All eyes focused on Serena and met her revelation with shocked silence.

Captain Stone did not need to ask the question that came to mind. They all thought it. What were Atlantean markings doing in Peru?

Serena sighed and started to trace the pictures with her index figure and read aloud. "Here doth rest Osiris, entombed deep in the bowels of the Netherworld, forever hidden from mortal gaze. Yet, heed this warning: should any soul dare to disturb these hallowed remains, a beast most dire shall rouse and wreak its wrath upon the earth. Tread not upon these consecrated lands, lest the world itself bear the brunt."

Captain Stone rested one hand on the hilt of his sword and wrapped his other around Georgette's waist as he looked around them.

The air felt unusually still, and when he dragged his boot across the dusty floor, he could not see any markings. "Do you think the remains are beneath us?"

"The bowels of the Netherworld…doesn't that mean the Underworld?" Prince Edward asked.

"We were just there." Georgette gasped and held her hand to her mouth.

Serena huffed and dragged her hands through her hair as though she thought that she was surrounded by imbeciles.

Captain Stone did not doubt that was truly what was on her mind.

She tied her hair back and met gazes with each person. "It is not literal. Stone is right. The remains are below us." She dropped to the floor like a cat and pressed her ear to it. "I can hear vibrations. Listen…"

Everyone crouched and strained to hear. Sure enough, even Captain Stone could hear something.

In the heart of the crypt, the sounds of battle grew more intense, echoing through the ancient corridors.

Serena, her ears finely tuned, caught a distinct cry amidst the chaos. "I can hear Ava!" Her voice laced with urgency. "The beast is awake, and they need our help!"

The group scrambled, and Stone searched desperately for a path to their companions as he pondered their options, and his tactical mind raced.

"We may need to retrace our steps; they likely fell through a different route," he suggested, his voice steady despite the mounting tension.

Georgette shook her head, and her expression turned grave. "The tunnel we came through is too steep. Climbing back would take hours, and even then, there's no certainty of where we might end up."

Captain Stone, ever the pragmatist, knelt and swept his hand across the crypt's floor, seeking any hint of a passage or a clue.

Instead, his fingers traced a faint crack. Without a second thought, he slammed his fist against the stone.

The crack widened, and a spiderweb of fractures spread from the impact.

"Hurry. We need to break through." His voice echoed in the chamber.

Georgette looked at the fissure with apprehension. "But how far might we fall? Is it wise?"

Before anyone could respond, a violent roar shook the walls and floor, a sound so fearsome it stilled their hearts for a moment.

They had to act. Now!

They formed a circle around the crack.

Captain Stone took the lead and spoke with the determination he felt inside. "On the count of three." He met each of their gazes.

Everyone nodded, their expressions a mix of resolve and determination.

"One...two..." Captain Stone's voice rose over the din of the distant battle. "...Three."

The formidable quartet slammed their fists against the ground with all their might.

The combined strength of Triton and Siren lineage surged through their blows.

The rock floor shuddered and crumbled beneath them, giving way to the void.

The ground disintegrated, and they plunged into the abyss, freefalling toward the calamity below.

AVA

*A*va moved with a dancer's grace, and each calculated step evaded the terrible jaws of the Hydra.

The beast's heads, a nightmarish bouquet of serpentine horrors, lunged at her relentlessly. Each head grotesquely mirrored the others—scales that shimmered with a sinister sheen, eyes like molten orbs of hatred, and fangs that dripped with venomous spite.

Inside Ava's chest, fear pulsed not for herself but for Hercules. She could see him, a steadfast warrior, fighting near the beast's underbelly, dwarfed yet undaunted by the monstrous creature.

Summoning her magic, Ava focused her energies. Her hands wove intricate patterns in the air. She managed to lock eyes with one of the Hydra's heads, and its gaze became glassy as her hypnotic spell took hold. But with four heads to contend with, her task was Sisyphean.

As she subdued one, another would break free.

Their relentless assault never ceased.

Ava's arms burned with the strain of her magic, a dull ache that seeped into her bones.

She wondered, amidst the chaos, how much longer they could endure.

A shower of loose rock cascaded from above, pelting the Hydra and drawing its furious attention upward.

Amidst the debris, four figures descended in a whirlwind of motion, landing with precision on the creature's back.

Captain Stone, Serena, Georgette, and Edward's arrival turned the tide into pure chaos.

The crypt filled with roars, screams, a cacophony of battle cries and the clash of steel.

Ava struggled to keep track of the unfolding melee.

Her heart raced as she watched her companions engage the beast with fierce determination.

Then, without warning, the Hydra jerked

violently, and its massive body shuddered under the relentless assault.

With a final, deafening crash, it collapsed to the ground, and its many heads fell limp.

Everyone leaped off the beast and quickly regrouped on the crypt floor.

Ava felt a surge of relief and joy as she saw her friends, unharmed and victorious. But her gaze quickly turned to the Hydra.

Her heart flew into her throat as she hurried forward, scanning the tangle of long necks and limbs for Hercules.

Then, in a display of sheer might, Hercules hoisted the Hydra into the air.

He looked strong and powerful, a titan in his own right, effortlessly holding the belly of the beast.

With a final heave, he tossed it aside, striding forward with purpose. He picked up his bloodied mace and re-joined the group, and his presence felt like a reassuring symbol of their triumph.

Ava took in his body. All his bulging muscles damp with sweat and blood.

His brow creased, and his eyes glinted as adrenaline soared through his whole body.

Ava inhaled, and his rich masculine sent made her heart and stomach flutter. Without saying a word, she flew into his arms, grabbed his cheeks, and kissed him.

He stiffened momentarily, but then the mace fell with a thud, and his broad hands grabbed her waist as he kissed her back.

The demigod tasted salty from sweat with the metallic tinge of blood. But then his tongue roamed her mouth, and a new sensation flooded her.

Ava closed her eyes and dragged her hands through his damp hair while his hands roamed her back and slid down to grab her bottom.

The charged moment formed an unrivalled passion and victory between them.

When he pulled her in for a full body embrace, his hard shaft pressed against her stomach.

But then an awkward cough seemed to snap him to his senses, and the next thing Ava knew, Hercules pushed her away again.

Her heart beat faster than the wings of a hummingbird as she blinked several times and pressed her fingers to her tingling lips.

She met the amused stares of their comrades, and her cheeks burned.

"It's good to see you both getting along…" Prince Edward smirked. "But perhaps we should look around for those remains?"

Ava wiped the sweat from above her lip and the back of her neck. She coughed, avoiding Hercules, who stayed unusually quiet.

She wondered if he already rethought his actions.

But before she could wrestle with her thoughts, Serena marched around the fallen beast and disappeared behind it. "Over here."

Ava and the others joined her in front of a pair of ornate doors. Atlantean writing etched into the frame.

"Retreat forthwith, lest thou unleash the specter of death upon the world." Ava pointed at the writing.

"You read Atlantean?" Serena asked with widened eyes.

Ava raised her brows at her. "I may not have been raised in Father's city, sister. But Isis did teach us many secrets. As is our birth right to know."

Georgette folded her arms and frowned at the door. "There are no handles. Should we break through?"

"And unleash the specter of death upon the world? Perhaps we should think about this first." Prince Edward's eyebrows knitted as he glared at the door.

Serena pointed at the dead Hydra. "I do not think

we need to worry about that anymore. The specter of death is quite… un-alive."

Hercules pointed to two portcullis mechanisms fixed to the wall either side of the door. "Stone. Help me with this." He marched over to one.

Captain Stone followed suit, and before anyone could argue, they wrenched the portcullis into action.

Wood groaned and crunched as they began to move. Slowly, the doors thrust open, and a beam of golden torchlight poured over them.

As they walked through, Ava lifted a hand to shield her eyes.

When her sight adjusted, she beheld a vast room.

The vast temple loomed before them. Its ancient grandeur remained undiminished by time. Flaming torches lined the walls, and the fire flickered in a way that felt comforting. Two massive doors greeted the group as they stepped inside.

Mystery veiled each door.

Captain Stone, ever the brave soul, took the lead.

"Get down!" Hercules bellowed, and they all ducked just in time, the arrows whistling overhead.

Captain Stone straightened up, brushing off his coat with a chuckle. "Ah, I see. Booby traps." He exchanged a knowing glance with Georgette.

The realization dawned on them that the floor was a maze of potential triggers.

Serena's eyes scanned the markings. "These writings... they're a guide," she murmured. She pointed at the plate that Captain Stone had stepped on. "This symbol is for Anubis, most commonly associated with the word 'death'."

She hummed and looked around them. "Maybe we should only step on the symbols that mean 'life?'"

Georgette frowned and hugged herself. "But how can we possibly know which ones mean life? We can't all read these ancient scripts."

Ava surveyed the markings. She pointed at one. "There! 'Vita' is the Latin word for life." She stepped forward and everyone waited. But nothing happened.

Serena beamed, obviously triumphant that her theory was correct.

Ava gestured to the others. "I can guide us. Stone and Georgette, follow Serena's lead. Edward, Hercules, come with me."

As they navigated the perilous floor, Ava felt the weight of their safety on her shoulders. Each step became a calculated risk, but her knowledge of the ancient languages guided them true.

She hopped onto the word Balāṭu, then Lif.

Hercules and Prince Edward followed, while the

others crossed the treacherous floor with Serena as their guide.

"Ḥayāh," she whispered, skipping to the last one.

Finally, they reached the other side.

They looked around and let out a collective breath.

Now they faced two identical ornate doors, each sporting a brass handle.

Without hesitation, Edward and Captain Stone each stood in front of a door and rested a hand on the handle.

"Prepare yourselves, we don't know what other traps might be waiting for us," Hercules warned.

Captain Stone thrust open the door on the left and everyone ducked on instinct.

But there was nothing but a dusty closet with a broken bucket sitting in the corner.

There was a collective exhale, of part relief that nothing deadly flew out and part disappointment at the dead end.

Everyone turned to Prince Edward.

"Ready?" he asked.

The group braced as the hinges squealed, and dust expelled from within as he thrust open the door.

Inside, was a simple arch, like the frame for a wall mirror. But instead of glass, a strange veil of energy was in its place. Prince Edward reached out, apparently drawn to its power but he halted at Serena's warning shout.

"Have you learned nothing? Do not stick your hand into some unknown magic. For all we know, it'll be the last time you see it."

Prince Edward hummed as he scratched the back of his neck.

"I think I can squeeze around it, there seemed to be another room back there…"

Before Serena could argue, Prince Edward sidled around the arch and disappeared from view.

The group gasped.

"Edward!" Serena shrieked.

"That's odd."

Ava jumped at the sound of Edward's voice, and she exchanged looks with Georgette.

"Edward? We can't see you," Captain Stone said.

"There's nothing back here, just an empty closet. But I think if I just walk through the—"

"No!" Serena shrieked, but it was too late.

Prince Edward emerged through the arch, like an apparition.

Everyone held their breath.

But Prince Edward stood, seemingly unharmed. He frowned at them all.

"Nothing happened," he said, his voice laced with defeat.

Serena ran up to him and slapped his arm. "I had my heart in my mouth, thinking the worst."

But Prince Edward seemed too distracted to notice. He pointed at the tiles. "The words... look different."

Ava frowned. "What do you mean?" She followed his line of sight, but they were just as they appeared moments ago. "Nothing has changed."

"Wait." Georgette turned to Prince Edward, looking suspicious. "Walk back through the portal."

Prince Edward did as she said and sidled around the frame to rejoin the group. Then he pointed at the tiles. "The writing is back to normal."

"Perhaps we should all walk through. I'm sure more secrets will be revealed," Captain Stone suggested.

Carefully, everyone walked through the portal.

As Ava stepped out, she looked around the room. Sure enough the lettering on the tiled floor appeared reversed. "It's like we've stepped into a mirror."

"Look around, there must be something new," Serena said.

In the dimly lit chamber, Ava watched as the

group, invigorated by her insight, embarked on a thorough search.

Each member looked engrossed in their task, examining the walls, the floor, and even the ceiling for clues they might have missed.

The shadows cast by the flickering torches danced across the ancient stone, lending an air of mystery to their endeavor.

Captain Stone, with a soldier's precision, methodically tapped along the walls.

A hollow sound echoed back under his firm touch.

He carefully pried a stone loose, revealing a hidden niche. Inside, lay a small, ornately crafted key, its surface catching the light with a subtle shimmer.

Georgette's eyes lit up at the sight. "Brilliant!" Then she looked around the room. "Now we just need to find what it opens."

The room, initially seeming straightforward, revealed its complexity under their persistent scrutiny.

They moved tapestries aside, uncovering hidden alcoves and ancient frescoes that spoke of a time long forgotten.

Each beautiful tile covering the mosaic floor spoke of untold stories.

Ava and the others examined each one with a reverent attention to detail.

Serena stared at a tapestry that depicted celestial alignments. "I discovered something—an anomaly."

Pulling it aside, she revealed a lock embedded in the wall, and its design mirrored the key's intricate patterns.

Prince Edward, with a practical air, handed the key to Serena. "Let's see if the past can unlock the future," he said in an optimistic tone.

Ava held her breath as Serena tried the key, but it refused to turn. Disappointment filled the chamber.

Hercules had a keen insight. "The portal, perhaps it changes more than our perception. Let's try walking back through again."

As a unified team, they stepped through the portal, re-entering a room that now felt subtly altered after being in the mirrored one.

The key, now in Serena's hand, seemed no different. But she ran to the lock anyway.

This time, the lock yielded smoothly to the key with a satisfying click.

The ground began to tremble beneath them. The deep rumble emanated from the earth itself.

Dust fell from the ceiling as the floor shifted, revealing a large sarcophagus rising from its hidden depths. Ancient symbols and hieroglyphs adorned the ancient tomb.

Ava stepped forward, her voice barely above a whisper. "Osiris..."

The group exchanged looks, a mix of awe and the realization of the gravity of their discovery.

"Gents..." Hercules placed his mace on the ground and unsheathed his knife.

Captain Stone and Prince Edward followed him to the stone coffin, as each took out a knife, and the three men stuck the tips into the groove.

"We should prepare ourselves," Ava suggested, watching the men struggle to open the sarcophagus. She stood beside her sisters, and they braced for whatever they might face.

Slowly, the stone slab sealing the coffin slid free, and the men peered inside.

"Well?" Serena asked, her voice hopeful.

Ava and Georgette joined her as she hurried forward.

Everyone looked down, and Ava's heart sank. "It's empty!"

Hercules hummed. "Perhaps we should try the portal again?"

Without question, everyone walked through the

portal but discovered the sarcophagus was just as empty as it was before.

"Maybe someone has already been here and taken them?" Prince Edward suggested.

Ava frowned. "No, the Hydra would surely not have been alive if that were the case." She looked at Hercules, searching for answers, but he looked back at her just as mystified.

Georgette gasped and climbed up inside the empty tomb.

"What are you doing?" Captain Stone asked.

Everyone watched in bewilderment as Georgette dropped inside. The sound of her boots thudding against stone echoed around the temple.

Georgette, with an unexpected boldness, disappeared into the sarcophagus.

Ava watched, her pulse quickening, as the younger woman's actions broke the spell of disappointment that had settled over them.

"What are you doing?" Captain Stone's voice echoed with a mix of concern and curiosity that replaced the bewilderment from the first time he asked.

Georgette responded in a series of muffled taps.

The sound of hollow stone resonated, a tell-tale sign that more secrets lay hidden within.

Ava leaned closer. Her instincts told her that Georgette was onto something.

"There's a compartment here," Georgette's voice rang out, filled with triumph. "Pass me the key!"

Serena, with quick steps, handed the key down to her.

All eyes fixed on Georgette as she inserted the key into an unseen lock.

A soft click followed, and the sound of shifting stone filled the room.

With a heave, Georgette lifted a wooden crate from the depths of the sarcophagus.

Holding it aloft like a hard-won treasure, Georgette climbed out and presented it to Ava.

The group gathered around, and each face became a canvas of hope and apprehension.

Ava held her steady hands out as she received the crate, though her heart raced. She had been preparing for this moment for all of her life. But if this was another trick and another dead end met her, she wasn't sure if her heart could handle it.

She carefully pried the lid open, and nestled within, lay a skull. Time etched its ancient bone as a silent testament to the eons it had endured.

"Osiris," Ava whispered.

The room fell silent, and the weight of history filled the air.

Ava gazed at the skull with reverence and solemnity in her heart. The moment felt suspended in time, a connection to the divine and the mystical past.

Finally, a rush of hope filled a void in her. Perhaps after all this time they would succeed in their mission.

"It's really him," Ava whispered, and her voice filled with awe.

The discovery sent a ripple of excitement through the group. They had found what they had been seeking, a relic of immeasurable importance.

Hercules stepped closer, appearing deep in thought. "Good. We should take this back to Isis."

Prince Edward nodded, and he turned to Hercules. "I don't know about anyone else, but I'm exhausted. Do you think you can make us a portal? It would save us a long journey back to Imerta."

"That certainly sounds like a good plan," Georgette said, while Captain Stone helped her out of the dusty coffin.

Chuckling to himself, Hercules waved his hand to create a portal. But when nothing happened, he frowned.

"What is wrong?" Ava matched his frown.

"I can't feel anything."

Serena held out her hands. "Neither can I. Not even a tingle."

Ava handed the skull to Hercules and waved her hand, but it moved in a way that did not feel like her own.

"Perhaps our magic is suppressed in here," Serena said.

"We should go outside and try again." Hercules carefully placed the skull back into the box.

Prince Edward raised his palms. "I know we've all been through a lot since we arrived, but have you all forgotten what is waiting for us out there?" He pointed to the open doors.

Captain Stone, ever the pragmatist, looked at the skull and back at the group. "I don't know about you, but I'm feeling rather invincible after what we've just achieved. I say, let's take our chances with them."

Serena hissed at him. "A rather bold statement, considering the fact you ran like a piglet from battle, while Edward—"

"Edward would be dead if I hadn't carried him away from the scene," Captain Stone cut in, and his eyes flashed dangerously.

Georgette stood in-between Serena and her husband. "Enough of that. We all need to rest and hold our tongues."

She glanced at Hercules and nodded to Ava. "We can sneak out. We only need to get out of this crypt to make a portal. I'm certain we shall not even see a Viking."

The group, weary yet resolute, made their way through the narrow opening and emerged into the dimming light of day.

The mouth of the cave brought them several yards away from the waterfall, and to their surprise, the area looked deserted.

The Vikings had gone.

The group cautiously navigated their way through the dense foliage of the Peruvian jungle.

The air thickened with the heavy scent of damp earth and lush greenery. The towering trees, ancient and majestic, formed a verdant canopy overhead, and their leaves whispered secrets in the gentle breeze. Vines draped like curtains from branch to branch, creating a tapestry of life in every shade of green.

The warmth of the jungle enveloped Ava in a humid embrace that clung to her skin.

Sunlight filtered through the dense canopy in golden shafts, dappling the ground with a mosaic of light and shadow. The vibrant calls of exotic birds echoed in the distance in a symphony of natural sounds that underscored the untamed beauty of their surroundings.

As they drew closer to the waterfall, the roar of rushing water grew louder. It became a powerful and constant presence that resonated through the air.

Ava found the waterfall to be a breathtaking sight as it cascaded down from a great height. Its waters foamed white against the dark rocks.

The Vikings' ambush abruptly shattered the tranquility of the scene.

The sudden appearance of these fierce warriors seemed at odds with the peaceful jungle backdrop. Their weapons gleamed menacingly in the filtered sunlight, and their cold, determined eyes spoke of a resolve as unyielding as the ancient trees around them.

They caught Captain Stone unaware from behind and swiftly seized him.

"In the name of the All-Father, you are sentenced to death for the murder of Hakon." The Viking leader, a formidable presence, stood out starkly against the lush greenery. Tattoos covered his face, and a single braid fell down from the base of his skull, leaving the rest of his head shaven. His proclamation of Captain Stone's sentence hung heavy in the humid air as oppressive as the jungle heat.

"No!" Georgette cried, clutching her face in terror.

"Shut up, wench, or I'll gut you and feed you to your friends," a bald Viking snapped.

A thunderous smack met his words as Ava's fist collided with his cheek. Her heart roared with anger at these repulsive beings. She still could not wrap her mind around the fact that Vikings existed. She refused to stand by and let them insult her sister.

But then a pair of hands grabbed her from behind.

Hercules thrashed about, sending several men flying in the air, and he punched the man who clutched Ava. He stopped at the sound of Captain Stone grunting.

The Viking leader held a knife as white as bone to his neck. The tip was painted black, and everyone knew what it was.

"Come with us without a fight, and we shall spare your lives long enough to witness justice," he snarled. "Or make another move, and I shall carry out said justice right here, right now."

Hercules looked around the group, and they all raised their palms in defeat.

The tension that followed was palpable, the group's surrender a stark contrast to the wild freedom of their surroundings. The jungle, which had felt like a sanctuary, now seemed to close in on them, and its once comforting embrace turned into a constricting grip.

As the Vikings led them away, the vibrant life of the jungle continued unabated around them.

Monkeys chattered in the treetops, oblivious to the human drama unfolding below, and the occasional flutter of a brightly-colored bird cut through the dense air.

The jungle, with its untamed beauty and inherent dangers, became a reminder of the precarious balance between life and death—a balance now hanging in the balance for Ava and her companions.

CAPTAIN STONE

*I*n the dense, sweltering heart of the Peruvian jungle, Captain Stone, his usual charm undiminished even in the face of death, stood defiantly as the Vikings prepared his pyre around him.

He was bound to a pole by his feet, his chest, and with his arms stretched upwards, his hands were bound tightly.

The air thickened with the scent of damp earth.

"Who are you? What is the name of your clan?" Hercules boomed, throwing his shoulders back with authority. "Who are you to insult a god, such as I?"

A wave of derisive laughter followed his words. "You? A god? We know all about you, Hercules. The broken demigod subjected to one thousand years of solitude, all over a broken heart."

The laughter grew louder as Hercules's eyes narrowed.

But then a hiss brought everyone back to silence.

They looked at Ava, who had transformed. Her claws swiped the air and her teeth like knifes flashed on show. "How dare you speak such atrocities to the mighty Hercules?" she hissed.

Captain Stone watched with mild amusement as the surrounding men grabbed Ava, and Hercules threatened to tear them limb from limb.

It reminded him of Georgette on that old ship, surrounded by filthy pirates before he slaughtered all of them for her. It was a simpler time.

He longed for one more day with Georgette—alone. Perhaps they should have taken a page out of Hercules's book and opted to live on a deserted island for a thousand years. It would have brought them far more happy memories; of that he felt certain.

"Enough!" the leader shouted. "You ask who I am." He stood a foot away from Hercules and glowered at him, even though he stood at least a foot shorter than the demigod. "I am Jarl Rognik, leader of the Ulfshjartr clan. Our former Jarl, Hakon, was brutally murdered at the hands of this pathetic pirate."

"Oh." Captain Stone lifted a finger. "It has been so long since anyone called me a pirate. I was beginning to forget who I am. Thank you for that." He closed his eyes, reveling in the moment.

But the others continued their conversation as though he had not spoken.

"The Ulfshjartr clan is as deadly as a viper, and as quick as a leopard."

"Then I'm curious, why don't you call yourself the Deadly-As-A-Viper-Quick-As-A-Leopard Clan?" Captain Stone teased. "I suppose it does not roll off the tongue, huh?"

"Quiet, pirate," Rognik snapped.

Georgette shot him a troubled look, but Captain Stone took the moment to try and send her a message. He jerked to his trousers and mouthed, "Come here."

As Hercules continued to argue with the Vikings, Georgette slipped through the rows of people and came to his side.

To feel her breath on his neck one last time was pure ecstasy.

"In my pocket, quick," he whispered.

Georgette rummaged in his trouser pocket and gasped when her fingers wrapped around something.

"Pull it out," he instructed, giving Georgette a serious look.

She withdrew a hissing viper.

Captain Stone nodded again.

Georgette hovered the viper to his exposed forearm and dangled her fingers in its eyesight.

When the snake lashed for her, she moved just in time for the snake to bury its fangs into Captain Stone's arm.

He bit his lip at the hot pinch, but already a surge of power soared through his blood.

Georgette cradled the snake in her arms and snuck back to the group just as Rognik finished a speech. "… and after you see this man die. We shall extend mercy to the rest of you, and let you take his body home."

All attention returned to Captain Stone as a line of Vikings began to chant and marched forward with flaming torches.

"Really, gentlemen," Captain Stone began, flashing a rakish grin despite the ropes binding him, "is all this necessary? I've always enjoyed a good campfire, but isn't this a bit much?"

The Vikings, stoic and unyielding, paid no heed

to his humor. Their faces, illuminated by the flickering torchlights, set in grim determination.

Ava, with fire in her eyes, stepped forward, her voice laced with desperation and fear. "You can't do this!"

Prince Edward's deep voice resonated through the thick jungle air. "I have money. Let him go, and I shall give you riches beyond your wildest dreams."

Captain Stone felt an overwhelming sense of gratitude and love for his companions.

The Vikings, however, had their orders, their code, and their pleas fell on deaf ears. They were unwavering and would have no more negotiating, that much became clear.

Captain Stone just had to hope that the venom in his blood would give him enough strength to break free and kill as many Vikings as possible.

Turning to Georgette, his voice stayed gentle yet filled with emotion.

The odds had been stacked heavily against him, and if this would be the last time he saw his beloved, he wanted to make sure she knew how much she meant to him.

"My dearest Georgette, my life with you has been an adventure like no other, filled with laughter, excitement, and the deepest love one could ask for. I regret nothing."

Georgette's eyes brimmed with tears. Her hand reached out, trembling as it stopped mere inches from him. "But I can't... I can't let you go," she whispered as her voice broke.

He met her gaze with all the love and resolve he could muster. "You'll never lose me, my love. I'll be with you, always." His voice softened. "Now, do not watch, my darling. Do not watch me burn. I do not want you to remember me this way."

Rognik stepped forward with a torch raised above his head. "If you try to escape, I'll be the first to slit your wife's pretty neck," he muttered, and Captain Stone's heart sank. Whatever hope remained in his soul just dissipated into the atmosphere like a wisp.

He cast his sights over the people he had grown to care about.

From his brother, Edward— who had once been so young and naive and had now become solemn and strong—to his spirited wife, Serena, who shared Georgette's steel confidence and headstrong nature.

Hercules and Ava, who looked unified, stood side by side with matching expressions of concern.

And finally, he looked upon Georgette again. Her

arms wrapped around herself, and her face twisted into horror and despair.

He mustered one last cheeky smile for her, and a single tear slid down her ashen face.

Peace flooded his heart at the bittersweet knowledge that Georgette was not alone, and that she would be all right. She'd found a family who would do anything for her, and he would watch her with love and pride from the stars.

A drumbeat picked up, and Captain Stone shut his eyes, ready for death to come.

The Vikings, chanting with more excitement now, set the pyre alight.

The fire crackled to life, casting eerie shadows across the jungle's canopy. The flames began to creep up toward Captain Stone, and the heat grew more intense by the second.

Flames smothered his legs and feet, and within seconds, sweat clung to his temples. But the smoke gripped him in a choke hold.

He coughed but suppressed the next impulse, trying to make the experience less traumatic for his love.

An inordinate amount of pain tore the skin from his feet and shins, as the fire roared all over him.

Something between poker-hot burning and ice-cold freezing.

It felt maddening as the pain crept up his body at the worst, most agonizing pace.

Before the flames reached his face, Captain Stone opened his eyes to catch one last desperate look at his wife.

Something extraordinary occurred.

Georgette, perhaps driven by a mix of desperation and love, tapped into something primal and powerful within herself.

She raised her arms, her voice rising in a powerful howl that seemed to shake the very Earth.

The sky above responded immediately. Clouds gathered as if summoned by her will.

The Vikings stopped chanting to look up at the sudden change of atmosphere.

Then, to everyone's surprise, a deluge of rain poured down, each drop a testament to her fierce love for Captain Stone.

The torrent of rain quickly extinguished the flames that had started to consume Captain Stone's body. It left only smoke and the scent of wet ash. And a mighty gust of wind blew the smoke away, clearing Captain Stone's vision.

The sudden turn of events appeared to have left

everyone, Vikings and companions alike, in stunned silence.

The downpour, seemingly a divine intervention, had saved Captain Stone from a fiery end, a miracle none had anticipated.

He shuddered under the downpour as his body went in shock from going from one extreme temperature to another. But with the snake venom soaring through his veins, his body was already healing.

And nothing could dampen his mood.

He grinned at Georgette, standing amongst the commotion of confused Vikings, she slumped over, panting, as though utterly spent.

Captain Stone wrenched his arms free from his weakened bonds, snapping the remaining ropes in the process.

He stumbled over to Georgette and pulled her into his arms.

Georgette trembled when he pulled back to look at her.

The small viper's head poked out of her shirt.

On her collarbone were tiny pin pricks of the snake's bite.

Captain Stone finally understood. "Good boy, Robert," he muttered.

He pulled his wife in for another hug and caressed her cheek.

Georgette pushed back to look at him with a mixture of surprise and amusement. "Robert?" she repeated.

Captain Stone pointed at the snake. "I told you I wanted to keep one as a pet. Robert is his name."

Georgette let out a weak laugh, but then her eyes narrowed as everyone went quiet.

Captain Stone turned around to face a sea of shocked and furious stares.

"Who are you? A warlock?" Rognik pushed people out of the way to stand nose to nose with Captain Stone.

"No," Georgette barked. "He is a chosen one. Everyone in our group was chosen by the goddess Isis for a sacred mission."

Rognik scoffed. "Do you always speak in riddles? What is this, talking about a chosen one?" He stepped forward and raised his dagger to Captain Stone's throat. "You won't burn, but I bet you bleed."

The ground suddenly trembled, and everyone staggered to keep on their feet.

Rognik spun around as his men backed away to open a path.

The clouds faded enough for one golden beam of

sunshine to land on a lone cow standing on a small patch of red flowers. The cow sported a headdress and several floral leis.

Captain Stone, barely grasping the reality of his near execution, stared in disbelief as the cow adorned in a headdress and flowers caught everyone's attention. "Hathor," he whispered.

He placed a hand over his heart, and his eyes reflected a mix of wonder and reverence.

Georgette's fierce demeanor momentarily softened as she turned to him. "How do you know Hathor?"

Captain Stone stared, transfixed at the cow as the memory replayed in his mind. "I'm sorry, my love. I should have told you, but so much happened. There was never a good time…"

Georgette grabbed his arm, snapping him out of his trance. "Tell me what? If you bedded her, I swear to Zeus, I will set you on fire myself."

Captain Stone smiled at the flash of jealousy in her eyes. "No, my love. She saved my life when Isis tried to have me drowned."

Before Georgette could react, the cow transformed seamlessly into a woman of captivating beauty, with caramel brown skin and deep, soulful eyes. Her voice resonated with a divine boom, echoing through the dense foliage, and piercing the hearts of all present.

"In the name of Odin, I command ye, Rognik, to let these people go."

Rognik, leader of the Vikings, stepped forward, his posture a mixture of respect and skepticism. "Other clans may recognize you, Hathor. But mine only obeys Odin, himself."

As if summoned by the challenge, a deep, thunderous bellow rolled from the heavens. "Hear my voice and let your body tremble under my power. Do not dare to dishonor Hathor, the goddess of beauty and fertility. Lest your testicles shrivel to raisins and your bloodline die with you."

The Vikings, once resolute and unyielding, fell to their knees in unison, their faces etched with awe and fear. The presence of the goddess, conveyed through the powerful voice from above, left no room for doubt or disobedience.

"Yes, All-Father. Of course. As you wish." Rognik raised both palms to the skies. "Forgive me, Hathor. Forgive us."

HERCULES

𝒰nder the watchful gaze of the Peruvian jungle, Hercules stood tall amidst the Vikings, feeling the resurgence of magic in the air.

The Vikings, now their unexpected allies, offered them an array of food and weapons.

With a sense of gratitude and mutual respect, the group accepted their generosity.

Hercules, finally regaining the sense of the familiar hum of magical energy, concentrated and waved his hand to create a portal.

The swirling vortex of light and energy formed effortlessly.

Stepping through the portal, they found themselves back in Imerta, the land overseen by the goddess Isis.

The transformation of Imerta was nothing short of miraculous.

In their absence, Isis had erected a new palace.

The majestic structure stretched high into the heavens, and its spires pierced the sky. The palace, adorned with intricate carvings and shimmering with an ethereal glow, stood as a testament to her divine power.

Around the palace, the land of Imerta was a vision of utopia.

The abundant wildlife looked vibrant with birds of exotic plumage flitting between trees and animals that roamed freely in the lush greenery. The magnificent trees held leaves in a tapestry of green, and their branches arched gracefully toward the sky. Streams and waterfalls added to the idyllic scenery. Their gentle murmurs harmonized with the soft rustling of leaves.

The group walked to a resurrection circle—an area marked by ancient symbols and a tangible sense of sacred energy. At its center stood an altar, around which the air thrummed with potential and power.

Isis, regal and serene, greeted them in her lair. She was the embodiment of divine elegance, and her presence felt commanding.

To Hercules's surprise, she reminded him of

Georgette, though he'd never noticed the resemblance before.

"You have been gone so long I was beginning to worry you had forgotten about me." Isis reached to give Ava a hug. "My oldest daughter. I trust she pleases you, Hercules?" Isis looked up at him expectantly.

"She does." He nodded.

Ava's cheeks reddened.

Isis held out her hands. "Well, where is my dear Osiris?" She looked around them all with wide eyes.

When Georgette handed her a small wooden crate, she looked up at Hercules with repulsion. "This is it? You haven't brought me all of him?"

Captain Stone stepped forward. "Arguably, we brought you the best part of him."

Serena stayed unusually silent, and by the narrowing in her gaze, it was clear to all who wanted to see that she harbored a silent grudge toward Isis.

But Isis paid Serena no attention. Isis looked to Georgette. "You have been gone for weeks. What have you been doing all this time?"

"It's not been easy." Prince Edward kept his tone mild-mannered. "We have faced much adversity."

"Did you know Vikings still walk the Earth?" Ava asked.

Isis's nose wrinkled at the word as though she'd cursed. "No. I did not."

She lifted open the lid of the crate and smiled fondly at the skull inside. "Hello, my darling," she whispered, stroking it with her index finger.

She walked down the path toward the resurrection circle and placed the skull on the altar.

"Nine burial sites, and after all this time, you have been to just one." She turned around, and her lips turned into a thin line as she shut her eyes for a moment. "At this rate, it shall take years to recover his remains."

Serena huffed and began to pace, but she seemed lost for words.

Isis ignored her. "You may rest here and gather supplies, but I expect you all to continue your quest in the morning."

"With respect," Hercules said. "I have a request."

Isis's eyes widened for a moment, but then she turned impassive and waved a hand. "What is this request?"

Hercules glanced at Ava, before he looked at Isis again, determined. "I wish for your hospitality for three nights, before we begin our next journey."

Isis pursed her lips and blinked at him.

The soft breeze flowing across the island let her

hair move like it had a mind of its own, waving like ripples of sunlight. At first, it seemed that she formulated an argument, but then she looked at Georgette's messy hair and bloodstained shirt. Then she hummed.

"I suppose you have done well…" She looked at the skull again with fondness. "And I gather that you have not enjoyed a comfortable place to bed your new wife, Hercules." Isis glanced at Ava, who blushed.

Hercules maintained composure, even though it surprised him that Isis had immediately picked on the one thing he had in mind. It was true, he had yet to take Ava to bed.

He promised her he would not take her innocence unless she asked. But as he grew to know her, it began to stir forbidden feelings.

He had overheard her comforting Georgette one evening, and she was the most compassionate member of the group. Always reminding everyone to drink or rest. She had an inner strength that bolstered him. It was not her siren fury or the way she faced the Hydra with no shred of fear that called to him the most.

He had almost overlooked what truly captivated him. Yet now, as he looked at her on the beautiful island of Imerta, where she hugged herself, keeping quiet and reverent in the presence of her mother, his heart swelled.

Ava embodied pure kindness.

He felt certain she did not possess a selfish bone in her body, and after all they had been through, he yearned to indulge her in as much pleasure as possible.

Isis hummed again as she tapped her finger on her lips.

Meanwhile, Serena watched the exchange with her hands balled into fists. Though Hercules could not understand what put her into such a foul mood.

He looked at Isis again to find her studying him intently. "Very well," she said finally. "Three nights. The cottages up on the hill are waiting for you all."

She began to walk away but stopped to touch Georgette's cheek and give her a beaming smile. Then she walked past Serena as though she was not even there.

When she left, Serena broke out of her furious silent state and raised her arms. "Am I invisible? Why does she hate me?"

"She doesn't hate you at all," Ava said, defensive, but she stopped under Serena's glare.

Georgette shrugged. "Isis is a complicated

woman. Who knows what her motivations are for ignoring you…"

Serena frowned. "So, you saw it too? She didn't even look at me!"

"I know, which is strange… she even winked at me, and she's tried to kill me. Ttwice," Captain Stone offered.

But Serena scowled at him, and Georgette elbowed him in the ribs.

Ava reached for Serena to hug her, but Serena shoved her away. "I demand to know why she continues to reject me."

"She hated me too… until I threatened to kill her. She seems to respect that kind of aggression," Georgette offered.

Serena just gave her a cold stare.

Hercules glanced at Captain Stone, who shrugged back. No one had any answers for her, it seemed, and comforting Serena was the last thing on Hercules's mind.

Evidently, Prince Edward had other plans for his beloved.

He wrapped his arm around his fiery red-headed wife and did not withdraw when she protested.

"Do you want to know a secret?" he asked her in

a quiet voice, but not so quiet that no one else could hear him.

Serena gave him a glum look with her arms folded. "What?"

Prince Edward picked her up, and she let out a shriek of surprise. "I love what it does to me when you're angry." He said it louder than he likely meant to.

Everyone grinned as they watched him carry his grumpy wife up the path to the line of cottages on the hill.

Captain Stone winked at Georgette before he leaned in to murmur to Hercules, "The one at the very end toward the willow tree is your dwelling." He jerked his head to Ava and grinned at him. "See you in a few days… Good luck."

With a final salute, he took Georgette by the hand, and the two broke into a run to their house.

Ava clasped her hands in front of her and blushed deeply when Hercules looked at her.

"Do you want me to…?" he started.

"Only if you want to?" She spoke a little too fast to sound sincere. Her eyes twinkled at him, and she tucked a strand of soft hair behind her ear with a smile.

Hercules looked upon Ava, and his heart danced. "Stone says there's a house…"

"Mine is… well, I'll show you." Ava walked away.

Hercules couldn't help but notice the exaggerated sway of her hips as she moved.

"It was a gift, from Isis," she called over her shoulder. "My usual abode is quite humble."

She led Hercules to a pretty cottage, decorated with red roses lining the roof. A pair of baskets hung on either side of the blue door, which had 'Ava' carved into it.

She stopped and traced her index on her name with a smile.

Then, she hovered her finger over the door and began to write in the air. The words "and Hercules" appeared under her name.

Inside the cottage, little streams of sunlight settled on the humble furniture.

Hercules had to duck to enter the room, and his head almost touched the ceiling.

Ava giggled as she shut the door behind them.

"Oops, I misjudged how big you are." She waved her hand, and the walls stretched, pushing the ceiling closer to the sky.

Hercules gave her a lopsided smile and removed

his shirt. "I guarantee you will not be misjudging my size again."

He reached for her hair.

Ava's breath grew short, and she froze while he fisted her soft locks and dragged her head to the side, exposing her neck.

He leaned forward and breathed on her.

She shivered and shut her eyes, prompting him to grin.

"Is this what you want?" He murmured the words against her skin.

Ava's eyes snapped open, and she looked at him with mild alarm. "I want…"

Hercules took a step closer and found her hand, intertwining his fingers with hers. "Yes?"

"I want…" She closed her eyes and lifted his hand to rest on her collarbone.

Her heart raced beneath his palm, and when Hercules drew circles over her thigh with his other hand, she almost passed out from breathing so fast.

The woman was not lying when they first met. Truly, she had not been touched by a man before.

"Why are you doing this?" Ava gave him a furtive look.

Hercules inhaled to steady his nerves.

Part of him had no idea what he was doing, let

alone why. He just knew that being with her healed his aching soul, and she'd earned the right to be worshipped.

Somehow, the words in his mind could not make the journey to his mouth.

He swallowed.

"I want to tell you…" Hercules stepped back to give her space.

Ava looked at him, blinking.

He walked her to the small bed, and he sat and pulled her into his lap.

She yelped and straddled him.

He lazily zig-zagged his finger over the fastenings on the front of her cotton dress.

"You enchant me," he said. "I've never seen anyone stand up to Hades like you have, and the way you handled yourself with the Hydra…"

He loosened the fastening, and the neckline of her dress gaped open.

Ava's teeth glittered as she beamed at him.

When his finger touched her cleavage, though, she wriggled in his lap, and it rubbed him in the most pleasing way.

Hercules shut his eyes for a moment and gripped her thighs.

Ripples of pleasure shot through his senses.

He couldn't wait to worship this siren. He would cherish and savor every single moment, willing the world to stop turning just so he could take all the time he'd need.

"You awakened something in me that I thought was forever lost," Hercules muttered into her ear, stroking her hair back from her face.

Her milky exposed skin made him lick his lips, and he longed to kiss every part of her.

"What is that?" Ava's voice sounded too high-pitched.

Her hands roamed over his pectorals, and his muscles tensed under her touch.

She sighed, throwing her head back as she shut her eyes. Apparently, she adored every moment of this closeness.

At that moment, Hercules understood that Ava had been just as lonely as him. Yet, she had never experienced love before. No one had ever shown her what it felt like to be cherished and to be complete.

He would change that. It had become his new mission.

He took her chin with his thumb and index figure and brought her to his lips. "You awoke a hunger in me that can only be quenched by you," he whispered against her mouth. Their lips brushed, and everything zinged.

"You're going to eat me?" Ava grinned at him, and amusement laced her voice.

Hercules picked her up and turned around to toss her on the bed. Then he took a few moments to just look at her.

Ava fell back, and her wavy hair splayed out across the pillow like rays of sunshine. The soft peaks of her breast rose and fell, and her beauty was enough to bring any man to his knees.

But her eyes truly captivated him. They looked like two magical portals, swirling, inviting him into another world—a world where pain and grief did not exist. Instead, only pleasure and belonging existed there.

"Yes, Ava, I am going to eat you. And you are going to enjoy it very much."

Hercules growled and crawled up her body to find her mouth. He brushed her hair away from her forehead and kissed her.

Ava melted under him, and her body molded into the bed.

She dragged her nails down his back and lightly dug in while he stroked her tongue with his and kissed her with every passion of his soul.

She kissed him back and did not even try to come up for air for longer than Hercules expected.

When they finally broke apart, beads of sweat appeared on her upper lip.

Smiling, he wiped it away with his thumb. Then he peppered her face and neck with kisses.

She moaned when he brushed his lips over her collarbone, and he resisted moaning back as he inhaled the sweet aroma of her.

She wanted him, and he wanted her.

For that moment, nothing in the world mattered more.

He moved, slow and tender, careful to touch every part of her with his mouth.

He tugged on her gown and kissed her shoulder, before moving to the other one.

Her breaths came quick and sharp as he reached inside the neckline of her gown and fondled her breast.

Hercules had to keep reminding himself to take things very slowly. After all, Ava was innocent, and all of this was new for her.

He waited for her breaths to return to normal before he tweaked her nipple.

But just the one pinch had her panting again.

Her body arched against him, and her hands greedily found his manhood through his shorts.

He throbbed under her touch through the material. He jerked against her, his body reacting entirely against his will now.

But then he pulled away, taking himself out of her reach, and Ava grumbled something incoherent.

Hercules grinned, happy to be back in control.

He pulled out a small knife from his holster and dragged the iron blade over her neck.

Ava sucked in a breath with a hiss and stayed still, her eyes wide with panic.

But then he cut the front of her dress and tore it open with one swift motion.

Ava yelped, but she did not resist when he cut through her undergarments too.

Finally, she lay beautiful and bare, like a Grecian goddess on the bed. Sweat clinging to her skin like jewels.

He roamed over her body with his mouth, feasting on her, until every drop had been sucked away.

Ava shivered, dragging her hands through his hair as he enjoyed her. "I can't bear it anymore. There's a terrible ache…"

Hercules removed his shorts and sighed at the

release of arousal that had been restrained for so long.

Ava's breath hitched, and her eyes widened when she looked at it.

"Do not worry, my love," he growled into her ear as he rubbed her core with it.

She mewled, arching into him.

Hercules pinned her down by the wrists. "I will take the ache away and give you a new one. Do you trust me?" He pulled back to look into her ethereal eyes.

She blinked and gaped at him. But then she gave him a resolute nod.

He took it slow, knowing that it would hurt.

Ava cried out and gripped his shoulders as though she had fallen off a cliff, but Hercules stayed right there, cradling her.

"It's all right," he whispered, edging in deeper. "I will not let you come to harm."

Ava shut her eyes and tensed under him, so Hercules started to kiss her neck again, and sure enough she loosened under him.

Then he fully entered her, and he just held her and waited.

Sweat dripped from his chest to hers, and Ava

clung to him like he was a lifeline, adjusting to this new sensation.

Then, finally, she tentatively began to rock her hips.

Her widened eyes looked so innocent, as though she curiously tested something new.

She wrapped her legs around his waist and rolled her hips again.

This time, she shut her eyes and let out a shuddering groan.

Gloriously, she took matters in her own hands and began to buck against him, growing more confident with each move.

"You are a force, my darling." Hercules enjoyed the tremendous waves of pleasure that soared through his body.

Making love to Ava lit his soul on fire, and his heart burned with joy.

He picked her up and sat on the edge of the bed, lifting her up and down, with his hands on the globes of her bottom.

She rested her hands on his shoulders and sighed.

Hercules kissed her mouth and nibbled on her bottom lip.

It seemed to send Ava over the edge, because everything tightened, and she cried out for a long time. When she finished, she collapsed against his shoulder.

"So, that is what it feels like…" She kept her eyes closed.

Hercules held her as she recovered. "What does?"

Ava lifted her head to smile at him, and her eyelids drooped. "Oneness."

Hercules caressed her cheek, falling for her even harder.

After an entire life of loneliness, she finally felt connected to another person, in both body and spirit. And he had not experienced this closeness for more than one thousand years.

He never once believed he could be this vulnerable again.

But there he was. Succumbing to another woman, letting his guard down and inviting her to touch the most hidden parts of his soul.

And it empowered and terrified him all at once.

Hercules made love to her all day and all night, and she never tired of him.

When he did break apart from her, she clawed at his back, pulling him back to bed once more.

They moved like two broken souls, connected in a way that healed their hidden wounds. Neither of them wanted to be apart.

Indeed, Hercules thought about telling Isis to forget about the mission. He would have to spend the next thousand years with his wife in solitude. After all, they would never be alone again. And the rest of their days would be nothing but unrivalled passion and devotion.

However, on the second night, Ava started to complain that she felt raw. Just the slightest touch made her wince.

So, Hercules just held her instead, and they lay in the bed listening to the wildlife outside the window.

Her body fit so perfectly in his arms. He cradled her close, breathing in the floral scent of her hair, and they breathed in unison.

When Hercules slept, the ghosts of the past no longer haunted his dreams. Instead, they reflected his days with Ava.

He'd wake and feel her wriggle against his chest. It prompted him to hold her tighter.

He began to believe his lot in life would be too good to last. But their passions entwined with their bodies, and Ava's presence brought him nothing but eternal bliss after a millennium of suffering.

Until the night before the third day, he was proven right.

"Will you tell me what happened to her?" Ava

whispered, snuggled into Hercules's protective embrace as she stroked his arm.

Hercules stiffened. "Who?"

Ava paused, and her index finger hovered over the hairs on his arms.

Then she finally said the word that ripped open the wound all over again.

"Megara."

Hercules's eyes burned, and his chest tightened at the name.

Sensing his mood, Ava rolled over to look at him. "Let me in, Hercules. Let me know…"

She reached for his cheek, and Hercules knew she planned to enter his memories, just as she had done before.

But he flinched and backed away. "No."

Ava's eyes grew misty as she watched him jump out of the bed. "Even now, you carry this burden?" She sat up and held the covers to her bare chest. "Hercules, if you are ever to move on, you need to tell me…"

"Everything was fine. I was fine," Hercules roared, pacing the room now.

It felt like millions of tiny daggers had split all the most tender parts of his soul. Flashes of memories flooded his mind like a virus, and he clenched his jaw.

"Hercules," Ava whispered. She hurried out of bed and shuffled to him. "Please don't shut me out. You care for me. I know you love me as deeply as I love you." Her voice sounded soft and gentle, like a healing balm.

Hercules looked at her and anguish filled his heart. "I am nothing but a broken vessel of a man, a shadow of a god. Hades is right. It is consuming me. Soon, there will be nothing left to love."

Ava took his hand. "Very well. I shall take it."

Hercules frowned. "Take what?"

She moved in to rest her head on his chest.

He wondered if she could hear his heart crying, pounding faster than the hooves of a runaway horse.

"My dearest Hercules, I accept you as you are now. If you don't want to talk about the past, don't. If you never heal from this, then very well. I shall take the broken parts of you and cherish them until truly, there are no more parts left to love."

Hercules cradled her face and pressed his forehead to hers. "Can we just stay here and pretend there is no world outside? That it is just you and me, forever?"

Ava rested her palms over his chest and nodded.

Then she straddled his waist and kissed him with unbridled passion.

"But I thought you were sore?" Hercules asked, when she began to roll her hips over him.

She pulled back to give him a soulful smile that shone like the morning sunshine and warmed his soul.

"I don't care anymore; I need to be close to you one more time before morning arrives."

Hercules enjoyed one last sweet sleep with Ava in his arms and pretended that nothing else existed but her.

But the next morning, the couple had to face reality and re-enter the real world.

Hercules did not expect the stench of smoke to wake him. Frowning, he shook Ava's shoulder. "Wake up. Something is wrong."

Ava jumped and dressed as thick smoke seeped in through the open window.

Hercules pulled on his clothes and boots and picked up his golden mace from the table.

When he opened the door, a cloud of black smoke flooded the cottage. He reached back to grab Ava. "Try not to take deep breaths." He coughed into his shoulder.

They stumbled out of the cottage, and when the wind blew in the opposite direction, Hercules and Ava stared in horror at the island.

Captain Stone came up beside them. "What on earth…?"

"The whole island is on fire." Ava's eyes glistened with tears.

Georgette emerged from her dwelling and looked just as bewildered as Hercules felt. "Who did this?"

The treetops billowed with thick smoke, and giant flames roared, burning everything in its wake. Low, black clouds hung in the sky, and the reflection of the fire sent an orange glow over them.

Just as Hercules tried to formulate a plan, Prince Edward ran into view.

His face looked clammy and gray as he coughed and panted. "Have any of you seen Serena?" he asked between raspy breaths.

Everyone shook their heads, and Prince Edward sank to his knees, while dragging his hands through his dark hair. "She's gone."

SERENA

*P*rince Edward attempted to distract Serena in all manner of ways—from trying strange new positions in the bedroom, to using everyday objects to tickle and arouse her.

But by the second night, the pain of her mother's rejection roared to life as she lay in bed unable to sleep, while her husband snored softly into her back.

She replayed the memory of Isis always greeting Georgette like she was the most precious creature on Earth.

Now, Ava was in her favor, having pleased the great Hercules.

And what did Serena do that impressed her mother?

Had she not done enough to warrant any praise?

She stood up to the Vikings, racing into danger when she saw Georgette and Captain Stone had been captured. She deciphered the ancient writing in the old crypt.

But her fierce spirit and knowledge of ancient writings seemed to be too insignificant to be mentioned. Her comrades stayed silent, happy for Ava and Hercules to take all of the credit, instead.

She could have lived with that if Isis had not snubbed her.

Serena barely blinked, staring at her mother with such intensity, willing her to look her way. She would have given anything for a flicker of a smile in her direction.

A simple, "hello," would have sufficed.

But instead, she caressed Georgette's cheek, looking adoringly at her twin sister. Then Isis dropped her loving gaze to the ancient skull in her hands.

Serena seethed as she thought about it.

She replayed the conversation with her father, Poseidon, when she had learned of the curse Isis put upon her own bloodline and then sent Serena away to be raised in Atlantis.

She thought things would be different now. After

all, Isis had welcomed Georgette back into her life after growing up in England. Georgette had no idea she had been born a siren. And yet, she had already won favor with their mother.

Perhaps the fact that she looked just like Isis made the goddess love her more—with their matching long, golden locks and intense eyes.

It made her want to hate Georgette.

Why did everyone love her sister? Prince Edward once called out her name while they made love. Serena would never forget it.

Captain Stone would destroy anyone and everyone who dared to threaten his beloved Georgette.

Even Ava took her under her wing and acted like a loving big sister.

But what about Serena? What made her so unlovable?

Hot tears clung to the corners of her eyes, and Serena sniffed angrily, willing them not to fall.

She would not cry over these people. None of them loved her. Not like her father and her brothers.

She thought about the Tritons down in Atlantis and wondered what they were doing. Had they decided to finally take part in the war? Or did they remain stuck in their old ways of endless training and hiding?

Did her father miss her?

Prince Edward stopped snoring and stirred, prompting Serena to wipe her eyes and slide out of bed.

She took a pillow and positioned it where she had been. As planned, Prince Edward draped an arm over the pillow and slept on.

The weakest light of the morning sun peeked through the cracks in the shutters while Serena waved a hand over her body and draped herself in a silver cotton dress.

She tied her red hair back and yanked on her ankle boots.

Today everything would change. Serena would no longer be the rejected twin. She would show Isis what a formidable enemy she could be.

After all, Georgette suggested that Isis's respect for her had been born when Georgette threatened to kill her.

The rage swirling within Serena propelled her to do something unthinkable. Even if it meant she would never bear a child.

She stopped outside the cottage as a gust of cold air hit her cheeks. She placed a hand over her hollow stomach and imagined a bump. Inside, a baby kicked and moved.

Serena clung to the dream her entire life.

But the anguish over being rejected by her own mother over and over again returned full force.

Even after she crossed the world, going to hell and back, for her mother's sick mission.

And the thanks she got? None.

It made something inside of her snap. And whatever snapped would be the last thing holding her back from unleashing her powers and destroying Isis once and for all.

She marched down the hill and ran light and fast, like a cat, across the path to the palace.

No guards patrolled the area, not like the city of Atlantis. The large palace doors stood ajar.

She pushed them open and scaled the sweeping staircase.

Finally, she found her mother's room. Isis lay so poised and peaceful as though she could not fathom a reason to lock her door or be guarded.

Was Isis so narcissistic that she truly believed no one wanted her demise?

Serena stared at her sleeping mother. The fire within her burned so brightly that it seemed to set her hair alight.

She opened her palms, willing the heat to transcend from her spirit to her body.

Serena had only read about the magic in the depths of Atlantis--called a siren's flame.

If a siren got scorned and grew bitter, their wrath would take over in the form of a fireball. She could then, as a phoenix, explode into fire and rise from the ashes anew.

The books also talked of powers to destroy worlds.

Serena looked out of the window at the beautiful, tropical island scenery.

Everyone slept on, unaware of the torment writhing inside of her. She wanted everyone to wake up and for them to feel pain and fear as she had.

She let the intensity of the fire build and thrust her palm out, sending a blast of fire outside.

A soaring energy gripped her, and Serena liked the way intense power thrummed through her blood.

She sent another blast and another, condemning Imerta to burn in hell.

"Huh?"

Serena turned, balls of flames swirling above her palms as she looked upon Isis, who sat up and blinked at her.

"Are you happy now, Mother?" Serena hissed at

her. "Your island is burning. You will burn. And all because you made me."

Isis leaned forward to look at the fiery inferno outside. She took in the sight of her daughter's trembling hands.

Finally, Isis looked Serena in the eye, and she beamed at her, clasping her hands together. "Glorious." Her face brimmed with pride. "I knew you had power beyond any of your sisters. It just needed to be triggered."

Serena hesitated, frowning at her mother's words. "What did you say?"

The balls of fire extinguished, and she curled her fingers to make fists. "Is this another trick?"

Isis shook her head. "Oh, my spirited Serena. Come." She stretched out her arms.

Serena hesitated, but finally ran to her mother.

Isis held her and stroked her hair. "My dear Serena. No one in this world bears the fire in your soul. This is why I choose you to take Imerta."

Serena pulled back to frown at Isis. "Take Imerta?"

"Yes, child. Once I bring back my beloved Osiris, two curses will be broken. The one on you and your brothers and sisters." She rested a hand over Serena's belly. "And the one keeping me trapped here."

Serena shook her head as she tried to process the information. "How could Osiris's resurrection break that curse?"

Isis smiled and looked out the window. "Osiris is the most powerful force in the world. Even more powerful than you," she said. "In him, anything is possible. And I intend to be free of this island and go to my home in Egypt with my love. Luckily, I have other gods on my side."

Serena looked down at the silk sheets in thought. "Hathor rescued Captain Stone from the Vikings."

Isis nodded. "She is quite fond of him. She believes he will be key to getting what we want. You see, I have my allies who share my desire to bring back the ancient world."

Serena looked at her mother, startled. "Bring back the ancient world. What does that mean?"

Isis caressed Serena's cheek. "Worry not, my darling. All will be clear in due time. But let me ask you one thing: do you know what sacrifice you made binding yourself to a human?"

Serena stiffened. "My immortality."

Isis blinked. "Do you love him to live with him for eternity?"

Serena shrugged and rubbed her arm as she thought about her prince. "It may take that long for me to forgive him," she muttered. She looked up at her mother. "But yes, my heart belongs to him. If anything were to happen to him, it would be the end of me."

Isis took her hands in hers and exhaled. "Then what do you say if I promise to give you and Edward immortality, along with Imerta?"

Serena held her breath for a moment as the question registered. "You can do that?"

Isis leaned forward to grin at her. "With Osiris, nothing is impossible." She cocked her head. "You see how important this mission is, now?"

Serena nodded, and her heart lightened.

"I've set the island on fire."

Isis nodded to the window, and Serena looked out with surprise at the heavy downpour of rain. She turned back to Isis.

"Georgette has got it under control." Isis's eyes twinkled. Her expression suddenly sobered. "Remember the feeling you had today. Now that you have awakened the flame, you will be able to summon it again. And now I have no reason to be cold to you anymore."

Isis pulled Serena in for a tender hug, and Serena savored her mother's tenderness.

She did not know if this was another manipulation. But in the moment, she didn't care. She needed nothing more than the warmth of her mother's embrace.

"You must not tell the others about my offer or your new powers, not even Edward," Isis said when they broke apart. She gave Serena a hard look. "This will be our secret."

Serena smiled at the word. She liked the idea of that, and she reasoned that if the others knew what she had done, they would never trust her to join them on their mission.

"Our secret. Very well," she whispered, but then she frowned. "The others are not fools. They will know this is me." She gnawed on her lower lip.

Isis laughed. "Then make me the villain in your story. After all, everyone else likes to paint me as one."

Her words gripped Serena's heart like a vice, and for the briefest moment, she caught a flicker of pain in her mother's eyes.

Had she read her all wrong? Was this woman just a heartbroken soul, yearning to be reunited with her lost love?

Or was she a master at manipulation?

Serena did not care to find out.

"Go. The others are calling your name. They're so worried about you." Isis squeezed Serena's hands.

With a final nod, Serena slid off the bed and released Isis's hands. She stole a final glance at her mother's warm smile before she hurried out of the room.

AVA

*I*n the aftermath of the calamity that had befallen the island, Ava and her companions trudged through a landscape that had been transformed into a ghostly shadow of its former self.

The relentless rain drenched them to the bone, adding to the surreal and somber atmosphere.

Georgette, visibly drained, struggled to catch her breath. It seemed that the effort of summoning yet another rainstorm to quell the flames took its toll on her.

"Have all the sirens left the island?" Captain Stone's voice barely sounded audible over the steady drumming of the rain.

Ava strained her ears, trying to reconnect with the distant voices of her sisters.

For so long, she had tuned them out, and their presence had been relegated to the back of her mind. Now, she focused, sifting through the cacophony of the storm. "I can hear Serena... and Isis. They're talking, but I can't make out the words. The rain is too loud." She sighed and tried to push back her frustration.

At her words, Prince Edward's expression turned desperate. He swiftly approached Ava, grasping her arms with a mix of urgency and fear. "Is Serena all right?" His eyes, bloodshot and wide, searched Ava's face for any clue, any hint of reassurance.

Around them, the remnants of Imerta's once vibrant greenery stood, charred and smoldering, a stark contrast to the verdant paradise it had been. The earth underfoot had soddened and blackened, and the air carried the pungent scent of burnt wood and wet ashes.

"Do you think Serena did this?" The question Georgette asked weighed heavily on everyone's mind.

Only Prince Edward dared to shake his head and answer. "No."

But the way he said it sounded far too defensive to be convincing.

Hercules stopped, and everyone halted, looking at

him. "She was irritated about something when we arrived. Edward, did you... pacify her?"

The question turned Prince Edward's forehead to a deep shade of red. He coughed. "Of course. She was fine... in good spirits, on second thought." He avoided Hercules's discerning look and marched forward. "Someone has taken her. She'd never just—"

"Edward..." Captain Stone cut in, with a tone like a concerned older brother. "Serena is many things, but she's not weak. Who could possibly capture her here of all places?"

"Isis."

Everyone spun around to find Serena leaning against a tree, catching her breath.

Prince Edward ran up to her and wrapped her up in his arms. "My love, I was so worried."

When he pulled away, Serena met the stares of everyone in the group. "Isis trapped me. She asked if I wanted to join her for a morning stroll..." Serena looked down. "And instead, she told me terrible things, and she almost killed me." She lifted her bandaged arm.

"I can't believe this..." Georgette whispered, reaching closer.

A faint look of repulsion took hold of Serena's

face for a splinter of a second, before her expression sobered again. "Tell me you have not been tricked by Isis and almost perished because of it."

Captain Stone laughed, which broke the tension in the air. All eyes focused on him, and he shrugged. "She has a point; I can attest to that." He pulled open his shirt to reveal the scars across his chest.

Ava took in this information, stunned. "I thought she had changed. You're part of the prophecy, Serena. Why would she try to harm you?"

Serena glared at her. "Why did she trap Georgette in a cave and cause an earthquake? Why did she try to drown Stone? Who knows what twisted thoughts motivate her actions."

"So, Isis did all this?" Hercules gestured to the charred forest.

Serena folded her arms. "She wanted to send us a message."

"And that is…?" Prince Edward asked.

Serena walked down the path and rested a palm on an old sycamore tree.

With blackened bark, it had become a shadow of its former glory.

Serena's eyes held pain as she stared at it. Finally, she turned around. "She says time is ticking. Her patience is wearing thin, and if we do not hurry up and retrieve the remains of Osiris, she will unleash her fury and burn the entire world."

A chill crossed Ava's entire body at Serena's words, and she hugged herself. Those warnings certainly did sound like something Isis would say.

Ava stepped forward, and her heart filled with determination. "We should split up. I've mapped out every burial site. If we each tackle two, we'll regroup and wrap this up in no time."

Georgette's eyes darted around, and a flicker of concern passed over her face. "But what about the guardian beasts at each site? We always needed Hercules to stand a chance against them."

Captain Stone wrapped an arm around her with a reassuring grin on his face. "Fear not, my dear. We have more than just brute strength on our side now. We have divine backup."

"Divine backup? You mean those fickle Egyptian goddesses?" Georgette retorted.

Captain Stone looked around for support but found none.

Ava bit back a smile, leaving him high and dry.

He sighed dramatically. "Fine, fine. And let's not forget Athena. Speaking of which, Isis still owes me a golden axe."

Hercules raised an eyebrow and kept his stance

firm. "Golden axe? And just when did you become a Greek hero?"

Stone folded his arms defiantly. "Athena herself gifted it to me. I used it to slay a foe and present his head to Isis who then… stole it from me. Typical."

Hercules's expression became unreadable as he clearly mulled over Stone's words.

Georgette broke the tension. "Another goddess, Mannington? Just how extensive is your… acquaintances list?"

Prince Edward winced. "For the love of the gods, don't answer that."

Georgette shot him a glare before turning back to Captain Stone, and her nails extended slightly. "Why am I always the last to know about these escapades?"

Hercules, sensing the brewing storm, subtly stepped back, and his hand found Ava's hip. "On second thought, Stone, perhaps retrieving that axe isn't the worst idea."

Prince Edward cut through the mounting tension. "What about Isis? Should we confront her directly?"

Serena shook her head, and her expression turned grave. "No. She's in no mood to see anyone. I barely escaped with my life." She raised a finger to pre-empt Edward. "And killing her would only make our curse permanent. We must focus on retrieving Osiris's remains."

Captain Stone cleared his throat. "I need to hold a gathering with my pirate lords in Tortuga. I need to see how the war's faring."

"I'll come with you," offered Prince Edward.

Georgette and Serena exchanged a look before Georgette spoke up. "I've got a different plan. I need to master my powers in Atlantis. It could speed things up for us."

Serena raised an eyebrow. "But we just decided to prioritize the mission for Osiris."

"It's just a brief detour," Georgette insisted. "I only need a few books."

Serena shot her a firm look. "You think you can just waltz into the ancient library and borrow a few tomes? You'll never be allowed in, and if you do find a way to sneak inside, you'll have the army of Tritons ready to punish you."

Georgette shot back, "Then you should come with me. They are the brothers who raised you, after all. Perhaps you can appeal to their soft spot."

Serena opened her mouth to argue, but before the debate could escalate, Ava interjected. "Actually, that works. The next burial site is in Atlantis."

Everyone stared at her with widened eyes, lifted eyebrows, and gaping expressions.

"It is?" Serena asked.

Ava sighed, pulling out the maps. "Does no one read these?"

They group exchanged sheepish looks.

Ava listed off the locations. "Peru, Atlantis, England…"

"England?" Prince Edward perked up. "Perhaps we should tackle that one together, brother."

Stone raised an eyebrow. "Don't tell me it's guarded by the Loch Ness Monster."

"That's Scotland, you fool," Edward muttered, but they both chuckled.

Captain Stone scanned the group. "All right. We'll regroup at the fourth burial site, which is…?"

Ava met Hercules's knowing smile. "Athens."

Edward's expression turned solemn as he shifted to Serena. His hand caressed her cheek. "I'm going to miss you. Without a portal, it could be weeks."

Captain Stone pulled Georgette into a tight embrace and spoke in a low voice low. "Join us in England when you're done."

Ava found Hercules's hand.

Despite their fight, she felt grateful they did not have to be parted from each other. Just feeling his hand in hers gave her a strength she so desperately needed.

Her mind reeled at Isis's betrayal. She had truly believed that her mother had changed. She disagreed with the conniving plan to treat people like puppets.

Ava had to cling to the hope that when Osiris returned, it would restore her mother's good nature and bring her back to the light.

With their plans set and their farewells exchanged, the group prepared to embark on their separate paths. Each step taking them closer to unravelling the mysteries that lay ahead.

GEORGETTE

*I*n the heart of Atlantis, just outside its city walls, Georgette stepped through the portal.

Immediately, the stunning city in front of her overwhelmed her senses. It looked as if they stepped into a world made of light and water, where the buildings shimmered with an ethereal glow, and the air itself sparkled with suspended droplets of the sea.

Ava held out the map in front of her. "The burial site is not far from here... in a cave."

Serena leaned forward to look at it over Ava's shoulder. "That tiny thing? There's nothing in there." Serena waved her hand dismissively. "Are you sure about this? I've spent all my life exploring Atlantis, unravelling the mysteries of the city and the outer parts. It's beautiful, but there's no ancient burial sites."

Georgette held her tongue, but Ava said the very thing on her mind.

"Did you ever think that the burial site would be…hidden?"

Undeterred, they continued walking as the path descended into a steel decline.

The air felt cool and crisp as they ventured toward the mouth of the cave. The small entrance meant everyone had to walk sideways. Its walls shimmered like the inside of a pearl, and as Georgette dragged her fingers over the glossy surface, it reminded her of the time Captain Stone took her to a cave not long after he forced her to marry him.

She smiled to herself. Back then, she hated the pirate captain.

Had she known what would happen next, she might not have been quite so troubled.

They traversed deeper into the cave.

The path wound and narrowed until it opened out to a space large enough for everyone to fill.

Hercules looked around the dark cave and placed his hands on his hips.

Georgette stumbled into the space, quickly followed by Ava and Serena.

Ahead of them loomed a dead end.

"See? I told you. There's nothing here." Serena's voice echoed in the confined space.

"Perhaps there's a clue written somewhere…" Georgette brushed the sides of the cave, hoping to uncover ancient text.

Everyone followed suit, but when they came up empty-handed, Ava huffed with frustration. "I don't understand, I was certain…" she muttered.

Hercules, looking unimpressed, leaned against a nearby rock, which to everyone's surprise, began to glow with a soft, pulsating light.

"That's never happened before." Serena furrowed her brow.

The ground beneath them rumbled, and an opening appeared.

Everyone exchanged nervous looks. With cautious steps, they moved forward.

The ground sloped and they stumbled over the slick rock floor.

When they finally ended up in a vast cavern, refractions of light dazzled the rocky walls and a Leviathan stood in front of them: a guardian of Atlantis.

The cavern echoed with the sound of the

Leviathan's deep, resonant growls, and its massive form coiled like a serpent of the sea.

The creature's scales shimmered in the dim light, casting prismatic colors on the walls. Its eyes, deep and mesmerizing, fixed on the group with an intelligence that suggested it was more than just a mindless guardian.

Ava stepped forward with a focused expression. "Let's try not to hurt it. Remember, it's just protecting its home."

Hercules nodded, hefting his mace. "Agreed, but let's not end up as fish food either."

Georgette's eyes reflected the Leviathan's iridescent scales. "I will try to find its weak spot. Keep it busy."

The Leviathan roared, a sound that reverberated through the cavern, as if the very walls trembled at its fury.

It lunged forward, its enormous jaws snapping shut inches from Hercules, who deftly rolled aside.

Hercules, poised for combat, eyed the Leviathan warily as it lunged at him. "I could make quick work of this," he said with a half-grin, dodging another mighty swipe. "Shall we just end this swiftly?"

Serena, with her usual fierceness, nodded in agreement. "Normally, I'm all for dispatching any creature that poses a threat," she said, readying herself for a fight. "I say we take it down."

But Ava, her voice steady and calm, interjected. "Wait! This creature…it's not just a mindless beast. There's a sense of goodness in it. I believe I can reach it, maybe even hypnotize it."

Hercules paused, and his gaze shifted to Ava.

In that moment, his expression softened, and he gave a small nod. "Alright, Ava. We'll try it your way." Deep trust resonated in his voice.

Georgette watched the exchange, and a sense of awe filled her.

The connection between Hercules and Ava felt palpable. It looked as if they were two halves of the same entity, moving together with an effortless harmony. Their bond was so strong, Georgette could not imagine a world where one existed without the other. Their unity, their understanding of each other, was something rare and beautiful, a testament to the depth of their relationship.

Ava, concentrating, began to hum a soft, hypnotic melody, and her siren song wove through the air.

The Leviathan paused, and its eyes momentarily lost their fierce glow.

"Is it working?" Serena asked, with her sword out, ready to spring into action.

"It appears the beast is tiring," Georgette said. "Keep singing, Ava." She watched the mystical beast.

After a few moments, the Leviathan shook off the drowsiness. Its gaze sharpened as it focused on Serena.

With a speed belying its size, it struck, forcing Serena to leap back. Her nails extended into sharp claws, but she grinned. "I think it's quite safe to assume it is not working," Serena called out, darting around the beast and bracing for another attack.

"We need to exhaust its defenses," Hercules said.

Georgette conjured a burst of water and aimed it at the Leviathan's eyes.

The creature reeled back, momentarily blinded.

"Goodness, I am surprised that really worked." Georgette looked at her hands as she felt a rush of power from her palms.

Hercules swung his mace with precision, aiming not to wound but to distract the beast further. "Come on, fishy, look at the glittery gold stick!" He danced about, waving the mace above his head, and the Leviathan's eyes moved with it.

All the while, Ava sang her song and raised her hands, focusing on the task.

The Leviathan stilled and looked at Ava, almost cross-eyed.

Ava's song grew louder, more insistent.

The Leviathan, caught in the battle on multiple fronts, began to sway. Its movements slowed, and its eyes rolled.

"Keep it up! We're wearing it down!" Hercules's eyes gleamed with the thrill of the fight.

Finally, the Leviathan lay before them, breathing heavily—not dead but asleep. Completely subdued.

The group, panting and exhilarated, looked around with smiles.

"That was...amazing," Ava breathed, and her eyes shone with adrenaline.

Serena, still poised for action, relaxed her stance. "Well, I stand corrected." She reached forward and touched her palm to the Leviathan's face. It snoozed on, undisturbed. "There are still secrets to uncover here."

Georgette followed the group as they delved deeper into the cave.

The walls, etched with ancient runes and glowing with a soft, otherworldly light, guided them further into the heart of Atlantis.

As they ventured deeper, they came across a chamber, grand and imposing, with a large stone dais in the center. Intricate carvings adorned the dais, depicting scenes of Osiris's life and death.

Hercules peered closely at the carvings. "Looks like we've found the right place, but where's the entrance to the tomb?"

Ava stepped forward, and her eyes scanned the cryptic symbols. "There's a riddle here. 'Only through harmony of the three can the lost be found.'" Her eyes flew to Georgette and Serena. "It must be referring to us, the three sisters."

Georgette stared at Ava in shock as she processed it. "Who do you think wrote this? And how did they know we would be here…?"

Ava shrugged. "It does not have to be literal. Three is a very sacred number, and it would stop people with ill-intention from coming alone and stealing the bones."

Serena leaned in, examining the carvings. "So, we sing? Is that it?"

Georgette frowned. "A song to open a tomb? It sounds a little too simple."

Ava nodded. "It's more than just a song. It's a siren song, a melody of ancient magic. We need to harmonize our voices."

Hercules chuckled. "Well, I'm out of this one. My singing could wake the dead, but probably not in the way we want."

Serena smirked. "Don't worry, Hercules. We can do this."

The sisters positioned themselves around the dais, and each took a deep breath.

Ava began the melody, a haunting, lilting tune that resonated with the very stones of the cave.

Serena joined in. Her voice wove seamlessly with Ava's, adding depth and richness to the melody.

Georgette, hesitating for a moment, finally let her voice soar higher than the other two, completing the trio.

Their voices melded into a perfect harmony, echoing throughout the chamber.

As they sang, the carvings on the dais began to glow, and the light pulsated in time with their song.

The ground trembled under their feet.

Hercules, watching in awe, murmured, "I'll never doubt the power of music again."

The chamber filled with a warm, golden light, and the dais slowly slid open, revealing a hidden staircase that led down into darkness.

Ava's voice softened as the song reached its crescendo. "The tomb of Osiris."

The group descended the staircase, and the air grew cooler as they went deeper. Hieroglyphics lined the walls, telling the story of Osiris's journey to the afterlife.

At the bottom of the staircase, they found themselves in a vast burial chamber.

In the center lay a sarcophagus, ornately decorated and shimmering with an ethereal light.

Hercules approached the sarcophagus cautiously. "This is it."

Excited, Ava and Georgette joined Hercules and carefully opened the sarcophagus.

Inside, they found a small bundle of bones.

"It looks like a pair of feet," Georgette thought aloud as she tilted her head and looked at them from different angles.

"Hurry, then. Put them in here." Serena held out her satchel.

"That seemed to be easier than I expected." Hercules rubbed his chin.

As the group emerged from the hidden tomb, carrying the bones of Osiris, an ominous chill crept over Georgette.

The light in the chamber seemed to dim, and a sense of foreboding filled the air.

From the shadows, a monstrous form emerged. Its shape shifted and undulated as if made of darkness itself. It let out a guttural roar that echoed off the cave walls, sending shivers down Georgette's spine.

"Ah yes," Hercules muttered. "It appears that I spoke too soon."

Georgette braced herself as she watched the monstrous being darting around them.

Hercules, always ready for battle, swung his mace with a mighty roar, but it passed through the shadowy beast as if it were mist. "It's no good trying to attack. Our weapons will go right through it."

Ava struck up her siren song, hoping to soothe the beast, but the melody seemed to dissipate in the heavy air. "There's nothing but pure evil in this one…" she shouted.

Serena, quick and agile, darted around the creature, slashing with her nails. But like Hercules's mace, her attacks had no effect.

"What are we supposed to do now?" she cried out with frustration.

Georgette unleashed a torrent of water, but it only seemed to anger the beast further. Its shadowy tendrils lashed out, striking them with brutal force.

The beast threw them backward, and Georgette's body ached as she fought to catch her breath.

"It's impossible!" Georgette clutched her bruised arm. "We cannot beat this!"

As despair began to set in, a mysterious figure appeared at the mouth of the cave.

Cloaked in green, with black leather boots, the stranger had a dark, brooding presence. His black hair framed a stern and striking face.

Without a word, he stepped forward, raising his hands toward the shadow monster. A powerful aura surrounded him, and the air crackled with energy.

The beast turned its attention to the newcomer, roaring and lashing out with its tendrils.

But the man, undeterred, chanted in a language they didn't understand.

Light emanated from his hands, forming intricate symbols that floated in the air. The symbols glowed brighter, weaving together to form a barrier between them and the beast.

The shadow monster thrashed against the barrier. Its form became more erratic and unstable. The man's chanting grew louder, more insistent, and the air vibrated with the force of his magic.

Ava, Hercules, Georgette, and Serena watched in awe as the man wrestled with the beast.

His power seemed inexhaustible.

The shadow creature let out one final, ear-splitting roar before it imploded into a cloud of dark mist, which the man swiftly dispersed with a wave of his hand.

The man lowered his hands, and his chest heaved as sweat covered his face.

Georgette rushed over to him, followed by her companions, and each of their expressions held a mix of gratitude and curiosity.

"Who are you?" Ava's eyes widened.

The man gave a tired but warm smile. "A friend." His voice sounded deep and reassuring. "But we can talk later. Right now, you need to get those bones to safety."

Emerging from the cave, the group turned to face their enigmatic savior.

He stood tall and confident, and his brown eyes glinted as he introduced himself. "My name is Loki, and I am a god. It seems you've all become quite the topic among the deities."

His revelation brought a mix of surprise and skepticism from Georgette.

The air charged with a newfound tension, the kind that always accompanied the meddling of gods.

Georgette exchanged nervous looks with Ava. As much as she felt happy not to have been destroyed by the shadow beast, she did not entirely trust him.

Loki slid his gaze lazily over them with a smirk on

his face. "You see, your quest has become something of a celestial spectacle. Gods and goddesses are watching. Some have even placed bets on whether you'll succeed in gathering all of Osiris's bones. I daresay, we haven't had this much fun since the fall of the Roman Empire."

Georgette, her curiosity piqued, stepped forward. "And which side are you on?" Her gaze fixed intently on the god.

Loki's expression morphed into something impassive, but then he smiled, and his eyes twinkled with mischief. "Perhaps," he mused, "you should invest your energy in asking more pertinent questions."

Despite the cryptic nature of his response, Georgette couldn't help but feel a sense of gratitude toward him.

"Thank you for your help," Ava said.

Hercules nodded in agreement, a rare gesture of acknowledgment toward a figure of Loki's ilk.

Loki waved them off. "Just don't go spreading the word. I'm not exactly supposed to be lending a hand," he said.

Georgette, her mind already racing ahead, turned to Ava and Hercules. "I need to get to the library. Wait for me here, at the city gates. I'll be back with the books we need." Determination colored her words. She nodded to Serena. "Are you still coming with me?"

"As much as I wouldn't complain if my brothers locked you up in the dungeon...yes. I'll go with you."

Ava and Hercules exchanged a look, and a silent understanding seemed to pass between them.

"We'll be here," Hercules assured her.

"Thank you again, Loki." Georgette gave a slight bow. "We owe you a great debt."

Something about the way Loki smiled back at her made the hairs on the back of her neck stand on end.

"No, thank *you*. You've helped me more than you know."

After a troubled moment, she turned around and followed Serena toward the golden gates.

SERENA

*S*erena approached the towering gates of Atlantis alongside Georgette, and a sense of foreboding enveloped her.

Serena's eyes narrowed as an eerie, unsettling silence met them, broken only by the gates creaking open without a touch.

"This is not normal." Serena's voice barely sounded audible over the sound of their cautious steps.

The stillness of the deserted streets amplified Serena's growing anxiety—and Georgette's, judging by her trembling hands.

As they moved through Atlantis, the scale of devastation appeared into view. Buildings that once stood proud had now become mere skeletons with weak and crumbling structures. The streets, once teeming with life, had been blanketed with debris and an overwhelming sense of loss.

"This...this can't be," Georgette stammered. Disbelief colored her tone. "Where is everyone?"

Serena shook her head as her eyes scanned the horizon for any sign of life. "It's like the city just...vanished."

They quickened their pace toward the palace, the heart of Atlantean power.

With each step, the destruction grew more pronounced, and the air thickened with the scent of ruin.

Reaching the library, Serena's heart sank.

Georgette's face fell as if hit by extreme sadness.

The hallowed halls that once housed ancient wisdom had morphed into a graveyard with scorched pages and remnants of what once existed.

She picked up a charred scroll, a sense of mourning in her voice, reverence in her touch. "All this history, gone."

"Let's check the throne room," Serena suggested with grim determination.

The throne room, once a beacon of Atlantean majesty, looked like a scene of tragedy.

Serena fell to the cold floor, shaken at the sight.

Poseidon, the mighty ruler of Atlantis, lay motionless on his throne, a green spear lodged in his chest.

The hilt of the sword bore an emblem of a scorpion that resembled the one on Loki's cloak.

Georgette gasped. "Loki's spear...but why did he do this?"

"We've been deceived." Serena's heart filled with a mix of anger and fear that made her body tremble. "Loki is not who he claims to be."

They raced back to the city gates.

Serena's heart pounded as fear and urgency propelled her forward alongside her sister. The realization that their friends might be in grave danger weighed on her and grew heavier with every step.

But nothing could have prepared them for the sight that greeted them.

Where Ava and Hercules had been waiting, only a haunting pool of blood remained.

"No, no, no," Georgette's eyes widened with horror.

Serena dropped to her knees beside the blood, and her hands trembled. "What happened here? Where are they?"

Georgette scanned the area frantically, searching

for any clue, any sign of their friends. "We have to find them, Serena. We have to!"

"I don't understand." Serena cried as her voice broke. "Why would Loki do this?" Serena's mind raced, trying to piece together the fragments of their encounter with the god. "He said the gods have a wager...maybe this is part of it?"

"But at what cost?" Georgette's eyes filled with tears. "At the cost of our friends? Our mission?"

"We need to act, and fast." Determination seeped into Serena's voice despite the dread that clung to her heart.

Georgette nodded, wiping away her tears. "You're right. We have to continue the mission. For them."

They stood in silence for a moment.

The weight of their situation pressed down upon Serena.

"We need to warn the others." Georgette sucked in a deep breath. "We need to tell them about Loki's betrayal."

"And we need to find out what happened to Ava and Hercules." Serena's resolve hardened. "We can't leave them to their fate, whatever it may be."

PRINCE EDWARD

*I*n the shadowed depths of a dimly lit tavern in Tortuga, Prince Edward sought refuge.

His troubled thoughts swirled like the storm outside.

The tavern, a haven for pirates and misfits, buzzed with the low hum of hushed conversations and laughter, and the air thickened with the scent of rum and tobacco. Flickering candles and oil lamps cast an eerie glow, throwing dancing shadows across the walls and onto the faces of the patrons.

Prince Edward sat with a half-empty glass of strong liquor as his only companion. His mind became a tumult of worry and strategy.

As he brooded, a woman approached. Her dress

clung seductively to her curves, and her red lipstick looked bold against her pale skin.

She leaned in close and whispered in a sultry voice, "How about you join me for a night you will never forget?"

"I'm married," Prince Edward replied in an icy voice as his gaze fixed on the dark liquid in his glass.

The woman shrugged, unfazed. "Most of my clients are married. What's the difference?"

A flash of anger sparked in Prince Edward's chest.

He stabbed his knife into the table, and the sound echoed through the tavern. "The difference," he growled, "is that my wife would send you to the depths of the ocean if she heard your offer."

The woman retreated quickly, sensing the danger in his tone. She found solace in the arms of an old pirate.

Pirate lords surrounded Captain Stone on the other side of the room, which drew Edward's attention.

Their conversation sounded intense, and concern etched each face.

As the meeting disbanded, the lords melted into the shadows of the tavern, and Captain Stone approached Prince Edward. "It's good news and bad news." Stone fell into a chair across from Edward with a deep frown on his face.

"Give me the good news first." Edward braced himself.

"The pirate lords are with us," Stone began. "They've agreed to keep to the seas and avoid any entanglements with the Navy. No one's interested in hunting sirens."

Edward nodded, and a flicker of relief passed through him. "And the bad news?"

Stone's expression darkened. "The King of England is dead. And the new King... it's Uncle Richard."

Edward's heart sank. "What does that mean for Mother?"

"She's married him." Stone's voice thickened with unspoken implications.

Edward abruptly rose, and his chair scraped against the wooden floor. "She married our father's brother, the most ruthless man in the kingdom?"

Stone nodded solemnly. "Exactly. So, we have to—"

Stone cut his words short as he glanced out the tavern's window. Something had caught his attention.

He stood and rushed out, and Edward followed him. The chill of the night air bit his skin.

Outside, a small, winged figure awaited them.

The man, if he could be called that, looked like something out of a myth with wings on his sandals and a scroll in his hand. "I am Hermes, messenger of Olympia," the figure announced. "I bring a message from Zeus."

Edward and Stone exchanged glances.

"To those who seek the remains of Osiris: cease your search immediately. You risk unleashing the fury of the titans and bringing about the destruction of the world."

The words hung in the air, heavy with portent.

"There's a postscript," Hermes added. "Trust no one, least of all, the gods."

Before they could respond, Hermes took to the air. His wings beat rapidly as he disappeared into the night.

The gravity of the situation hung in the air.

They had to warn the others, to regroup, and plan their next steps.

They hurried to prepare their ship. But as they readied to set sail, a fleet of Royal Navy ships appeared on the horizon, cutting a menacing figure against the dawn light.

Edward stepped forward, his voice commanding. "Stand down! I am Prince Edward of England!"

The navy men laughed derisively. "Prince Edward is dead. Who do you think you are?"

The ridicule stung, but nothing prepared them for the shock that followed.

From the lead ship, a familiar figure emerged.

Their father, supposedly dead, stood before them, his presence commanding and unmistakable.

"Hello, my wayward sons," he said, his voice resonating with authority. "We need to talk."

HERCULES

"Two sites down... seven to go," Hercules muttered once Georgette and Serena disappeared in the distance. He set his mace down and reclined against a bolder, happy for a break.

But then he eyed Loki with interest. "You're still with us, I see?"

Loki lifted his palms. "If I am not welcome, then by all means... I can leave..."

"No," Ava said. "We wouldn't be here without you. Perhaps we can persuade you to join us at the next site?"

"I may have a better idea. Ava, if you'll tell me where the next burial site is, I'll go for you. That way, we'll finish much quicker." Loki gave Ava an expectant smile.

She glanced at Hercules before she smiled back. "Of course. Let me just find a map. The main one is in Athens…"

While Ava fumbled in her satchel for a piece of parchment, Hercules opened up a portal. "Maybe we should send a message to the others—"

A muffled yelp made Hercules swivel round from the portal to see Loki holding Ava in his clutches, his dark red eyes like hot coals directed at him.

"What are you doing?" Hercules eyed the pocketknife pressed to Ava's neck.

Loki clamped a hand over Ava's mouth.

Before Hercules could move, the steel blade slid across her throat. The steel cut through her siren skin, and gushes of crimson blood spilled over her body.

"On second thought, I think I'll figure it out on my own." He pushed Ava toward a stunned Hercules.

He grabbed the bag of Osiris's remains and Ava's satchel. "Sorry, Herc. I need to ensure you don't follow me." He jumped into the portal, and disappeared.

Hercules felt too numb to care about Loki or wonder where he went.

His blood ran cold, and for a moment, his arms looked like two empty logs, hanging uselessly at his sides.

History repeated itself all over again.

His worst fear played out before him, and it took a second for his brain to move. Finally, when Ava slumped to her knees, he grabbed her.

Ava choked on her own blood as she bled out in Hercules's arms.

"I regret nothing," she breathed in a gurgle, lifting her fingers to his cheek. She trembled against his quivering body.

"This cannot be happening." He stared at her; eyes widened as he violently shivered.

When Ava caressed his cheek and shut her eyes, a montage of memories lit up Hercules's mind. But this time, they were not his.

They were *hers*.

She showed him every time he smiled at her, bold and cocky. when he looked up with a grin as he washed her body while they were in the Underworld. After battling the Hydra, he winked at her, striding forward with his mace propped on his shoulder.

Then she showed him every single time he kissed her. His eyes sparkled and darkened with passion.

It was the last gift she could give him. She showed him who he was through her eyes.

Not broken, but strong and worthy of love.

When her face came back into view, she was whiter than snow.

Hercules groaned like a wounded animal as he sank to his knees, and Ava fell limp in his arms. Her eyes became glassy, and a blue wisp floated out of her mouth and flew toward the sky.

Hercules watched it, remembering every detail of the day Megara died. He knew exactly where the wisp was headed.

But as grief poured through his body, a new sensation took hold of him.

"No," he said in an acid whisper. "You will not die today."

He cradled Ava's body and created a new portal. Then he carried her through.

He ran along the dark maze of the Underworld, following the blue wisp in its wake.

"Hercules? What in the... Oh no. Not again." Hades's voice floated to Hercules's ears, but he did not stop to look at his uncle. "Now let us not be hasty in making any rash decisions, nephew. It's too late. Look, she gone."

But Hercules paid Hades no attention as he hurried toward the river of the dead.

When they entered a vast cave, the silver waters stretched out before him.

"Hercules, you've already tried this before. She's gone. There's nothing you can do." Hades's voice sounded more panicked than angry.

Hercules tenderly set Ava's body on the ground, and he eyed the blue wisp that slowly floated over the fast-flowing river.

Hades ran in front of him and pressed his hand over his chest. "I cannot let you do this. You know what will happen if you're in there too long," he said.

"Let me pass," Hercules growled.

Hades took a deep breath and stepped aside. But as Hercules charged forward, Hades's final words echoed in Hercules's mind. "You'll be dead before you reach her."

Hercules sank into the cold waters and swam with all of his strength.

Countless souls floated aimlessly down the river. Their spirits clung to his body like leeches, sucking the very life out of him.

Hercules grunted, swimming further and further, desperate to reach Ava's soul.

It seemed ever out of reach.

Then suddenly, he faced the very last person he'd expected to find.

A wisp transformed into a human. Her eyes

looked like gemstones, and her dark hair waved in the water.

Megara.

His heart ached, and he paused for the briefest moment. But then his senses drew him back to the task at hand.

I have to let you go, Megara. It's time. Goodbye.

The truth of the sentiment scattered the illusion, but Hercules grew faint.

His lungs expelled of air, his limbs losing strength.

Soon, he would join the souls—fated to flow endlessly in the river.

But he could not succumb to it. Not yet. He just needed to reach Ava first.

She was too kind, too caring, too beautiful for the world to lose.

Her sisters needed her. If someone had to die, it needed to be him.

He outstretched his hand, reaching for the blue wisp of Ava's soul. Though it looked just like any other, it shone a little brighter, a little purer.

He knew her better than he knew himself.

And as his body waned and his senses grew dim, he allowed his final thoughts to be of gratitude. For having this opportunity to at least try to save her.

This time, he would not give up and swim out to

save his own life as he had done that fateful day Megara was killed.

He could not live with himself for not giving his own life. Even if it would be in vain.

He'd rather swim with his beloved in the river of the dead, than walk the Earth alone for eternity.

But just as black spots covered his vision, a wisp clung to his index finger. A surge of goodness soared through his soul.

Hercules turned and swam upward.

When his face broke the surface of the water, he met Hades, who cried out with relief. "I thought you were dead!"

But Hercules ignored him, holding up the wisp on his finger that glowed like a light in the darkness.

He walked over to Ava's lifeless body and lowered his finger to Ava's lips.

The light grew brighter and brighter.

"Hercules… what did you do?" Hades asked in a reverent tone.

They watched in awe as Ava's body glowed in ethereal beauty, and the cut on her throat healed before their eyes.

Hercules watched, and an otherworldly power flooded his body as he caught his breath.

"You're glowing." Hades pointed at him.

Hercules did not care, though. He could only watch Ava as she transformed.

Color stained her cheeks and lips, and her face filled with vibrancy that wasn't there before, even when she lived.

She took in a deep gasp, and when she opened her eyes, they shone at Hercules like two bright blue wisps.

"You were going to give your life to save me." She reached for Hercules.

He helped her up. "The only death is a life without you in it." Hercules pulled her into his arms.

Tears fell freely as he held Ava, and Hades looked on, apparently lost for words.

But then he regained composure. "All right, you two. As the god of the Underworld, I cannot just allow you to walk away…"

He held out a red jewel to Hercules as he approached. But Hercules, unaffected by it, punched Hades in the face and tossed the jewel in the water. "Your tricks do not work on me anymore, Uncle."

Hades rubbed his cheek, dazed, and looked at the red glow in the river of the dead.

Then he broke into a proud smile. "Finally, you have become the god that you were born to be."

Ava took Hercules's hand, stopping him from punching Hades again.

Somehow, her goodness flowed within him and softened his heart. "We should go," she whispered to him.

"I mean it when I say you can't just walk out of here. There are consequences..." Hades said. "God or not, you stole a spirit from the river of the dead. You think I will not punish you?"

Hercules lifted his brows. "Do as you wish, Uncle. I am taking my wife away from this wretched place. And if you come for her, I'll be there. Always."

Defeated, Hades dropped his hand and sighed. "All I've ever wanted for you is to find your purpose and be happy." He clapped Hercules on the shoulder. "But we are not done. I shall find you soon, for there are things you do not know. Things that affect everyone. Yes, even a god."

Hercules did not care for Hades's riddle. Instead, he conjured a portal, picked Ava up in his arms, and stepped through.

"I recognize this place." Ava looked at the rolling sea that moved in and out from the sandy beach.

Her eyes grew misty as she looked around, and it seemed as though a flood of memories washed over her.

She beamed at him. "We're back on your island."

"*Our* island," Hercules corrected, cradling her face. "My goddess."

Ava sucked in a breath before he kissed her.

She clung to his back, and their spirits entwined as they held each other.

When they pulled away, Hercules could not hold back the tears. "I thought I had lost you forever." He choked on the lump in his throat.

Ava touched his cheek and closed her eyes. "I'm so sorry," she said. "I'm sorry for the pain you have endured all these years. I'm sorry that you couldn't save Megara."

Hercules held Ava tightly, and for the very first time, the name did not sting his heart. But rather, it left a bittersweet feeling through his body.

He looked up at the cliffs in the distance and saw a woman standing on the edge. Her dark hair flowed in the breeze.

He rubbed Ava's lower back and kissed the top of her head as he watched the woman and knew exactly who it was. "I'm not." He looked at Ava. "I would go through it all again to bring me to this moment. Right here with you."

Ava rose on tip toes to kiss him again. It felt soft and sweet, like an unspoken promise.

When Hercules looked up at the woman on the cliff again, with a rush of wind, the vision of her faded.

It would be the last time Hercules saw Megara. For, in Ava, he finally found peace and healing.

After holding each other in silence for a long time, Ava lifted her head to look up at her beloved. "You know, we cannot stay here forever."

Hercules sighed, and the burden of responsibility weighed heavily on him. "I know, but for now, I want to be alone with you. No matter the consequences."

Ava nodded and rested her head on his chest again.

Hercules wanted to believe they could live out the rest of their days on this hidden island, far away from the dramas and chaos that came with mankind. But somewhere out there on the horizon, his friends still needed him.

And the world needed Ava's goodness.

But the future held more challenges and more perilous adventures.

He did not feel ready to face them, yet when he did, he'd face them with Ava.

Together, they would be unstoppable.

EPILOGUE

Hades

*P*ersephone lay in Hades's four poster bed like a sleeping princess. Her delicate hands folded atop each other and rested over her heart. Her exquisite bosom rose and fell with her breaths, and the sheer nightgown left very little to the imagination.

Not that Hades needed an imagination or a reminder. He had already memorized every curve and contour of Persephone's body.

His tongue, his fingers, his very soul, had touched

every part of her. And watching her sleeping so peacefully and ignorant of this fact drove him near to insanity.

Persephone had to be kept under a sleeping spell while he thought about his options.

The grand plan to finally rescue his woman did not go exactly as it should. After all, he thought Adonis simply kept her locked up in his palace against her will.

He had no idea the wretched man wiped her memories and seduced her into marriage.

The look of sheer devastation and hatred on Persephone's face stung as Hades stood with the bloodied mace in his hands. Pieces of Adonis's brain matter clinging to the spikes.

If Hades had known what Adonis had done, he would have thought of a different plan.

Now, Persephone was grief-stricken over the murder of her husband, and her heart felt cold toward Hades.

Without her memories, how could she ever accept the truth?

As far as she felt concerned, Hades was a monster who would stop at nothing to destroy her.

And in part, she was right. Indeed, he had committed monstrous acts. They both had. Together.

That had always been the charm of them.

She was his dark queen, his goddess. Some called Persephone more cold-hearted and ruthless than him.

He did enjoy destroying her, night after night, feasting on her flesh, making her mewl and melt under his hands.

He was the only person in all the worlds who could take her.

He licked his lips at the memory as he watched his sleeping bride.

His fingers twitched as he thought about dragging his hands over her scrumptious body.

He ran his tongue across his teeth as he considered biting her luscious thighs or tangling his fingers through her strawberry blonde locks.

This was a new form of torment. Perhaps this was Zeus's way of damning him to an eternity of hell: to have Persephone within his clutches once more but yet so far.

Days passed by, and he tried to wake her. He sent her gifts—her favorite dark lilies from the Hot Springs, a tiara of black and purple rhinestones with a large emerald in the center.

She screamed, howled, sobbed, and thrashed like a wild, wounded beast.

She shredded the lilies, scattering the petals all

over the floor. And she tossed the tiara so hard that it broke in two and smashed the floor-length mirror.

She moaned Adonis's name in her sleep.

No matter what gifts or how much time Hades gave her, she refused to calm down and listen to him.

"Just kill me," she demanded. "If I can only be reunited with my Adonis in death, then let me drink the bitter cup."

Hades cursed under his breath.

He would never allow his perfect Persephone to die. She was his eternal bride. He just needed her to remember.

After she had deceived him, and her newfound friends were safe in the world above, Persephone dropped her act and went back to being spiteful and angry with Hades.

As far as she knew, he was the villain, and nothing would change that.

In fact, as time went on, Hades began to believe it too.

While she slept, he poured over ancient scrolls and tablets from all corners of the world. He found a tea brewed in ancient China that dulled the senses and stilled the mind.

Some whispers said it could even wipe away memories.

He shook his fist at the dark ceiling of his boudoir, thinking of the wisp in his kingdom that belonged to Adonis.

The man had single-handedly destroyed him, and he would get his revenge.

But how could one carry out revenge on a dead man?

If he had known the extent of Adonis's crimes, he would have strung out the process. He would have locked him up in one of his torture rooms for a thousand years and let his Devil Men flay him just enough to heal, stick his eyeballs with pins, and break his bones. Smashing in his skull with Hercules's mace had been too kind and quick, too glorious of a death.

He clung to the hope that a siren could help him. After all, Ava had successfully hypnotized Persephone to follow her out of the castle.

But Ava was stubborn, and she did not wish to play a part in his plan.

He had attempted to break her, leaving her to rot in a cell with Hercules for weeks on end. But he'd gone too far. She had been left so broken, it seemed to diminish her powers.

So, he had been forced to let her go, hoping that when she and Hercules fell in love, she would be restored and of use to him again.

He paced the room, listening to Persephone's breathing.

He could steal another siren, though they were notoriously tricky to catch. Even for a god.

Sirens generally did not venture into the Underworld. Ava had been the very first one he came into contact with for more than a century. And though a war raged on, and scores of sirens' souls came down to the river of dead, they were as useful to him as a wet towel.

His mind raced back to the countless references in old fairy tales, promises of the magic that came with "true love's kiss."

He knew his chances were low, but he felt desperate.

With a deep, steadying breath, he approached the bed, and the mattress shifted under his weight as he sat beside Persephone.

She did not stir, too deep in a sleep to notice his presence.

He longed for her to open her pretty eyes and call out his name.

He'd even take an angry, scornful Persephone, if she'd follow up her tantrum with rampant love making as they had so often done in the past.

Hades found nothing more joyous than a round

of angry sex.

He brushed her soft hair away from her pale brow and grazed her bottom lip with his thumb. "Come back to me, my queen," he whispered and lowered his mouth to hers.

Persephone jolted awake at his kiss, and when Hades leaned back, he thought for one wonderful moment that it had worked.

Her pupils dilated when she blinked at him, and she rested her hand on his cheek for a brief moment.

But then, quick as a flash, she smacked him. "Get your vile hands off me, you murdering, soul-sucking, disgusting old man!"

She hissed and thrashed, clawing his face and chest with her nails that drew blood and trailed down his pectorals.

He grabbed her by the wrists and pinned them above her head. "Now you listen here," he growled.

Persephone's body stilled, and she held her breath and widened her eyes.

It gnawed at his stomach to see her react this way.

In years' past, this kind of act would have made her demand that he clutch her throat.

"I saved you." He gave her a hard look as Persephone's eyes welled up with tears.

He inwardly groaned. He could not handle more

crying. "Adonis hunted you, mutilated your mind, and locked you away from your family," Hades hissed, refusing to let her go.

Her face twisted under his words.

"He got better than he deserved, and if you possessed your memories, you would have commanded all the creatures from the Underworld to tear him limb from limb and devour him over a thousand years."

"Lies!" Persephone screeched. "He warned me. He said you'd do this! I hate you! I hate you!"

Hades grabbed her throat and squeezed just enough for Persephone to gasp and clutch his hand with a whimper. "You will not shed another tear for that man. He does not deserve it."

Persephone met Hades's hard look with a scowl. Then, she dropped her hands and went limp. "Fine," she whispered. "Choke me. At least I shall be reunited with my love."

Hades let her go like she'd scorched him. He staggered back.

He looked around the room from the fine antique dresser standing in front of the four-poster bed to the golden bath in the corner. A variety of fine gowns draped over a leather chair.

A thought struck him.

"You're not ready for this treatment." He turned back to Persephone. "I've been doing this all wrong. I see that now."

He caressed her cheek and withdrew just as she tried to bite him. "Very well, my love. I'll play your game."

He waved his hand and a pair of iron shackles appeared on Persephone's wrists.

"What are you doing?" she hissed as he brought her roughly to her feet.

The gaping neckline of her nightgown fell down one shoulder, and she stumbled as he urged her toward the door.

"Well, you have made it sparkling clear that you do not want any of this." He kept his tone steady even though his heart raced. "You think I'm your captor. The evil monster here to defile you."

They walked down the winding corridor, passing hooded men standing in the shadows.

He calmly opened an iron door and pushed her inside.

Persephone looked around the tiny cell. It had nothing but a bucket in one corner and a filthy little bed in the other.

"Is this better?" Hades asked. His gaze dipped to

her chest. "Cold, is it? Well, I'm sure your fond memories of Adonis will keep you warm."

Persephone's face reddened, and she glared at Hades like he was the most repulsive being in the world. "Go to hell," she shouted at him and spat on the ground at his feet.

Hades spread his arms and grinned, despite the fact his heart now bled at Persephone's rejection. "Oh, but my dear, don't you know? We're already there."

Then he turned around and slammed the door behind him, blocking out the sounds of Persephone's curses.

— *K*eep reading Hades and Persephone's story and see what happens next to the rest of our couples, in Vowed to Hades, book 4 in the Romancing the Seas series.

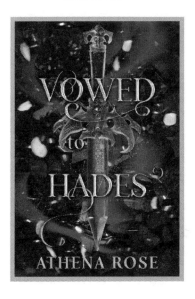

*T*hank you so much for reading! If you enjoyed this explosive story, then please consider leaving a nice review! Thank you so much, Athena Rose xoxo.